THE DUST OF

MELITA

—·—

CLARE HAWKINS

CAHILL DAVIS PUBLISHING

First published in Great Britain in 2023 by Cahill Davis Publishing Limited.

First published in paperback in Great Britain in 2023 by Cahill Davis Publishing Limited.

Printed and bound in Great Britain by Clays Ltd, Elcograf S.p.A

ISBN 978-1-915307-04-0 (eBook)

ISBN 978-1-915307-03-3 (Paperback)

Cahill Davis Publishing Limited

www.cahilldavispublishing.co.uk

And the rest, some on boards, and some on broken pieces of the ship. And so it came to pass, that they escaped all safe to land.

And when they were escaped, then they knew that the island was called Melita.

The Acts of the Apostles, vs 27:28 New Testament

Chapter 1

Malta, June 1940

The stream of his water darkened the white dust at the foot of the wall. From a gap between the stones, a gecko appeared, as though affronted by this insult, paused, then darted away. Frank buttoned up, hearing a noise in the sky that was spread like a tight blue sheet above him. His left ear tingled, burnt red by the sun, and he listened, squinting up and seeing them, five shining shapes, like fish swimming in formation, coming from the south. He scrambled over the low wall, dropping down and jarring his ankle as he landed on the other side, in sight of the machine gun position they'd been building. The others had seen the planes too and were staring upwards, standing inside the circle of stone.

They knew the Italians were coming, it was only a matter of time, and they'd all been flat out for a month, getting ready for the bastards. Now there were dark dots falling from the aircraft, little black lozenges in the sky. What were they doing bombing out here, for Christ's sake? He'd been shot at before but not bombed, and now, here they were, with nothing around but fields and walls and rock and no bloody Bren gun.

'Oi, get down,' Chalky was calling at him, waving his arms, as if Frank were an idiot and hadn't seen the planes. He turned back to see if the farmer was still there ploughing his field, as he'd been an hour ago, and there he was, plodding along behind his mule, in some other world, like in an ancient Bible picture.

'Get down. *Down*,' Frank shouted to the man, but he didn't so much as look up or turn his head, just kept moving on slowly over the ground. Frank yelled again. Was the bugger deaf or something?

Now there was a whistling, a high-pitched, nasal whine, then the ground a hundred yards to his left exploded in a thunder of spurting dust and broken rock. Frank threw himself flat on the ground and covered his head with his arms, hearing another pounding crack somewhere to his right. He crawled along at the foot of the wall, wondering whether this was a stupid action; these hunks of limestone might flatten him if the wall took a hit. But he stayed down, spying along the length of the low wall.

About twenty yards to his left, where the wall ended at a slab of solid rock, he saw the black hole of a small opening. Had it been there a minute ago? It looked a bit like the entrance to a shelter or store—some farmers carved them out of the hill sides, but it was pretty small. Big enough to shelter in though. Head down and doubled over, he scuttled along to the place, ducked his head into the hole and heard another explosion behind him. The ground shuddered. The whole bloody island was quaking.

Diving flat on his stomach, he hauled his body into the opening with his elbows, scraping his knees, finding there was plenty of room for the whole of him and more. From outside came the grizzling of aircraft engines, muffled now, and he tensed ready for the next explosion. It didn't arrive. He lifted his head, seeing that the rock roof was higher than he'd thought and that he was in some sort of tunnel. Twisting into a sitting position, he peered into the darkness where the tunnel penetrated further into the rock. He could only see about five yards ahead by the light from the small entry hole, so he shuffled further along, just to find out how far it went. His left hand groped ahead, over the

4

damp crust of the wall, his fingers creeping, stretching, as though he expected to catch hold of something or someone just out of reach. With his other hand, he fumbled for the matches in his breast pocket. He'd be able to see more with a little bit of light. Pausing, he struck a match and held it in front of his face. He was in a widening tunnel, its floor sloping down about another ten yards to a ledge, beyond which was a block of inky blackness.

The match burnt his fingers and darkness returned, so he struck another and held it above his head. An odour of mould rose in a wave from somewhere below him, and he knew that there was much more of this cave beyond the part he could see. The black cloak of the cave air was flung around him, wrapping him, tugging him on, and he struck another match, scrambling further along, on his feet now.

He found himself on the edge of a slab of rock that hung over a wide chamber. The far wall of this room-like cavern was flat and straight, like the side of a house. On it, he could see dense markings of some sort, or blotches of damp, he couldn't be sure. Hardly aware of what he was doing, he slithered over the edge, dropping down about four feet, landing with a jolt on the floor of the cave, and his match went out.

He crouched there, blind in the blackness, wondering what the hell had possessed him, coming all this way into a bloody cave. He fingered the last matches—Christ, only two left. What was he playing at? But he had to see what was on that wall. He stood up and edged his feet across the chamber, the tiny flame flickering against the flat surface, which was scored all over with writing of some sort. He reached forward, his fingertips touching the carved indentations, following them along one line and then the next. The match end stung his finger and thumb, and he cursed as darkness swallowed him again. But his other hand still rested on the intricate shapes carved in the rock. Who had done all this? Farmers? Not likely. What in hell *was* this place?

One match left, just enough to get him back up on the ledge again. Frank tried to steady his breathing and struck the match. But the flame flickered for only one brief moment before something snuffed it out. In this black pit, he heard his heart pumping, felt the sweat on his face and slid one foot forward. His boot crunched on something, and he lurched sideways, his other foot hitting a buffer of soft stuff on the ground. *Sweet Jesus, get me out of here*, he wanted to yell, but didn't dare.

Where was the fucking ledge? Shaking, he stretched out his arms, anticipating contact with the stone at any moment, but something nudged his elbow, like a guiding hand. He lunged forward, a scream stuck in his throat. As his foot hit rock, his hands grappled for a hold on the ledge. The air, soft and damp, crept around his neck, like the gentle passing of a silky cloth, enveloping his head, then a touch, a caress upon the cheek. Fear sucked the breath from him, but he thrust hard with his foot, jerking his body up onto the flat rock. He scuffled up the sloping floor like a terrified rat, catching sight, to his relief, of the hole of bright daylight at the cave entrance.

He elbowed himself furiously along the tunnel towards the circle of light. His head burst out into the sunlight, his chest heaving, his body trembling all over. Gasping the dry air, he lay for a moment trying to slow his breath, feeling the smarting of his grazed knees and elbows. The fading terror churned in his watery stomach. Then he remembered the others, his mates, ashamed to think that during his time beneath the rock, they might have been blown to bits. But Jesus Christ, he might have been better taking his chances with the bleeding bombs out here than being down there in that place. Before he had scrambled to his feet, a voice called his name.

Frank smiled to himself and tried not to laugh with relief—to mock his own stupid fear felt good. He made his way back to the others. They were all there, smoking, their rifles leaning against the wall of the stone sangar, as though they were taking a tea break in a routine day's work, intact, unhurt. The only signs of the raid were three craters in the fields nearby and a length of stone wall smashed and scattered in boulders all around. Their gun position remained unmolested.

'Where the bleeding hell were you? Thought you'd bloody bought it, Nixon,' said Farley.

'What about the farmer?' said Frank, turning round, glad to see the man still ploughing, plodding along, his stringy whip flicking at the rump of his animal.

'Bloody mad, these Maltese,' said Farley, scratching his ginger scalp.

'Perhaps they know the Eyeties couldn't hit a duck on a village pond,' said Corporal Myles with a laugh, but Frank saw that his hand was shaking as he dragged on his cigarette.

'Bastards were just dropping their leftovers on the way back,' said Chalky, gazing up at the sky.

The corporal stared at Frank. 'What's up with your hands and knees?'

'There's a cave under there,' he replied, sucking the blood from one of his torn knuckles. 'I went in it.'

He wanted to tell of his experience, half wondering whether he'd dreamed it: the damp darkness, the aura that had scared him to his bowels, the weird carved writing. Now that he stood out here in the blazing dry sun of a summer day, it seemed impossible.

'A what?'

'A cave?'

'There was writing on the wall,' Frank said.

'Come off it, writing on the wall?' said Chalky.

Farley and the three others were grinning, exchanging glances, stirring it up for a good laugh at his expense, as though to celebrate their escape, unscathed, from the bombs.

CLARE HAWKINS

'Seen the writing on the wall?' said Chalky, jabbing Frank in the ribs with a hard elbow. 'So, when are we for it? What did it say?'

'I don't bloody know,' said Frank, irritated now, wishing he'd never mentioned it. 'For all I know, could be saying, "Fuck off back to Blighty, you English twats".'

A silence hung in the air for a moment.

'Christ, I'm bleeding starved,' Coop grumbled, lighting another cigarette. 'Those buggers should've been here to relieve us by now.' He slumped down inside the rough wall of the empty gun emplacement.

Frank, glad that they'd lost interest in his find, decided to keep all his other speculations to himself. He'd ask Lieutenant Chambers, their platoon commander, when he got back to barracks. He was one of those university blokes. He'd probably know about history and foreign languages and that kind of thing.

'Look, here they are at last,' said Corporal Myles, dropping his cigarette butt and pointing down the track at a group of men on bicycles, about a quarter of a mile away.

'Well, they're not bringing the Bren, not on push bikes,' said Chalky, wiping his brow with the back of his hand.

Frank scratched his neck at the familiar itch of a mosquito bite.

'What's the point of this with no flipping gun?' said Farley. 'Thought we were supposed to be setting up more defence positions.'

'What do you expect?' Corporal Myles spat into the dust at his feet. 'It's the bloody army, after all. That would be too organised.'

Frank watched as four other members of their section came pedalling towards them, red-faced and glistening with sweat. Another followed some way behind, wheeling his bike.

Corporal Myles took a few steps towards them and shouted, 'Any damage done?'

The front rider drew near and dismounted, panting. 'Couple of holes in the ground, that's all,' he said. 'See you've had a few here too.'

'Yes, three of them got chucked down here, but no damage done. Nix here hid in a cave, so he was well out of it, jammy bastard.'

Frank, wanting to avoid more ribbing, watched the soldiers dismount, guessing that the one walking had punctured his tyre. In a moment of inspired opportunism, Frank quickly hunched his pack on his back, slung his rifle over his shoulder, ran forward and grabbed the bike from the second soldier of the arriving party.

'Someone's going to have to walk back, and it's not going to be me,' he shouted to the others.

'Oi, you, Nixon, come back here,' yelled the corporal, but Frank had already turned the bicycle round, stepped hard on the pedal and was gathering speed down the road, with wheels crunching and jumping over the stony surface. The breeze created by his movement cooled him a little, though the air still fanned warm in his face. He was glad to be away from the place.

It was a strange landscape, this island, a barren and dry-scorched lump of rock, criss-crossed by ancient stone walls of white limestone. These created little terraced fields where the farmers and villagers grew fruit: tomatoes, melons, oranges, lemons, pomegranates and God knows what else. And dotted on these arid slopes were clumps of prickly pear—which, to Frank, looked like desert cacti in a comic book—and olive trees, but precious little else at this time of year. When the Devonshires had first arrived, it had been spring, and flowers of pink and white and purple had coloured the slopes and edges of fields all over, but now it was dry and hot as a desert.

The houses dotted over the countryside were small white boxes, flat-roofed and built of blocks of this same pale stone that lay everywhere. The peasants went about in donkey carts and herded goats that boys brought into villages to deliver milk, fresh from the teat. It seemed to Frank that they had stepped back into some bygone time. The villages were small, tight clusters of narrow lanes between two-storey stone houses, with yards and enclosed courts where hens clucked and pecked under lemon trees. He wondered if the Devon countryside had really been as green as he remembered it, and longed at times to see its grassy fertility again.

The Maltese country folk were reserved at first, but helpful and friendly once efforts at communication were made on both sides. This was an island well used to the military but equally tied to its own rhythm of life and traditions.

Once, just outside the village of Naxxar, a young pretty-faced woman in a black dress and a strange hooped shawl on her head, like a lot of the country women wore, had given him a cup of water when he had fallen with exhaustion during a gruelling exercise on a scorching day. Her sad, dark eyes had watched him drink as he leaned, panting against the stone wall of her yard. He wished he had known how to say thank you in her language, though she had spoken to him in hesitant English.

Now he bumped his way over the road on the bicycle and heard his comrades behind him, feeling a moment's guilt for his speedy retreat and the poor bloke who'd ended up having to mend the puncture. He wondered if he should go back and help, particularly if the Italians were planning another raid. He was surprised at how quickly the fear had passed, perhaps because of the balmy day with the sea visible now, calm and silky blue. It wasn't right, the war coming to ruin the peace of this island and its people.

The great spread of St Andrew's Barracks was ahead of him now, sprawling like a town in its own right. He came skidding to the crossroads, just fifty yards from the north entrance, from which a Bren carrier, painted in patches to resemble the stony landscape, was emerging, turning to the right and grinding its way along the road towards the coast. A jeep carrying three officers crossed his path. He saluted the captain and two lieutenants, one of whom was Lieutenant Chambers. Frank hoped the officer would be off duty tonight and he'd have a chance to ask him about the cave. He had to admit that he'd nearly wet himself with fear in that place, but it was bloody fascinating too. It was a pity he couldn't have copied down some of the writing, but he'd had no paper or pencil and not enough matches. Probably someone educated would have been able to read the words, but not him. His schooldays were done five years ago at fourteen, with no chance of any books or learning since then.

Frank pedalled through the arched entrance, past the two blokes on guard, into the open square surrounded by three-storey stone-built blocks. The buildings of the barracks were magnificent in their way, Frank thought, a cross between a monastery and a palace, though he'd never seen real ones, only pictures in books. Built by the Victorians to house the whole machinery of British colonial government, the barracks had everything: churches, halls, a gymnasium, messes, school, married quarters, rows of elegant arched windows and cloistered walkways. It was all a bit run down, tatty and old-fashioned, but Frank liked the presence of the past in the solid, hefty elegance of the buildings.

He dismounted and wheeled his bicycle across the square to the range of buildings that served as a storage shed, ignoring the loud taunts of Coop, Farley and the corporal, who came rattling behind him, about his cheating victory. Their voices rose in mock sympathy for poor old Chalky, who'd had to mend the puncture and had promised to beat the hell out of Frank when he finally got back to barracks.

Frank headed quickly to the block where they bunked down. Some regiments in the south were billeted in cow sheds and pig huts, so his battalion of the Devonshires were lucky to be in a proper building, with its thick stone walls and cool flagstone floor. It was a relief to escape the sun, even though the bunkhouse was crammed tight with camp beds and kit bags, not to mention dozing soldiers and others cleaning their rifles and kit. Frank needed to change his shirt. He couldn't present himself to an officer like this. He nodded to two blokes from Marshall's section who were playing cards as Coop, Farley and the corporal clattered in after him.

'Here, guess what? Nixon's seen the writing on the wall,' the corporal said, laughing to the card players, who looked up with puzzled expressions.

'You mean he's seen an Eyetie bomb with his name on it?' said one.

The other player tossed down his card and muttered, 'It's not the Eyeties we'll have to bother about, it's the bloody Jerries. You just wait till the Luftwaffe get here. That'll be a different story. They're in a different class, them.'

Frank unbuttoned his shirt and threw it onto his blanket, then rummaged in his kit bag, found a cleaner, crumpled one and started putting it on.

'You reckon Hitler'll bother with this little lump of rock in the middle of nowhere?' said Coop to the second card player.

'It's not though, is it?' he replied. 'It's on the way to Egypt, right in the way of everything. Malta's the perfect base for attacking them, sea and air. The Jerries'll want it, you wait and see.'

There was the clang of metal on metal—the signal for grub. Every man in the bunkhouse leapt up, even those who had appeared to be sleeping like the dead. They wolfed their meal at long trestle tables. Frank enjoyed these dinners al fresco, mopping up the gravy with his bread. He'd lived much of his life in a state of mild hunger. He'd even gobbled all the food at St Augustine's home for waifs and strays, where he'd been taken, aged six. Now he ate army victuals without complaint or protest, unlike those who threw away burnt porridge or black-eyed potatoes. He swallowed the food, like the rules and orders he'd lived under all of his life, toed the line, mucked in with the lads, knew the boundaries and could mostly stand up for himself. As he ate, he hardly noticed what he was swallowing because he couldn't get that cave and the writing out of his head. He'd have to go and see if he could find Lieutenant Chambers as soon as he'd finished.

The officers' quarters and their mess were in a quadrangle in a towered block, about two or three minutes' walk away. There was a small crowd of officers on a terrace outside the main entrance, lounging around, chatting and smoking. Frank badly wanted a smoke himself but remembered he had no matches and he probably shouldn't light up in front of Lieutenant Chambers. He'd filch a box from someone when he got back.

Lieutenant Chambers was sitting on a deck chair, smoking a pipe and reading a book. He was a lanky sort with sandy hair and a pale moustache. Frank was unsure of his age but he wasn't old, though he had the rounded shoulders and limp figure of a man unused to exercise or sport, not exactly the soldiering type.

'Sir, could I have a word?'

The officer looked up and nodded. 'Yes, of course. What is it, Nixon?' His manner was relaxed, unhurried and less like an officer than most of them.

Frank was suddenly struck with embarrassment to be talking to an officer about something unrelated to military matters, to come to him with ignorant questions. Perhaps this cave he'd come upon wasn't anything special at all. Perhaps they were common on islands in the Mediterranean. But now he was here, facing the officer, there was no going back, and he could hardly turn and run. He caught a whiff of the lieutenant's tobacco and fumbled in the breast pocket of his shirt for his flattened packet of cigarettes. The officer was staring at him as he fidgeted.

'Do you need a light, Nixon?'

'Yes, sir,' he said, sheepish but relieved.

Lieutenant Chambers stood up, took a box from his pocket and tossed it to Frank, who lit up and took a grateful drag.

'Keep them, Nixon. Now, what's the problem?'

'No problem, sir,' said Frank, 'only, it's just that I found something today up near the coast, past Fort Madliena. We were working, building a machine gun post. We nearly got bombed.'

The lieutenant puffed on his pipe, then signalled with it that Frank should continue. So he told of his discovery, of the underground cavern and the writings, though he didn't mention the weird sensations he'd had, the daft terrors of his imagination, of course.

'This is most interesting,' said the officer, his eyebrows raised but not with disbelief or ridicule. 'Writing, you say? What language?'

Frank felt himself redden. 'I don't know, sir. It wasn't like anything I've ever seen before, but it was definitely writing carved in the stone. There were letters, shapes, some of them straight, sort of like capitals, and some more curved, a bit like on a gravestone. And the walls in the tunnel were rough, but the one with the writing was flat and straight, not natural... kind of manmade.'

Frank had stopped feeling foolish, as Lieutenant Chambers was clearly taking his story seriously, frowning with concentration.

'Could be a natural phenomenon caused by underground water, except for the writing. There are quite a few caves on the islands, some of them natural and some carved out by people—catacombs and things like that. And, of course, the Maltese islands have a very ancient history, dating back thousands of years, well before the time of the Romans: Neolithic temples in Zebbug and Mgarr and all sorts of different peoples, the Phoenicians, the Carthaginians, the Romans, Muslim Arabs, the Spaniards, the French and us, of course.'

Lieutenant Chambers was well into teacher mode now but with enthusiasm, not like the droning old toad Frank had endured at school who'd caned boys for not remembering all the kings and queens of England.

'So it's possible that these writings you've found might be pretty ancient, Roman or Byzantine. But then nobody knows much about what was happening during the Muslim occupation in the ninth century. Could be something from that time. Fascinating. You'll have to take me to have a look, Nixon.' His manner had become edgy with eagerness.

A shout interrupted the lieutenant's last words, then another, followed by the screech of the air-raid siren, the distant sharp whistle from a gunner and the sound of running feet, bursts of commands. Frank and the officer looked up at the darkening sky and saw the planes, six silver shapes.

'Sometime, Nixon,' said the officer, 'but I think we may have more urgent business for the moment.'

CHAPTER 2

JULY 1940

'Come on, Nix,' said Chalky, kicking Frank's outstretched foot, 'get your head out of that book.'

Frank shut the book Lieutenant Chambers had lent him, put it under the blanket on his bed and stood up.

'Yeah, professor. Got to get your hands dirty now,' said Coop.

Frank joke-punched his mate in the shoulder as he passed.

'Ow, leave it out. Who d'you think you are, a bloody school-teacher?' Coop said, laughing. 'I'll see you outside.'

'Stop your fucking larking about, you two,' the corporal said, 'and get a move on. There's a truck leaving in a minute.'

Though damage in the first Italian raids had not been severe, there were craters and holes in the airfield at Ta' Qali, which their platoon had been sent to fill in.

'Poor bloody infantry,' Corporal Myles muttered as they made their way out of their block. 'Poor bloody skivvies, that's what we are. If I'd wanted to spend my life busting up stones and filling in holes, I'd have gone to work on the railways.'

Outside, the sky was its usual unpunctuated blue, and although it was only nine o'clock, it was hot already. Frank wished he could have brought the *Historical Guide to Malta and Gozo* book with him to read when he had a break, but he didn't want to get it bashed about. He was caught up completely in the account of ancient civilisations in Malta. He didn't know what it was about history and things from the past that excited him. Perhaps it had started when he'd visited Exeter Cathedral as a kid. He hadn't been able to believe the sight of the mass of carved statues on the outside, saints and bishops. He'd been amazed by the inside of it too, the huge stone pillars soaring upwards as though they were holding up the sky. It was a day trip organised by a charity for the boys of St Augustine's. Some tall posh girls and boys from the local high schools had come with them on a bus, along with a few of the masters. Jimmy Spraggs had spent the whole journey chuckling about how he had seen one of the girl's titties through her blouse and had looked up her skirt. Then he was sick all over the floor and seats of the bus on the way back, on account of eating a whole bag of boiled sweets and four packets of chips. Frank had used all his money in the world—one shilling and three pence—to buy a guidebook of the cathedral and, holding his nose against the smell of sick, had read it from cover to cover twice on the bus home.

Reading Lieutenant Chambers' book excited that same sense of amazement in him. The astonishing fact that here, on this island, he was treading on the same ground and rocks where others had roamed thousands of years ago. He was touching stones carved by ancient builders; looking at sights seen by Phoenicians, Carthaginians, Romans; breathing the same dusty air as the famous Knights of St John. Even the juddering of the truck over the dirt roads hardly shook him from these imagined worlds back to the present. It was only when the driver crunched into a lower gear to go up a hill that he realised where they were: approaching the village of Naxxar. They were quite near that pretty woman's house.

He turned round in his seat, gripping the side of the truck, feeling Coop's body jammed against his. Dust rose from the road in spurts from the tyres. Chalky coughed drily, cursing between spasms. They were passing the wall of her place now, an olive tree bending over it and a huge bush of prickly pear, and Frank could see into the yard. She was there, a black figure, bare-headed this time, tossing food to a clutch of hens at her feet. Two little lads of around six or seven were scraping straw out of a wooden hutch onto the ground. The woman turned suddenly at the squeal of the truck's brakes as the driver slowed to negotiate the bend in the road. Her gaze met Frank's and, with his face burning, he smiled at her.

'She's a bit of all right,' said Chalky, whose eyes had been drawn to the woman too.

Frank longed to leap over the side, give her a proper respectful sort of greeting, but a moment later, they had passed on. If only he could have gone to help her with her chores in the yard rather than spending all day breaking stones and shovelling rubble in the heat. It was a stupid thought, he knew.

They rolled on through the square in the centre of the village, with its massive church. It had two tall towers, clustered with carvings and niches with statues of saints stuck in its walls. He wished he could go inside, but he hadn't had a chance yet. Magnificent for a village, Frank thought, but that was how big religion was to the Maltese. Just outside the village, the truck had to slow for a drifting herd of goats, big hairy black and white ones, bleating in random bursts, unhurried and untroubled by the throaty revving of the lorry pushing at their rear.

'Don't mind us, girls,' shouted Coop, standing up and looking ahead at the holdup. 'I ask you. What a place.'

Frank stood too, gazing at the sight of this herd of goats, with two small barefooted boys driving them. It could have been a scene from hundreds, maybe thousands of years ago, not this world of petrol engines, bombs and planes.

Out of the village, on the open road, they had to slow yet again, this time for a cluster of people on foot, moving slowly, weighed down with suitcases and boxes; a woman pushing a pram loaded high with clothing, pots and pans; several children straying about the road as they went. Their driver sounded his horn, and the people turned, then separated into two streams, moving to the sides to let the vehicle pass. As the truck pushed through, Frank looked into the forlorn faces of the refugees and saw that some of the children were crying.

'It's folk from the towns, getting out of danger,' said Corporal Myles. 'The places near the dockyards. Coming to stay with their country cousins.'

They passed two more groups of refugees, women and children mostly, and Frank wondered how the folk in the villages would cope with this influx of extra mouths to feed and bodies to accommodate. The truck juddered past them, the small gaggle soon left behind.

They were set to work as soon as their feet touched the ground at the Ta Qali airfield. There were two rough runways, with ranges of low-slung stone buildings, Nissen huts around the edges and a half-built stone pen containing three biplanes, the old Gloster Gladiators, which were the only airborne defences on the island. Frank had heard in the gossip of the mess room that these planes weren't quick enough to outrun the Italian fighters and that unless they sent Hurricanes soon, the island was likely to be blasted to hell and back. He hoped this was just a bit of scaremongering, but what did he know?

Today, as well as filling holes, they had to clear another stretch of runway and start building more of the protective pens for the new aircraft, when they arrived.

'Should have joined the bloody navy,' said Chalky, straightening his back and wiping the sweat from his brow. 'This is killing me.'

They were all burnt brown on the exposed parts of their bodies, apart from Coop, whose visible skin remained a freckled scarlet. He had taken to covering up.

As he dug and shovelled in the heat, Frank wondered when they'd next get posted to man the coastal defences. That would give him a chance to look for the cave again or even perhaps explore some of the places he'd been reading about in the book. He wondered if he'd ever get to know about the writings in the cave and whether Lieutenant Chambers had really been serious about wanting to have a look.

Another hour of toiling in the sun and Frank noticed how everyone had slowed down, like a film reel going wrong in the pictures. But the sound of a siren soon shocked them back into action, the corporal shouting the order to take cover. Frank, Coop, Chalky and a few others dived into the nearest slit trench and peered out from beneath their helmets. A piercing whistle called the gun crews to their positions, and a glance at the sky showed the enemy planes, five of them in formation. Then suddenly there was the rumble of engines from behind, a throaty, sputtering roaring, and a moment later, the three Gloster Gladiators racing along the runway, the first rising into the sky. The men in the trenches burst into a spontaneous cheer.

Then came the head-splitting sound of the ack-ack guns and the bombs thundering into the earth, blasting up the surface of the runways, crashing into one of the buildings, which burst into flames and belching smoke. The stink of burning fuel, smoke and dust arose out of the earth. Frank saw Coop's lips muttering curses, or perhaps prayers, during the whole time, his own ears and head blocked with noise. So this was it from now on, them down here, useless sitting targets for the bombers.

It was near dusk when they headed back to barracks, exhausted from their heavy labouring and the tautness of their fear during the raids. One of the Gladiators had shot down an Italian plane beyond the harbour at Valletta, so the pilot had reported on his return, and there had been some rejoicing amidst their toil. On the truck, going back to barracks, Frank's mind was empty with fatigue. The vehicle lurched along the road at a reckless pace until it had to slow for another group of civilians on foot. Frank glanced out as the vehicle steered past an old couple, the woman limping along with a stick, her bent husband at her side. In front of them was a boy weighed down by two suitcases and a little ahead of them a young woman carrying a toddler with another child attached to her hand. The old woman's swollen ankles, her husband's halting gait and the sight of the children struck Frank like a blow to the chest.

'Corp,' he said. 'Can we stop a minute? Let's give them a lift.'

'For fuck's sake, Nixon,' he said, but Frank saw him looking back at the pathetic family.

'Oi, Stan. Stop will you,' shouted the corporal to the driver, and then to Frank, 'OK, but you lot'll have to walk back.'

The driver stepped on the brakes, and the lorry shook, as though complaining at this unexpected halt. Frank, in spite of the heaviness of his fatigue, slid off the back of the truck and approached the young woman.

'Where are you going?' he said.

Her eyes glistened.

The boy quickly dragged his burdens to her side. 'Mosta.' He smiled up at Frank.

'Come on, then. We're going that way,' he said.

Coop and Chalky clambered down from the truck.

The boy's face lit up with a grin of delight as he rattled off something to his mother in Maltese. Behind him, the old couple raised their bent heads and tried to hurry forward. Coop lifted the suitcases into the vehicle while Frank hoisted the small girl, released from her mother's hold, into the back, though she whimpered in fear. Her mother replied in a soothing voice and

21

handed the toddler to Coop. Frank steadied her elbow and, with a hand on her waist, helped her up. She was a slim, good-looking woman, dark and attractive like many of the Maltese. She reclaimed her small child with a grateful smile at Frank and the others.

'Come on, Grandma and Grandad,' said Chalky to the old people. He and Frank hoisted them into the back of the truck with the rest of the family. The boy scrambled up eagerly last of all, as though he were about to set off on an exciting fairground ride. Frank and the other two stood on the roadway, watching the truck retreat down the road.

'How far do you reckon it is back to barracks?' said Coop with a sigh, though there was no resentment in it.

No one replied as they started trudging along the road, after the truck, which was hardly visible now behind the dusty cloud in its wake. The sky was glowing deep red, like coals in a brazier, turning the landscape a soft pink. Frank gazed as they walked, the others having fallen silent too, glad of some moments free from harsh and threatening noise. There were sounds—the gentle distant engine noise of the retreating lorry, thin bleatings from goats—but that was all.

'Stuck here like bleeding sitting ducks on this island,' said Coop at last.

'I reckon they'll bomb the hell out of us,' said Chalky.

Frank made no response, for even if this were to prove true, for the moment, walking in this place in the ravishing sunset, he didn't care.

'One day's leave. Better than a kick in the arse, I suppose,' said Coop, scratching his ginger head. 'I think I've got bloody fleas. Got any of that stuff, have you?'

Chalky was changing his shirt. 'Yeah,' he replied, tossing a small bottle to Coop.

'Let's get a move on, lads. You're beautiful enough,' said the corporal. 'Got to make the most of the day.'

'And the evening,' added Chalky with a snigger.

Frank ran his fingers through his hair and glanced quickly in his broken shaving mirror. Presentable at least, he thought, though he always imagined that there was something of the mongrel about him, like most of the lads in St Augustine's. There was a downcast look about his eyes, which smiling didn't seem to erase, but the matron had said to him on his last day at St Augustine's that he was a good-looking boy and not to get himself into trouble. He was as puzzled by her compliment as he was at her suggestion of its unfortunate consequence.

The tart he'd had in Plymouth, his first time, when he'd gone along with the lads, had said he looked like a film star, but she couldn't remember who. He wasn't too keen to go to Strait Street in Valletta again, where all the whorehouses were. He was sorry for the women, putting up with all sorts of blokes doing God knows what to them, although most of them seemed cheerful enough. It was a job and they needed the money, probably even more now it was wartime.

Frank and the others knew they'd have to walk to Valletta that day, as the bicycles were needed for patrols and there was no petrol available for non-essential journeys, so they started off across the yard towards the road. From around the corner of the officers' quarters, Lieutenant Chambers emerged, dressed in civvy shorts and cap with a walking stick and a bulky haversack on his back.

'Oh God, it's the fucking country squire,' said Coop, with a nod towards him.

The officer, seeing them, started in their direction with a purposeful stride, and they stopped and saluted.

'Off for a day out? Splendid,' the lieutenant said. 'I'm going for a spot of sightseeing. I'll try and find that cave of yours, Nixon, unless you'd like to show me the way yourself.'

Frank knew he'd gone red in the face, wishing he were anywhere else but here. What could he say? He badly wanted to go to the cave again, to find out about the writing, but he couldn't let on. He'd never live it down, choosing an archaeological expedition over a day of fun and entertainment.

'Don't know, sir. I... well...' he stumbled, wishing he'd just said 'no thanks' and turned away, but his hesitation had simply emphasised his error.

'No, no, don't let me spoil your plans,' said the lieutenant. 'I just thought with your interest in history. Well, have a good day.'

'Thank you, sir,' said Frank, feeling even more of an idiot. To his relief, the officer strode off quickly, his knapsack bouncing against his back as he went.

'Oi, Nixy,' said Coop, chuckling, 'what have you been up to with old boffin there?'

'You're well out of that one, Nix,' said the corporal. 'Down a cave with a shirt lifter. Not advisable, my son, unless you're one of them, of course.'

'Fucking shut up,' said Frank and threw off Chalky's hand, which he had reached out in an attempt to stroke his cheek.

Frank liked Valletta, with its elegant streets of white-yellow limestone houses, several storeys high, and coloured, glazed-in balconies jutting out over the street. From these windows, the gentry of old could survey the passers-by without suffering the sun and dust that would spoil their complexions and their clothes. Some of the buildings were a bit crumbling and old, but this made them more interesting to Frank's eyes. There were paved squares with cafes and bars, and the Upper Barrakka Gardens, planted with olive trees and flowering scented shrubs, overlooked the Grand Harbour with all its inlets. This was the

best vantage point from which to appreciate the sturdy fortifications of Valletta and the three cities on the opposite bank.
The cathedral, strangely named St John's Co-Cathedral, was a
plain-looking building on the outside, not a bit like Exeter, but
it was all gilt and marble inside, a glittering show of opulence and
arrogance on the part of the Grand Chambers of the Knights of
Order of St John, who had once ruled the islands. The paintings
and treasures had all been taken away for safety in case the place
was bombed.

He only knew what he'd read in the guidebook he'd bought the
last time they'd visited the city, about a month ago. He'd bought
a Maltese phrasebook too, thinking it'd be good to be able to
at least say 'hello' and 'goodbye', 'please' and 'thank you' to the
locals. This time, he wanted another look around, so he'd left the
others for a while in a bar down by the harbour, promising to
meet them again in a couple of hours.

He headed for the stone steps, at the foot of the bastion, passing an air-raid shelter carved into the foot of it. There were men
at work cutting out another in the rock a few hundred yards
from it. The tunnel of a disused railway had also been converted
to an air-raid shelter, and there were older caverns underneath,
according to the guidebook, once used to lodge or imprison
galley slaves. He gave a few pennies to some shoeless urchins who
were hanging about at the foot of the steps leading up to the top
of the walls of the fortified city.

Up high, he stood on the parapet of the Upper Barrakka Gardens, again gazing down on the waterways of the harbour, a
narrow entrance dominated by a promontory, with Fort St Elmo
on one side and the three inlets between the three cities, offering
anchorage for large numbers of ships. Once, it had been wooden
galleys, now there were grey warships, and this spectacular place
was the target of the enemy bombers. Already, there had been
some damage. Frank could see the fractured outlines of several

tall buildings in Senglea across the water and piles of rubble near the water's edge.

He made his way back to the Pjazza Kastilja, which was busy with civilians carrying gasmasks, going about their business, mingling with forces personnel, ARP wardens and gaggles of boy scouts hanging around the shelters. Quite a number of the shops were closed, with windows boarded up, their owners fled to the safety of the countryside. From here, he climbed down the many steps to the huge ditch at the foot of the great bastions and thence to the harbour to find the others he'd come with. Down by the waterside, it seemed remarkably normal. There were even a few fishermen landing baskets of crabs. Stone warehouses lined the harbour, their arched doorways boarded and padlocked. The bar had tables spilling onto the pavement, and he spotted his mates with some women at a table near the door.

'Here he is,' said Corporal Myles, looking up as Frank dodged his way through the tables towards them.

Their party included four young Englishwomen, probably from the offices of the Admiralty of the forces HQ nearby. Chalky and Coop were grinning with satisfaction at the arrangement.

'Makes a nice round number, girls, eh?' said Chalky.

The young women were smartly dressed, red-lipped, confident and smiling. Frank tried to smile back at them in a nonchalant way, but he knew he was blushing like a half-wit under their scrutiny.

'This is Nix. I mean, Frank Nixon,' said Corporal Myles helpfully before rattling off the girls' names: Doris, Vera, Lizzie and Myrtle. Frank couldn't be sure which was which, but the blonde one kept her smiling eyes fixed on him for a few moments.

'Your round, Nix,' said Coop with a grin, holding up his glass.

Frank went to the bar and edged his way in amongst the others waiting to be served. They'd fixed themselves up nicely with pretty girls for the evening. What would it be, drinking and dancing, a bit of a snog in the pictures or more? He was glad of this chance for an enjoyable distraction, but at the same time, he felt nervous and hoped that he wouldn't make a fool of himself with one of these bold-looking office girls. He'd never really known any women at all, apart from the matron of St Augustine's, but she didn't count, and the whore in Plymouth, but she didn't either. He had to admit to himself, as he watched the barman pour a stream of yellow beer from a bottle, that there was really only one woman he would like to get to know, and that was the woman in Naxxar. He didn't know why. She was married and foreign, for God's sake. Perhaps it was the way she looked, beautiful but lonely, and she was kind too. But this was just his hare-brained imagination again, thinking of the impossible.

He wondered what would have happened if he'd gone with Lieutenant Chambers to the cave. The officer wasn't a queer, surely. It was just the lads' banter because he was a bit of an eccentric. Frank believed that the lieutenant's curiosity about the cave discovery was based on his genuine interest and not any mucky motive. He appreciated the man's attitude too: not patronising nor dismissive of his ignorance. Lieutenant Chambers had made it seem that someone like him could still learn things, even now. He'd lent him a book and expected him to read it. Frank would go and find the officer the next time he was off duty, return the book, tell him how much he'd enjoyed it and ask, if he dared, if he could borrow another.

The barman was just pouring out two glasses of port and lemon when the howl of the air-raid siren deafened them all, a horrible wailing, which set a few people fleeing immediately for the door, the barman shaking his head.

Someone beside Frank muttered in an Australian accent, 'Oh buggery, buggery. Here we go again.'

Chapter 3

September 1940

T he sky was stark blue and the heat belted down, roasting them like meat on a spit. Sweat stung Frank's eyes, dripped from his nose and fell in drops on the ground. He thrust the shovel into the mound of rubble, broken yellow rock and lumps of tarmac again. He carried the shovelful two or three yards to the crater the bomb had made, a ragged-edged hollow in the runway. Chalky was following behind with his load. At another hole about a hundred yards away, the rest of the platoon was working. On the far side, Frank could make out the figures of RAF ground crew, beavering away fixing up the aircraft in the pens. All afternoon in the heat and they were ready to drop, with no sign that Sergeant Campbell was going to call it a day. At least there had been no more raids and the runway was just about fit for aircraft again.

At last they heard the sergeant shouting, and Frank thwacked the back of the shovel onto the dusty rubble he'd just packed into the hole and looked up. The sergeant was waving to them.

'Thank Christ for that,' said Chalky, ducking his head to scrape his brow on his shirt sleeve, his eyes red, irritated by the dust.

They shouldered their shovels and trekked across the expanse of the airstrip.

'God, what I'd give for a bloody beer,' Chalky said.

The inside of Frank's mouth was dry as sandpaper. 'Makes you wish you were back at the sea, doesn't it?' he said, thinking of their last posting on the coastal defences on the Marfa Peninsula, with the sea all around them.

Their platoon had been sent for a week to the north coast, with little to do but stare at the sea, bat off sandflies and mosquitoes and play cards. The islands of Comino and Gozo lay over a narrow strip of water, and they watched the odd fishing boat venturing out, a dangerous enterprise because of mines. No swimming was allowed. The beaches and shores were defaced with barbed wire barricades and concrete pillboxes, the whole coast bristling with defences. Frank and Chalky had climbed to the top of a stone watchtower. Frank didn't know how old it was, probably built by the knights in the sixteenth century or later. He'd wondered how many others had stood watch here on this cliff, even before the tower was built, spying out for ships bringing corn, armed galleys of pirates, invaders, friends and foes. Perhaps some Arab spotted the fleet of Roger the Norman from here, coming to reclaim the island for the Christians, or an eagle-eyed bloke first saw the Turkish warships coming and lit a beacon to signal to the fortresses. Now they, the British forces, centuries later, scanned the skies for bombers, and some folk said Mussolini was planning an invasion.

Frank had finished the second book, about the history of the Mediterranean, which Lieutenant Chambers had lent him, and he was eager for more. There had been no opportunity to see the officer, however, because of their deployment on the coast. But now they were back patching up bomb damage and based at St Andrew's Barracks again, there might be a chance to do some exploring on the island, even go and look for the cave on one of his leave days.

After marching the fifteen miles from the airfield on the most direct inland route, they reached the barracks by evening. Washed, fed and considerably recovered, Frank and the others were smoking and playing cards in the mess room when Corporal Myles came in with a murderous look.

'Christ, what is it now?' muttered Coop.

'No leave tomorrow, lads,' said Corporal Myles grimly.

'Fuck me,' said Chalky.

'No thanks,' said the corporal. 'Shut up and listen. We've got to help with unloading and delivering fuel.'

'Running a ruddy delivery service now, are we?' said Chalky.

'Shut it. I wanted a bloody day off too. We've got to go down to the docks at Vittoriosa, pick up some aviation fuel and take it to some caves or other in the south.'

'Caves?' said Coop, then with a jab at Frank's ribs. 'Caves. Did you hear that, Nix?'

'What are they called?' said Frank, ignoring Coop's banter.

'I don't bleeding know,' said the corporal, stamping off to the bunkhouse.

Just before dawn the next day, Myles' and Marshall's sections of the platoon loaded themselves into two lorries in a convoy of eight for the docks. They set off in the semi darkness to reach the port before any early morning raids. It was the Italians' strategy to bomb merchantmen unloading in the harbour. Ten stevedores had been killed the previous week in Kalkara Creek, working on a merchant vessel.

The truck rattled along the road, passing what used to be the Marsa racetrack, now an army camp filled with huts and tents for the Queen's Own West Kents, who were billeted there. Approaching via a road that ran south of the creeks of the Grand Harbour where the naval dockyards, ship repair yards and wharves lay, they saw some bomb damage. A whole street of buildings reduced to piles of stone blocks and rubble. This area had been the worst hit so far, and there had been some civilian casualties. But in spite of this, the Italians had not stopped the convoys getting through bringing in vital supplies. Even in times of peace, the island's population couldn't support itself, Frank knew from his reading. The Maltese had always needed necessities shipped in from elsewhere. Just a little speck in the Mediterranean, at the mercy of its neighbours, vulnerable to its enemies. This was not a comfortable thought.

They soon reached a row of large warehouses within sight of Vittoriosa. It was light when the first truck pulled up close to the open doorway of one of the warehouses, where two soldiers were on guard. The jeep at the front of the convoy halted, and the trucks drew up in a line behind it. One of the officers at the front was Lieutenant Chambers. He was speaking to another officer, who had just emerged from the doorway. The orders came down for them all to line up at the door of the warehouse. Looking in, they saw the task ahead: mountains of jerry cans piled high, all to be carried to the lorries. First, they tried the human chain method and filled the first two trucks, then resorted to two cans per man, running back and forth. Either way, it was tedious and tiring work, but Frank didn't mind, as he was thinking about their destination, these caves that were going to be used for storage. They'd have to be pretty big to take all this fuel.

The journey to the deposit point was about nine miles, through a couple of villages, but along roads where the convoy was easily visible to any half-decent bomber pilot. Frank and Coop exchanged no words. This was no time for talk, the air tight as a drawn bowstring as they listened for aircraft above. But there was only the growl of the vehicles' engines, the judder of the truck, the rasping of tyres on the dirt road. Frank thought he heard a collective sigh of relief as the convoy finally halted at the end of a long track, down which some civilians were trailing, laden with their belongings.

'What in hell's going on?' said Coop as he and Frank jumped down.

They looked up towards the head of the line of trucks, where an officer was standing in conversation with their platoon sergeant, Jock Campbell, and a group of civilians in front of a two-storey, flat-roofed stone building. Voices were raised in argument, women crying and others talking in Maltese. Frank and Coop joined Corporal Myles, Chalky and Farley, who had just climbed out of the truck in front, and they approached the building to get a better view of the altercation. A sign on the wall was just visible, and Frank squinted at it, reading the words, 'Ghar Dalam Cave and Museum', then moved closer to hear what was going on.

Lieutenant Chambers was surrounded by a group of civilians, mainly women. He was holding up his hands in a gesture of puzzled apology.

'Look, I'm frightfully sorry,' he was saying. 'You should have been informed by the authorities. The caves and the museum building have been requisitioned.'

A man came out of the doorway of the building and, frowning at the scene before him, hurried towards the group.

'I am the curator of the museum. These people are refugees. They were brought here from Birgu. Their homes were destroyed in the bombing of the docks. They were told nothing about moving out. I was not happy about them being here in the first place, but what else could we do?'

Lieutenant Chambers shook his head. 'I'm terribly sorry, but we have orders to store this fuel here. We've just brought it from the port, and we were told the evacuees would be gone.'

One of the women set up a wailing cry and was joined by a chorus of squeals from the children.

'Oh, good Lord,' said the lieutenant, his face reddening. 'Look here, my men will help you people to carry out your belongings.

Then, when they've unloaded the trucks, they'll take anyone where they need to go to find alternative shelter. It's difficult, I know, but these times are hard for all of us.'

The museum curator spoke rapidly to the women, whose protests fell away into looks of miserable acceptance. Sergeant Campbell turned and shouted out the orders down the line of men standing by the trucks.

'Come on, you lot. Help these people take their stuff out of the building and move them over to the side of the road, out of the way. Myles, get one of your men to go round these folk and find out who needs taking where.'

Corporal Myles looked at Frank. 'Nixon, you do it. See how many of them want a lift.'

Frank was startled at the order, unsure for a moment of how to go about the task. 'Have you got a bit of paper, Corp?' he asked.

'No, course I bloody haven't. Go in there and ask that museum bloke.'

The soldiers and civilians had now created a chaos of milling bodies in front of the building and alongside the line of lorries.

'You buggers, get away from those trucks if you're going to smoke, for Christ's sake,' yelled the sergeant to a group of soldiers who were lighting up close by.

Frank pushed his way through the clutch of people near the entrance to the museum and saw Lieutenant Chambers disappearing ahead of him. Inside was a central hallway, though it was not roomy and was full of refugees with suitcases and bedding, shoving and pushing to make their exit, while others were gathering up their belongings from beneath empty museum display cabinets pushed against the walls. The lieutenant was talking to the museum curator, the two of them hemmed in the corner by the crowd of civilians.

'Excuse me, sir,' Frank called over the heads.

'Ah, Nixon,' he said, beaming, 'this is a piece of luck, isn't it? Getting a free look at the Ghar Dalam cave. This is one of the most important archaeological sites in Europe.'

Frank could hardly believe that amidst this chaos, the officer was thinking about visiting a museum. He must be joking, surely, but then again, he didn't behave like a normal army officer.

'But, sir, I've got to—'

'Yes, yes, I know, but that can wait a bit,' said Lieutenant Chambers, his face eager, like a kid with a lolly. 'We can't do anything until all these people have got out of the place, and Mr Attard here has said he'll show us. Come on. You're interested in caves, aren't you?'

The curator led the way, pushing through the thinning crowd into a corridor beyond the central hall. This area contained more empty glass cases and a few remnants of the refugees' belongings on the floor. Beyond the empty exhibition cases was a heavy door. The man unlocked it with a huge key and swung the door open into the darkness beyond. Frank followed the lieutenant and, on taking only a few steps into the murk, smelt the same chilly dampness of his own limestone cave. Their guide paused and struck a match to light a kerosene lamp, which was sitting in a niche in the rock wall.

The passage widened further along, and there were great pale cones from the roof of the cave, hanging down, candle-like, liquid in appearance though they were solid or made of rock. Frank stared, marvelling.

'This was formed in the Pleistocene period,' said the guide, holding up the lamp. 'The Ice Age.'

'The Ice Age?' said Frank, amazed, his eyes travelling around the curves of the roof and walls. The formations were like ice cream smoothed by a giant tongue.

'130,000 years ago,' said Lieutenant Chambers. 'Marvellous, isn't it? And fossils of prehistoric creatures were found here too.'

'We've put them in storage, out of sight,' said the curator, frowning. 'We could not leave our pygmy elephant and dwarf hippopotamus bones on display. Not now.'

'Shame we can't see them,' said the lieutenant, looking up at the ceiling. 'But never mind. Aren't these stalactites splendid, Nixon?'

'Where did they come from, sir?'

'Limestone deposits over thousands of years.'

'And the animals—how did they get in here?'

'It wasn't always a cave,' said the guide. 'But, gentlemen, I'm afraid that's all I can show you. I've got to preserve the oil in the lamp and I must lock up and go back to make sure all the people have gone.'

'Yes, of course. It's very good of you to show us even this,' said the officer.

Frank stared at the walls and upper surfaces, still astonished at the sight, as they made their way out of the cave, along the passage, through the door and back to the outside world.

'What do you think, then, Nixon?' said Lieutenant Chambers.

'Amazing,' said Frank, 'but not really like the cave I found.'

'Different age, I should think. By the way, I didn't manage to find your cave after all. We must get round to it sometime. Yours might have been some sort of shelter, perhaps made out of an existing cavern. This limestone is soft enough to carve, even with flint tools. People are hacking out air-raid shelters in all sorts of places at the moment, and jolly good shelters they make too.'

The officer's eyes were alight with enthusiasm, but his expression changed when someone called across to him from the door of the museum.

'Sir, we're ready to bring the stuff in. Shall I get them to start?' said the sergeant.

'Yes, yes, go ahead,' said Lieutenant Chambers irritably, as though he'd been interrupted in the middle of a tasty dinner.

'Sir, sorry, sir,' said Frank, suddenly remembering his mission. 'Do you have a bit of paper and a pencil or something I could borrow?'

The officer plunged his hand into his pocket, rummaged for a moment, then pulled out a small notebook with a pencil attached. 'Borrow this, but mind you give it back,' he said, distracted now by his pressing duty. He strode out of the door.

Frank was grateful but aware that he should have started his task by now and that Corporal Myles would likely give him a hard time for delaying. He hurried to catch up with a middle-aged woman and a young girl who were on their way out of the building. They shook their heads dumbly at him when he asked if they needed transport anywhere and so he moved on to some others. They mostly spoke some English but just said the name of the town or village they wanted to go to. Struggling with the spelling, Frank sometimes had to ask them to write down the name and pronounce it for him—Mqabba, Qormi, Mgarr, Xemxija—though he knew some of them through field exercises and postings they'd done on the island. Next, he had to organise different trucks to go in different directions, so he begged a map from one of the drivers and allocated vehicles for a number of destinations, noting these in the book. There were only a few empty pages left in the lieutenant's notebook, the rest being filled with tiny handwritten notes and neat pencil drawings of buildings and coastal landscapes. Frank studied them with admiration.

The soldiers were carrying the fuel cans in twos into the museum and so Frank moved down the length of the queue of lorries and found another group of civilians sheltering under a clump of olive trees, a little away from the roadway. An old woman cried when Frank spoke to her, pouring out her story in garbled English. Her house in Senglea had been destroyed and the whole street gone. God had saved her but not her young neighbour and her children. The husband had come back from work at the docks and found them all buried under the stones.

Frank stood listening, feeling awkward but moved by sharing in her distress. He waited with her until she took up her rosary and started praying. Some others crossed themselves and kept looking up at the sky. If Frank had believed in praying, he would have joined them, but he'd stopped all that stuff when he was about eight years old because it didn't work. His mother never came back for him. The Maltese seemed to get something out of it, but they were Catholics and signs of their faith were everywhere on this island, in their churches, wayside shrines and holy statues. He admired the strength of their belief, envied it too in a way.

He hurried back into the museum, in search of any other civilians he might have missed, and saw that the curator had swung open the heavy door into the cave now to accommodate more of the fuel cans. They were soon nearly ready and loaded, and Frank ran back to find Corporal Myles to tell him about the destinations of the refugees.

'Nice work, professor,' said the corporal, listening to Frank's explanations and looking at the lists he'd made.

'Better watch out, Corp,' Chalky said with a grin. 'He'll have your stripe next.'

Frank and Chalky boarded the truck with a couple of very small boys, their mother, an old man and another woman with a tiny baby tied round her body with a shawl, heading for Mosta. They talked quietly to each other and seemed grateful for the lift.

'You beat Hitler and Il Duce?' said the old man to Frank.

'We'll try,' he said, and the two wide-eyed little boys stared at him and Chalky. One of these toddlers, crouched on the floor of the truck, stretched out his hand and started to play with Frank's bootlaces.

The baby grizzled, and its mother rocked it, whispering with her lips close to its face.

There were two other trucks in front on this route, with Corporal Myles, Coop and Farley in the one ahead of them. They'd be turning off to Mdina soon, but just as the lorries approached the crossroads, they heard a siren from somewhere over on the east.

'Hell's teeth,' said Chalky. 'No bloody shelters around here. Any ditches?'

Frank leaned over the side of the truck and peered along the road, seeing the leading vehicles ahead of them, the one in front about fifty yards away. It pulled in and stopped. The driver of their own vehicle braked hard, and it scraped to a halt.

'Quick, let's get out and take cover,' said Frank, grabbing one small boy under each arm. He jumped down, out of the back, onto the roadway as one of the children squawked with glee.

Chalky and the driver rushed to haul the others off, the boys' mother whimpering a stream of prayers, followed by the woman with the baby, with the old man coming last, his legs buckling as his feet hit the ground.

'Come on, down in the ditch,' Frank yelled, still clutching the children under his arms, plunging into the hollow.

There was a whistling, and he didn't dare look up, but he saw that at least everyone had made it into the ditch.

'*Down*. Keep your heads down,' he called to them.

The whistling intensified, then, with a terrible bang, something punctured the ground ahead of them. The truck in front exploded like a rocket of yellow fire, spurting black shards in all directions. Pieces of metal leapt through the smoke above their heads and a rain of rubble, stones and splinters spattered and hailed onto them. The praying woman, only yards from Frank, shrieked, speared in the shoulder by a spike of shrapnel. Frank saw the blood fly out of her in a straight jet. Beyond the screaming

38

outline of her head was the burning truck, red and yellow flame and black smoke bulging out in a cloud.

The children were whimpering in Frank's arms, and he knew he had to release them, but he felt paralysed. He saw the shape of their driver lying motionless in the ditch and Chalky crawling towards the wounded woman, who was howling in pain. Frank willed himself to move and loosened the boys, pushing them behind him and staggering to his feet, feeling blood on his face. He scrambled out of the ditch, ran to the lorry and dived into the driver's cab, grabbing for the first aid box and pulling the fire extinguisher from its clip. Bolting back to Chalky and the woman, he saw that she had, mercifully, fainted. The other civilians were hunched in the ditch, bound together in mute terror. Chalky took the box and snapped it open. Frank leapt up again, sprinting back towards the burning truck with the fire extinguisher, a pathetic little cylinder, squirting foam, which fizzled in a limp spurt against the flames. But it created a hole through which he glimpsed the dark shapes of the cindered bodies: Corporal Myles, Farley and Coop, along with five civilians.

CHAPTER 4

F rank was on his own, driving the lorry, crawling through the blackness of the countryside, with the faintest light of the moon his only hope of not ditching the vehicle, trying to remind himself to breathe. In the urgency of the aftermath, someone had told him to bring the truck back to the barracks. Two lorries from the convoy had returned to the burnt-out wreck, one to rush the injured woman to hospital—along with their own driver, who had a deep shrapnel wound—and the other to take the remaining civilians. Frank gripped the wheel, felt the bile rising in his throat and knew he was going to throw up again.

He was coming to a village on rising ground, the pale shapes of buildings on either side of a narrow street. He must keep on. He hit a boulder, which bounced the lorry to the right, clutched tight to the wheel and managed to steer it straight again, just in time to pass through between the houses. His stomach heaved. He'd get out of the village, away from the houses, then he'd have to stop. Slowing to steer round a bend in the road, he realised he knew the place. It was Naxxar. His hands were stuck to the wheel. He'd have to go on just a bit further, get out on to the open road.

But he couldn't, not with the image of those blackened bodies springing into his head. He jammed his foot on the brake, fell out of the cab and onto the road. He staggered over to the side, where he vomited painfully, his whole body shaking. On his knees, bent double, he wept, squeezing his eyes shut against the tears.

A soft shuffling noise, footsteps on the road, told him that there was someone coming. There was a swaying light too. *Christ in heaven, make me move*, he said to himself, but it was no good. He couldn't even turn his head to look.

'Can I help you?' said a woman's voice.

She could only have been a few yards from him, and he dared himself to glance to one side, seeing a black skirt or dress, slim legs and feeling a touch upon his shoulder. He wanted to rise from his knees, but couldn't make his body work. He couldn't stay like this, not answering the woman's question. He had to say something or do something.

The woman's lamplight turned a patch of the roadway pale in front of him. 'Come to my house,' she said. 'Rest and have water. You will be better.'

Frank shivered, his brow stinging with icy sweat, but he managed to stand up and turn towards the woman holding the lantern. She had taken a few steps away from him, and he saw her figure, small and slight, her head covered by a dark shawl. He knew she was the one who had helped him before. Had she really invited him to go into her house? On this dark night? She turned back to see if he was following her.

His stomach had settled a little and the sick sweat of his face was drying as he went after the woman to her gate and then across the small yard towards the door of the house, which stood open. He followed her into a dimly lit kitchen with a table in the centre. The only light was from a candle that stood on a stone shelf jutting from the wall, beside which was a chair occupied by a dark, motionless figure. Frank did not want to peer too deliberately, so flicked his eyes back to the woman, who gestured that he should sit at the table.

'Tea? I will make you tea?'

'Yes, thanks,' he said, hesitating by the chair she had indicated.

He lowered himself onto it, aware of the strangeness of what he was doing but feeling calmer now in this quiet place. The sound of water splashing from a jug, the clunk of the kettle lid, the faint throaty breathing from the seated figure in the chair were comforting.

The woman said nothing while she gathered two cups and a tin from the shelf, placing the kettle on top of the meagre flame of a small tin kerosene stove.

'The bombs. I heard the bombs far away,' she said. 'They killed some people?'

She moved to the table and stood opposite Frank, looking at him in the dim light. Her face appeared smooth and serene, like one of those holy statues or paintings of the Madonna he'd seen in the cathedral. She was hardly more real to Frank in his numbed state than a painting, and he wondered if in fact he was dead or semi-conscious. With an effort, he made himself speak, his voice coming out surprisingly normal and dull.

'One of the trucks,' he said, feeling the phlegm gathering in his throat.

'Soldiers? Your friends?'

Her voice was soft, accented, and Frank feared he might weep again because of her gentle manner. He swallowed hard. She sat down at the table, reaching for his right hand, which lay, he noticed, twitching like a dying animal on the tabletop. Her grip was firm, the skin rough and, in this hold, he was steadied. He stared at her dark eyes and felt a leap of gratitude. They sat like this in silence for some minutes, Frank unable to hold her gaze for long, bowing his head but feeling his control of himself gradually return. His breathing had steadied and his chest was losing its tightness.

The kettle whistled, and the figure in the corner chair groaned and shifted.

The woman released Frank's hand. 'Grandmother will wake now. She will not miss a cup of tea.'

Frank thought he saw a smile, heard the tone of her voice lift a little too, and he wished he could see her face more clearly than the poor light allowed. She rose and poured the boiling water into a teapot, bringing it to the table, saying something in Maltese to the moribund figure of her grandmother, who replied quietly and drowsily.

'You like sugar?' she asked Frank. 'My husband liked many spoons of sugar in his tea, to give him strength, he said.'

'Yes, sugar, please, I mean if you've got enough,' said Frank, noting the mention of her husband so clearly in the past tense. He focused on the stream of liquid splashing into the cups, feeling a desperate thirst come over him all of a sudden.

'He was in the Royal Navy,' she said as she poured another cup of tea. 'His ship was sunk in the north, your North Sea, last year.'

Frank, startled by his ignorance that Maltese men served in the British Royal Navy, blushed, glad that the light was too dim for her to see. He knew that the Royal Malta Artillery manned nearly all the defences of the island and that the King's Own Malta Regiment had recently been recruiting men of the islands, but he hadn't realised about the navy.

'I'm sorry,' said Frank. His tone sounded lame and useless, though his pity was painfully real inside.

The woman went to her grandmother, who was heaving herself into a more upright position in her chair.

'Grazzi, Manwela,' Frank thought he heard the old woman say, though he was not sure.

The tea was sweet and delicious. He had never drunk anything so gratefully and with such relief as this. The sweetness softened his mouth, seemed almost to reach the aching fatigue in his bones. He tried not to drain it too quickly, but he wanted more, wanted her to sit by him again, wanted her to touch his hand.

43

'Your children? You've got kids?' he said, feeling an urgency to prolong this time with her.

She left the old woman's side and returned to the table, sat down and drew her cup of tea in both of her hands towards her. 'Yes, I have my sons, David and Joseph. They are good boys and help me. But they are only little boys. I have my sister and her family nearby too and good neighbours.'

Frank wanted to ask her more, to know her name, to offer his help, his rations, anything, however pointless, just so that he had a reason to stay. Was it rude to ask her about herself? He drank the last of his tea, knowing that he would have to go soon. The lorry was outside. Lieutenant Chambers might have heard about the incident by now. They might even have sent someone out in search of him. He went to stand up, but the woman had already left the table and had moved closer to him.

'What is your name?'

Frank was thrilled that she was bothering to ask him. 'Private Francis Nixon, 15687, of the Second Battalion Devonshire Regiment.'

He bolted it out, an automatic response, and immediately felt a fool. She wasn't a sergeant major; she was hardly going to be impressed by his military status. He found himself squirming like the frightened six-year-old he'd once been, standing in the headmaster's office that first day at St Augustine's, when he'd realised that he was never going home again.

'Some people call me Frank,' he said, as a weak afterthought.

'You have a family, a wife and children, at home in England?'

He shook his head. 'No, there's no one. My mum—my mother—she's dead, and I never had... never knew my father. I was brought up in a children's home.'

Why was he telling her this? He sounded pathetic and feeble. He saw in the dull light that she was frowning.

'That is very sad you have no family,' she said. 'I know what it is like to lose parents. I will pray for you.'

He didn't know whether this was something he should thank her for or whether she thought he was doomed or cursed in some way. He'd never had a lot of time for God or religion. He didn't find it comforting in the least to think that his fate was in God's hands. If this were true, then God was a bastard to chuck people to their deaths whenever he felt like it, little children even, like those poor kids in the truck, like the corporal, Coop and Farley. But this woman obviously believed in all that stuff, and her sympathy didn't seem phony to him.

'Thanks for the tea and...' He couldn't find what he wanted to say; instead, he blurted out, 'What's your name?'

She smiled again. He could see her smile now, he was sure, even though the light was so poor. The old woman in the corner was making sucking noises as she drank her tea.

'I am Manwela Vassallo,' she said, 'and I am very pleased to meet you, Frank.'

Frank woke the next day, discovering that he had lain in his clothes all night, hardly remembering how he'd made it back to barracks. He pulled down the blanket and peered around the bunkhouse. There was a quiet gloom, almost tangible, like a fog hanging in the air. Some men were dressing on the far side, and Frank glimpsed the three empty beds of his dead mates, then the humped form of Chalky, still lying there. It was late—eight o'clock by his watch. They should've been up long ago, but perhaps it would be different this morning because of what had happened yesterday. It was. Lieutenant Chambers was coming in, and Frank, with an effort, shot his legs out of the bed and stood up in his crumpled khakis, feeling gritty inside and out. His body was stiff all over, and he felt a tightness and tender swelling in his right arm and on his cheekbone.

The officer made his way down the row between the beds towards him. 'At ease, Nixon.'

'Sir,' said Frank, seeing that the officer was holding his cap in his hand.

'Bloody awful luck,' the lieutenant said. 'They were good men.'

Frank nodded as Chalky's face emerged from the blankets on his bed, behind where the officer was standing.

'Do their folks know?' asked Frank.

'I'll write to their families today. Will you and White collect all their effects? Can you do that, Nixon, and bring them to Sergeant Cox?'

'Yes, sir.'

The lieutenant paused, eyeing Frank in a different way, as though to mark his change of topic. 'That cave you found, Nixon, we'll get back there some day and have a proper look. The more I think about it, the more I'm convinced it's Roman or Byzantine. The writing may be in Greek. I've been reading about the burial chambers and catacombs. Anyway, you and White have a day's leave. Go off and relax somewhere for a bit. Then report to Captain Miller about your promotion.'

'Sir?' Frank was bemused at first but quickly realised it could only mean he was to be given a stripe.

'You've earned it, Nixon. It's not because of... you know. Congratulations are due, I think,' said the lieutenant solemnly.

The officer hovered, awkwardly fingering the brim of his cap, and his continued presence triggered a reminder in Frank's mind: the matter of books and the library he'd seen in Valletta.

'Sir, I'd like to read more, you know, about the history of Malta. I saw a library—'

'Closed, I'm afraid.' Lieutenant Chambers shook his head. 'I wanted to borrow some material too, but it's all been locked down and the most precious items removed. No one's allowed to borrow a thing now. Pity. But look here, I've got a couple more books that might interest you. Then when you've read those, I don't know what to suggest. I'll ask around. Even the chap who owns the bookshop's closed up. Rum deal really for those of us of a bookish disposition, don't you think?'

Frank felt himself colouring. Lieutenant Chambers was talking to him like he was educated or something.

'Drop over later and I'll lend you the other ones,' said the officer. 'There's a good one about the siege of Malta by the Turks in the sixteenth century. An amazing feat of endurance, that was.'

'I need a bloody drink,' Chalky said after he and Frank had delivered the three kitbags of belongings to the sergeant. His face was true to his name.

'Let's go to Valletta,' said Frank.

'Yeah and get pie-eyed.'

They joined two others from Marshall's section, Williams and Bunter, on the road to the city. At Pieta, they passed a few wrecked houses, their white stones blackened, and as they came to Floriana, outside the city's main fortifications, they saw worse.

Frank thought of Manwela and her house in the village of Naxxar. He still had peculiar doubts about whether his encounter with her had really happened; however, he could, with almost no effort, remember the taste of the hot, sweet tea, the grip of her hand on his and the holy look of her face. He hoped they would be sent on more repair jobs to the airfield at Ta Qali, which was quite close to Naxxar. He had to see her again. Her village might be more vulnerable to attack than others, being on the way back for the bombers and up on a ridge, he thought in a moment of unease, but it was not as dangerous as the city, surely. This island was so blinking small, there was simply no place where you wouldn't be bombed.

'Fancy a game of footy?' asked Williams, a sturdy type with a blunt head and stick-out ears. 'The Malta boys, the Royal Malta

Artillery, want to take us on. Sunday afternoon? Do you fancy it, any of you?'

'Yes,' said Frank, 'all right, if we're off duty.'

'Sure you don't want to read a book instead?' said Chalky with a grin.

'Shut it,' said Frank. 'I could run rings round you anyway, you donkey.'

'In your dreams. I was on a trial for Plymouth Argyle Colts once.' Chalky took aim with his right foot at a loose stone on the road and kicked up a shower of dust.

'Bunter did a trial for Leyton Orient, didn't you, mate?' said Williams to his companion in a show of one-upmanship.

Bunter, with the build of a light-weight boxer, nodded and grinned.

Frank was keener, if he was honest, to get started on the books that Lieutenant Chambers had lent him than to play football, but he was glad to see Chalky more cheerful and didn't mind the idea of a bit of running about.

In the centre of Valletta, more buildings had been reduced to stone skeletons and mounds of rubble had been bulldozed up at the side of the street. But people were out and about their business as usual, it seemed. Frank and his companions passed several busy cafes and bars on Triq San Pawl as they returned to the one on the quay, where they had last gone with the corporal, Coop and Farley. Frank was uneasy about revisiting the place, but Chalky pushed ahead, down the steep steps, and the rest of them followed. The four girls were there again, too, as though they'd been waiting. Frank caught the eye of one, the one called Myrtle.

'These your girls, then?' Williams asked Frank.

'No, just had a few drinks with them the last time,' he said, 'then there was a raid, so that was that.'

Another of the women, the tall redhead, Vera, stood up as soon as she saw them approaching and waved in an exaggerated gesture of welcome.

'Is that the one I'm getting,' murmured Bunter in Frank's ear.

'What have you done with Myles and the others?' called Vera. She sank back down into her seat, however, when she saw Frank and Chalky's expressions, the other girls exchanging embarrassed glances.

The men pulled up chairs and sat down in an uncomfortable quietness. Williams coughed, introduced himself and Bunter, then, in a comradely gesture, offered to go for the drinks.

'When was it?' Vera asked Frank and Chalky.

'Yesterday.' Frank felt the phlegm in his throat, not looking at her.

'Oh God.' Vera clutched her chest. 'All of them?'

Frank nodded.

'You never know when it's going to happen, do you?' Doris said as Chalky struck a match and lit her cigarette.

Frank stared out across the harbour at the dockyards opposite, watching the small figures of men at work on the deck of a ship, seeing the barrels of the anti-aircraft guns sloping up at the sky. He sensed the shared release of tension when Williams returned with a tray of drinks.

'In memory of Myles, Coop and Farley. Brave boys. May they rest in peace,' Myrtle said in a steady and solemn voice.

Frank was grateful to the woman for taking charge.

'I spent all night in a shelter last week,' said Doris, her mouth in a mock pout. She was a chatty girl with a round face and generously daubed red lips. 'It was pretty grim, I can tell you. Cram-packed full and the smell of you-know-what and the noise, then there weren't any raids after all. Next time, I'm going to take my chances in my room and just go into the shelter if it gets really bad.'

'Those big ones are the worst,' said Myrtle. 'The one under the walls. It used to be tunnels or something.'

Frank thought he'd read about these. 'They'll be the tunnels and chambers dug out by the Knights of St John in the sixteenth century or before.'

'Oh God, here he goes,' said Chalky, laughing. 'It's the professor. Excuse him, girls. He can't help it. We're in for one of his lectures.'

Frank blushed when he noticed everyone's eyes on him.

'Really? You're never a professor. You're too young,' said Doris with a giggle. 'Professors have big, long beards and glasses, and you don't look any more than eighteen.'

'I'm nineteen.'

'Well, well, well,' she said, smiling, her fingers creeping over the table towards him. 'Tell us about the tunnels and the knights. I'd like a knight in shining armour to protect me.'

'Don't encourage him,' said Chalky, rolling his eyes.

Myrtle directed a frown at Chalky and Doris. 'Oh, do shut up. Some of us are interested.'

Frank scraped his boots on the ground under the table and looked down, wishing he'd kept his mouth shut. 'I don't know much about it, only what I've read in a book.'

'Well, it's more than he could do.' Williams jabbed Bunter in the ribs. 'He can't read, him.'

Frank looked back up in sympathy with the supposed illiterate. 'Those underground chambers were the quarters for the galley slaves. The knights had a huge fleet of ships.'

'Who were the slaves?' asked Myrtle.

'Anyone that was captured,' said Frank. 'The knights took prisoners—Muslims, Turks, Jews, anyone. They needed men to row their warships. And it worked the other way round too. A Christian could end up a galley slave on a Turkish ship. The knights kept their slaves in the underground tunnels here, when they weren't chained on the ships, having the hell beaten out of them.'

'Just like the British army, then,' said Chalky with a laugh.

'I met a WRAF last week who spends her whole time underground in an office, the operations room. Terrible. I couldn't stand it,' said Vera.

'Me neither,' agreed Doris as the yowl of a siren started up.

Myrtle sighed. 'Bloody hell.'

Under different circumstances, Frank would have been glad to go into the shelter, to examine one of the ancient tunnels. But now he and the other soldiers were helping to wave civilians from the streets towards the door at the foot of the bastion. This had formed part of the Knights' fortress all those centuries ago. And here it was again, ready to take another bombardment, Frank thought, with admiration for those sixteenth century engineers who'd built the fortifications and the warriors who'd defended them. The siren still wailed all around and the crack-cracking of anti-aircraft fire from the harbour had started up.

'Hurry up. Get a move on,' shouted a warden as people filed in, many looking more bored and irritated than frightened.

Frank helped an old woman in with her bags, a group of boy scouts came scurrying along with a pram and Chalky scooped up an escaping toddler, handing him to his mother. Frank and his companions squeezed themselves in last as a warden closed the door.

The roof of the shelter was about a foot above Frank's head, and in a niche in the wall, near the entrance, stood a small holy statue, the Virgin Mary and a candle burning, its flame flickering with the movement of bodies passing. It was a tight fit, so Frank and a few others moved deeper into the cave, back to where some new work of excavation had recently begun taking place to enlarge the shelter. Two kerosene lamps glowed dimly near the entrance door, but it was gloomily unlit at this rear end. There was a pile of stones, crumbled and heaped up, with some picks and shovels lying around where the tunnellers had left them. A smooth ledge of rock ran along one side, forming a long bench. Frank sat down on it and listened as the bombardment began outside.

Even deep in the rock, he could feel the shudder of the ground, hear the thunder of falling buildings, the manic rattle of anti-aircraft fire. Some people stood huddled together. The Maltese civilians were praying quietly, some mouthing the Rosary in audible whispers. Dust and grit powdered the air, dropping in sporadic showers from the roof. The light of one of the lamps sputtered, then went out, and someone spoke insistently in rapid Maltese. The back of the shelter, where Frank was sitting on the stone bench, fell into a deeper murkiness, and the people standing nearest to him edged away towards the remaining light, leaving him alone.

He leaned his head back, feeling the smooth stone of the rock beneath him, running his hand over a surface that had surely been crafted to serve as a sitting place many years or centuries ago. It was indented too by the bodies of generations of others, of slaves, who had sat festering here in the dark. Black hummocks of rubble lay at the back of the cave and the air was grey and damp. The shapes of the others, crowded together near the door, were silhouettes, outlined by the glow of the lamp and the small flame by the Virgin Mary.

Frank heard his own breathing, a strange sound, like a wheeze in his chest, though it seemed somehow apart from him, not of his body. He consciously steadied his inhalations and exhalations, feeling his lungs expand and shrink again. Another shuddering and a dull blast came from outside, but Frank detected a smaller, closer noise too, the repeated faint clang of hammer on metal. He looked around for the source of this sound, some child with a toy in the shelter perhaps, but it was too dark to see.

Then came a sigh, a waft of air and the rasp of dry breath close to his ear. He batted at it with his hand, thinking it a stray insect's buzz, but his hand touched something, a solid, fleshy mass, the sweating, naked shoulder and arm of someone sitting beside him, breathing hoarsely, moving the weight of a heavy body against him.

CHAPTER 5

MALTA, MAY 1565

I am a Christian... I am a Christian... Demetrios chanted in his head until the rhythm numbed his brain. *Mother Mary give me strength.* His hand flitted like an anxious bird, making the sign of the cross once, twice, though none would see in the darkness where they lay. He needed to tell them again, these knights fighting in the name of Christ, make them hear him, make them understand that he was not an infidel. All was blackness and heat in the cavern where he and the other enslaved ones lay. Was it a day ago when they were driven here? He could not be sure. He shifted and felt the pull of the shackle on his ankle, the chain taut where the next man had twisted in his sleep. Demetrios heard the rasp of his breathing, smelt the nauseous odours of their own filth.

Then someone was beating a drum in loud, dead blows, and a light came dancing, a torch flickering on the pale walls around him and over the shapes of bodies slumped, crooked, dozing or dead. A whip crack split the air, and his body clenched in readiness for a sharp cut, a searing burn, but not this time, and he thanked God for this deliverance.

'Get up, you infidel dogs.'

A slave master moved past, kicking at the limbs of those close to his feet. 'Sons of whores.'

Demetrios knew this insult in the many different tongues of their jailers and masters. Strange that 'infidel' was used by Christians too against those of the Mahometan faith, amongst whom he now languished in chains. This was not the moment, however, with the whipmaster alert and ready to pounce, to plead his case again, to tell of his devotion to Christ the Redeemer and Mother Mary, to recite the prayers that he knew by heart from his early childhood in the monastery.

He had the scars still from trying to speak of his faith after the bloody engagement at sea. The Knights of the Holy Order of St John had won the day against the Turks. They had dragged him, a galley slave, along with the surviving soldiers of the Sultan's army from the captured Ottoman ship. They had flogged and enslaved him, deaf to his entreaties that he was of their faith, branding him an infidel.

It was his lot to be a slave, he saw that now. He must suffer as the Lord Jesus Christ had suffered: pain, injustice, indignity, false accusations. Jesus had endured this with patience and had taught humility and forgiveness of his enemies. He, Demetrios, must follow his Lord's example.

He made to stand up, as the man on his left was already on his feet, tugging at his chain. Demetrios nudged the prone figure of his nearest companion, a hulking, scarred warrior of many battles, the one alongside whom he had toiled and sweated these past weeks but whose name he did not know. The man had spoken to him once or twice only, but Demetrios did not understand his Turkish tongue. The whip cracked again and met its target, the hard smack against flesh and they were on the move, rowing partners and galley slaves, infidels all in the eyes of their Christian captors. He was of no more worth or value than these Muslims, the sworn and hated enemies of Christendom.

The line of men, shackled by one leg and joined to a long chain, shambled along to the clanking of metal, a tuneless accompaniment to their progress out of the cave. More were following them, from darker depths into the startling sunlight, which made Demetrios' eyes smart.

The man in front of him held his face to the sun, closing his eyes. 'Allah, Allah,' he murmured and continued some chanting in his language.

The shout of the slave master dragged them all forward, and Demetrios felt his knee threaten to buckle beneath him, bruised and swollen, crushed in the chaos of battle when the galley had been taken. The ground beneath his feet, which he knew was solid, swayed and welled up with the imagined motion of the ship, just as the hypnotic agony of the thrust and pull of the oar still tightened the muscles of his arms.

They emerged from a pit into a scorching terrain of rock, of pale golden stone. In the distance stood a fortress built of the same stone with a tower pointing up from its centre, the pennant of the cross of the Order of the Knights of St John proudly fluttering. The walls of the fortress were straight and tall, and all along the base were the figures of men, like so many ants working. Lines of ox carts moved along with heavy loads over a network of pathways to and from the place.

Now they were being driven up a ridge towards the fortress slowly in their jangling train, with the slave master flailing at the rear of their line. Two horsemen, armoured and helmeted, with the red cross of their order bold across their tunics, rode by, dust rising from the hoofs in small clouds. A number of others followed behind. Then another rider, in extravagantly decorated armour, the general perhaps, came accompanied by a standard bearer. He reined his horse to a stop, speaking in a hard and rapid voice to the slave masters, pointing towards a deep trench where the multitude of labourers were hacking and pounding with picks and shovels some fifty paces before the fort.

The slave driver near to Demetrios turned to them and shouted, '*Sit*. Get down, you scum.'

Most of the men, stunned to hear such an order, halted, staring, and then, one by one, dropped to their knees or shuffled with their chains to sit upon the dusty ground, as Demetrios did. His swollen knee throbbed, so he rolled onto one side, feeling the sun beat down upon his skin. He wondered how long they would be let to lie here before starting their labours. The chief of these knights cast his eyes over them with a look of disgust. These preparations around the fortress spoke of an imminent threat, some fearsome attack to come, and it was clear that many hands were needed.

A man was driving a donkey cart alongside them, laden with several stone flagons and some baskets piled high with dried fish and lumps of bread.

'Eat, filth, and be ready for your labours, else you'll be thrown into the sea like dead dogs. Get up and fight for it.'

The slave master grinned at them and took a few steps back, his whip handle balanced on his shoulder. The men needed no exhortation at the sight of the food. Those at the end of the line had started scrambling to their feet, hauling others with them by their shackles, some falling over in their efforts to make for the cart and its burden. Demetrios, seized with a terrible hunger, surged forward but found himself propelled by the more powerful figure of the Turkish soldier, thickly bearded, black-eyed and desperate.

The slaves were a rabble around the donkey cart, causing the creature to buck and let out a hideous croaking bellow. In spite of the pain in his knee, Demetrios barged, jostled, pushed, then grappled with the multitude of grasping, desperate hands to pluck a piece of the grey bread and a fistful of hard scraps of fish. He clamped this treasure tightly, drew back and stuffed his mouth with it.

The pick struck rock again, the shock of it travelling up Demetrios's arms, loosening his grip. Closing his fists around the shaft again, his forearms tight with pain, he raised the implement for another blow. Close to him, lumps of rock, grit and dust arose as the heavy spikes flew up against the floor of the trench. It was by now about ten paces wide and in height rose above their heads. One man along the line keeled over in a faint, hitting his head upon a boulder as he descended, crumpling to the ground. A slave master leapt into the trench close to him and raised his whip, thrashing him until the sweat dripped from his face, but with no result except to draw much blood from the senseless man. Those chained to him paused in their labours, held by their shackles to his ankle. The slave master stopped too, to regain his breath, then in one smooth movement, unsheathed his sword and brought it down upon the man's ankle, severing the foot in a fountain of blood. The two others recoiled, one stumbling over, the other gripping his pick handle to remain upright. The slave driver shouted for another guard to help him haul the dying man out of the ditch while the others, heads down, kept to their digging.

Fatigue had reduced Demetrios to a state of half-awareness, worse even than all he had endured in the relentless agony of the Turkish galley. His eyes stung with dust and sweat, and he thought he must surely be losing his senses, for the pale walls of the fortress were changing colour before his eyes. They were turning pink, then, a moment later, staining to a darker redness. But it was the sunset, and he gave thanks to God. Nightfall would mean that they would have to stop. He would soon be able to lie down. Perhaps he would never rise again, a thought that lent him some small comfort.

But there was movement above their heads, on the land beyond the ditch. Horses were galloping, a drum was beating out its command for troops to rally and a trumpet bleated in urgent bursts. The slaves stopped, dropping their arms, releasing their grips on the digging tools. The slave masters too looked up, one clambering out of the ditch and joining his fellows with questioning shouts of, 'What's afoot?' Demetrios could not understand the words of all the exclamations, but knew well enough the sound of fear and hostility.

The Turkish slaves muttered and exchanged glances.

'*Up*. Up with you all!' shouted the slave master, flailing his whip down into the trench.

Demetrios scrambled with the others to the top of the trench. Squads of soldiers were running in tight formation towards the fortress; others teemed on the star-shaped bastions. High above on the ramparts of the fort were the barrels of guns pointing out to sea, their crews in position. The slaves stood, forgotten momentarily by their guards, as everyone stared at the lurid sky. The surface of the sea burned red in the sunset, a shining sheet on which, in the distance, like a huge swarm of bees, came a densely moving fleet of galleys.

'Holy Christ in heaven, they've come, the Ottomans,' said one of the soldiers, who now stood alongside the slave masters. 'Get these dogs back into their hole at once.'

This order led to a rapid rain of whipping, driving the slaves back down the ridge, towards the mouth of their cave prison. Demetrios stumbled, tripping on a stone, his knee giving way beneath him, and his face crashed into the dirt at his feet. Someone stood on his head and then a heavy body, a great suffocating weight, fell on top of him, pressing out his last breath. He choked, gasping a prayer, *blessed Jesus, my saviour, take me to your arms*. Through the blur of pain, he heard shouting and felt an iron grip clamp him under one arm and pull him upwards, something grabbing around his waist and his feet leaving the ground, floating, swimming in the air until he knew no more.

He was upside down, his nose against the sweating skin of a muscled back, his head dangling, jolting along, over someone's shoulder. There was muffled foreign talk buzzing all around. Demetrios felt his knee throbbing as the shackle round his ankle tugged, a wet trickle of blood upon his arm as it dangled over the shifting ground. He realised now that he was being borne along by the Turk and the clanging was the sound of the chains as the slave gang moved along. In that moment too, he knew that his unlikely saviour was this Ottoman soldier. But for this act, Demetrios would have been cut free of the chain and left for the dogs to devour.

The slave master twirled his whip and snapped it on the ground some ten paces in front. Demetrios, on the shoulder of the Turk, waited for the shout from the slave master, the order that he should be thrown to the ground and the life stamped out of him. He had never seen a slave bearing another, but there were, at that moment, more urgent matters afoot. Guards and slave drivers were running hither and thither, gabbling instructions, orders, curses. The pain was befuddling his brain, and they were talking too rapidly in an unfamiliar tongue. He caught fragments only: 'Get them into the cave... secure them... there must be no uprising... Kill if need be...'

Soon, they had reached the mouth of the cave, the wave of dampness swamping them as they entered the first chamber. They were driven to the back, where the roof was lower and it was solidly black. When full of bodies, it was cramped and rank-smelling, but there was a stone ledge, a bench where Demetrios felt his bearer lowering him with surprising gentleness, the big man kneeling because their shackles demanded it.

'Lie here, little Christian,' said the Turk, dropping down at his side on the rock bench, the next shackled man slumping to the ground. In the gloom of the cave, lit only by the remnants of light from its mouth, the slaves were black heaving bodies, groaning in their chains as they fell to rest upon the ground.

Demetrios was shocked to hear the Ottoman speak to him in his own Greek tongue. For a moment, he thought his mind so fevered that he had imagined it. He glanced at the dark form and, wincing with pain, squirmed to find a position that would enable him to speak to the man, even to lend him thanks.

'You speak my tongue?' he managed to utter.

The Turk's voice replied, 'Some, from long ago.'

'You are a Greek?' said Demetrios, amazed that the man had not revealed his identity until now.

'It was the place of birth. My mother's tongue. I remember little.'

'And now you are a soldier of the Ottoman army,' said Demetrios.

'Do not insult me, Christian. I am a Janissary,' he said. 'I am no common soldier. I am one of the Sultan's chosen men.' His voice rose in volume, so that Demetrios feared he might receive a blow from the fist that he saw tightening on the Turk's knee.

'Since a child, I serve Allah. I fight for the mighty Suleyman, God's shadow upon Earth. I kill his enemies.'

Demetrios shrank from the man, wondering if his purpose in carrying him back to the cave was for the pleasure of killing another Christian with his own hands. But why had he not done the deed before now? Why not dispatch a feeble Christian with one blow of the hand, like a servant swatting a fly? He could not fathom the motive of this warrior. But whatever he had been, he was now a slave, squatting here with the rest of them, shackled, helpless and disposable, at the mercy of the ones who held the whip and the key.

The Janissary sat up, his chest thrust forward, his body expressing something of his pride. 'The Sultan's forces come,' he said. 'Their ships are yonder, coming. Ali Pasha has one hundred, nay five hundred galleys. They will soon attack and kill these knights, these Christians, every man.'

'But the fortresses are strong,' Demetrios said. 'There are guns on all flanks, hundreds of armed men. Did you not see? The army is led by knights who will die for their cause, for God.'

The Ottoman snorted with laughter. 'And you think we will not die for Allah? Christians are nothing. Our guns and powder, hammer and rams can destroy walls, can break rock. It is nothing to the might of Allah. These knights will die.'

The Janissary's predictions might well prove true, Demetrios thought. He knew too well the might of the Turk. He and his brothers in Christ in the monastery had seen twenty ships, like prowling animals, their sides heaving with oars, moving towards their island of Patmos. They had watched from the bell tower of the chapel and seen their fate approaching. Father Abbot had led prayers in the chapel, where all on their knees had sought mercy from God on high. Demetrios had tried to keep his mind fixed on their pleas for intercession by the Holy Mother, while outside was the thunder of a stamping horde, the howl of a horn. Then he had bowed his head, clenched his teeth and named the saints with the power to turn the Sultan's troops from them. His prayers were trampled upon, as were the bodies of his brothers, those elders who were not young and fit enough to serve on the Turkish galleys. This same enemy was coming again. He had escaped with his life when most had not. This time, there could be only one end.

'I am a Christian,' Demetrios said, wishing only for a speedy dispatch by the merciful hand of this enemy who had saved his life.

The Janissary laughed. 'Not good to say. You bow to Allah and pray. Then you be saved.'

Demetrios was silent. 'Why do you not kill me?'

The Turk gripped Demetrios's wrist. 'We toil together in this hell. We are brothers,' he said, then laid his head against the stone bench and said no more.

In the stinking blackness of night, Demetrios heard the rattling of chains. Men shifted and moaned and there was a burst of murmuring talk. The Janissary was tugging at Demetrios's ankle, rising, calling to others of his tribe, questioning in a rising tone, insistent. His voice was joined with others to form a scramble of talk. Then he roared aloud, and silence fell. Demetrios felt himself being hauled to his feet, staggering to stand on his one good leg.

'The filthy dogs are gone,' the Janissary told Demetrios.

'The guards?' Demetrios said, unbelieving into the dark.

'Cowards have run to the fortress. We break free now,' said the Turk. 'We join our brothers in the Sultan's army.'

Again, the Janissary had to shout to quell the rabble of voices, the lunging actions of the slaves and, at his bidding, they subsided to a quieter grumble and ceased their struggling. Someone started pounding stone on stone, heavy blows, like a hammer on the anvil, again and again. They were breaking the chains of their shackles. On and on it went until a cheer arose, and through the grey darkness, which was now seeping in through the entrance of the cave, Demetrios saw two men rise and stumble their way towards the daylight outside. Others, impatient, shouted after them, and the pounding redoubled its speed.

The man shackled to the Janissary was freed, stood up, turned and pointed at Demetrios, his eyes flaming, jabbering something.

'Bow down to Allah,' said the Turk. 'All infidels die under the sword of holy warriors.'

Demetrios stared for a moment, fevered in the brain but seeing clearly what was to be his fate. 'Yes, my friend,' he said to the Janissary who stood above him, 'that is what Christians believe too.'

The man's eyes narrowed. He grabbed Demetrios by the throat. 'Pray,' he said.

'Holy Mary, Mother of God,' Demetrios began, though his voice was thin and he was choking.

The hands clamped tighter on his neck. His head filled with darkness, then with a rush of noise like the sea.

Chapter 6

Malta, March 1941

F rank woke to a thump on the nose and, half-awake, rubbed it. The book had fallen on his face, a heavy slab with hard covers, entitled, *Malta: The Islands and their History*. The thin shaft of moonlight from below the ill-fitting window blind had leaked just enough light to read by, so he'd carried on for an hour or so even though it had strained his eyes to make out the print. In his head, he could still see the Turkish fleet advancing on the island, with hundreds of galleys, coming to destroy the fortresses. *Bloody hell, nothing changes*, he thought. Now the Luftwaffe were doing the same thing, only in the air.

There was snoring all around him, and Frank knew that he should get more sleep. They had to be up at dawn to get straight to the airfield again. Not that anyone expected much sleep these days. A few hours snatched here and there between raids was all they often had. Thirty raids a day sometimes and then on into the night. He didn't know how much more the island could take without more air power to fend off the Germans. The supply ships were being sunk too.

He laid the book down on the floor and covered his head with his pillow to dull the sound of snoring and to stop himself thinking. It didn't work though. Now that he had a corporal's stripe, he was supposed to be responsible, to make decisions, order men about. It scared him, the thought of being in charge, and it would make him more of an idiot in the eyes of his mates. At least Marshall did the kit inspections, so Frank could avoid one way of getting up the noses of the men. He'd never been in charge of anything in his life. He was always the one to take orders, do as he was told. The only freedom he'd ever had was in his head, his imagination and when he was reading. He'd enjoyed comics like *The Boy's Own Paper* when he was a kid, then cowboy books and adventures stories like *King Solomon's Mines*, *Treasure Island* and *The Coral Island* from the school library, stories where plucky heroes fought off the forces of evil.

The wind was howling when he woke, having slept only in bursts. It was dark and he heard the rain lashing against the wall outside. The summers were boiling on the island but some of the winter days had been wilder and more miserable than anything he could remember back in England. He leaned over and slid out of bed, then went around the sleeping figures of his platoon, their numbers swelled by some men from D Company, which made up for the gap left by their dead colleagues, in the bunkhouse, if not in Frank's memory. Frank was still troubled with the image in his head of the burnt-out vehicle and the bodies. At times, he worried that he might be losing his mind. Some blokes went mad in war, shell shock and the like. The weird things he'd felt underground also made him anxious for his sanity, in the cave with the writing, then just the day before in the air-raid shelter in Valletta.

He kicked Chalky's foot that was sticking out the end of his blanket. 'Rise and shine.'

Chalky groaned as Frank shook others, pulled the blankets off some but didn't go near Green.

'Bastard,' someone muttered as he passed.

'Give us a break, Corp,' said another.

Frank flicked the switch, and a single light bulb lit up their end of the sleeping quarters. It was enough to wake the remaining men and get them staggering out of bed and into the toilet block next door.

'Bloody freezing.'

'Here we go a-fucking-gen,' said Green, one of the new ones, a cocky, contrary type who'd managed to sour the atmosphere within a week of being in their section.

Frank smelt his own stale sweat, sour on his shirt and armpits. His underwear was dirty too, but they could only get a few things washed per week because there was always a water shortage. He hated being dirty and had longed for more changes of clothes all his life. He'd read a book once where the bloke had so many shirts he could put on a clean one every day. What would that be like? It didn't matter so much now, he supposed, as standards for kit had needed to be relaxed a bit, with only a bucket of water a day for washing. Parades had been suspended too. All the lads were in the same stinking state, and you got used to it after a while.

In the light of the moon, with rain blowing in from the sea, they ran across the quadrangle to the canteen. Two trucks were waiting for them already.

'Eggs, that's great,' said one of the men.

The cook's assistant was lifting a huge draining spoon with boiled eggs onto a dish. Two big aluminium teapots sat steaming on the table, alongside the rows of white mugs.

'Eggs are going for ten bob a dozen,' said Chalky. 'Nice little opportunity there for someone with a couple of hens.'

'Poor bloody civilians,' said Frank. 'They're rationing sugar and kerosene and God knows what else.'

Sergeant Campbell sat down at the end of the table. 'Eat up. It'll get worse before it gets better, 'specially if the Jerries keep hitting the convoys.'

Frank had heard how only one merchantman had got through to the harbour last week and four others were sunk as soon as they'd entered the Med. This had always been the fate of the islands, he knew, as he'd read about it in the first history book. Even in Roman times, grain had to be imported from Sicily and the Balkans because the soil was too thin and poor. The knights had even built some huge underground stores in Floriana in the sixteenth century to store up supplies in the event of a siege. Sieges weren't all ancient history, though. Frank had never imagined he might be caught up in one himself.

'Only fair,' said Green, 'we should get decent grub. We're the fighting men, after all. Where would these peasants be without us?'

'Better off maybe,' said Frank. He hadn't meant to contribute to this discussion, having decided since he'd started reading to keep even the most interesting facts and ideas to himself. He'd grown a bit tired of the ignorant jokes and not being able to talk about things that excited him.

'What you on about?' said Green, sneering.

'Well, the only reason they're being bombed is us. If we weren't here, the Italians would just be using it as a base, and it might be an easier life all round for the Maltese. Better than being bombed to hell by the Luftwaffe.'

Frank could feel all eyes on him and wished he'd just kept his mouth shut.

'You best watch yourself, Nix. You'll get arrested for treason with that sort of talk, you will,' said Chalky, with a half-serious laugh.

'I'm only stating a point of view,' Frank said, wishing it were time to go.

'Only bloody point of view that counts is beating the fucking Hun and getting home,' said Sergeant Campbell. 'Get this down you, lads. We've got a job to do, in case you'd forgotten.'

The heavy clouds and rain were probably the reason for the lack of raids that morning, so Frank and his section worked untroubled in the drizzle for several hours. They were erecting protective pens out of old kerosene cans filled with dirt and stones for the Hurricanes. The airfield was a mess, with the burnt-out aircraft lying like animal carcases about the place. More potholes and craters had punctured the landing strips and new ones were created in the next raid as fast as the soldiers could fill them up.

By afternoon, the men were soaked and hungry, and Frank asked the sergeant if they could take a break. The sky was clearing and turning blue, so everyone knew what would appear before long: the familiar sights and sounds of a raid. And so they did, before the men had time to reach the canteen building. The siren wailed, the air crews dashed for their planes, frantic whistles called the gunners and ten enemy aircraft were soon clearly visible above, coming in low, with throaty roaring intent.

Frank and his men dived into the nearest slit trench and ducked down as they heard the ground ripping like a piece of torn oilcloth. The ack-ack guns deafened Frank, his head numb and thick, watching the showers of rock and tarmac fly up in a fountain. Two planes in their pens were aflame.

'That was a waste of bloody time,' said someone.

'I'd like to get at the bastards on the ground,' muttered another.

Four Hurricanes were up and in pursuit of the German bombers, which had now circled round and were heading north-east towards the sea and their base in Sicily. As the anti-aircraft guns fell silent, the engine noises retreating, Frank and his men climbed out to a new field of destruction. A fire truck was at one of the burning planes, hosing water onto it. Frank looked at the pitted surface of the airstrip in dismay, knowing that it was all to do again. They had to keep the runway fit for landing and take-off.

'Quick, let's get some grub and then back to it,' he said to his men. 'At least the canteen hasn't been hit. Fifteen minutes.'

'Who d'you think you are, General Bleeding Montgomery?' said Green under his breath but meaning to be heard.

Frank would have liked to punch Green in the face and was glad when the sergeant shouted to all the men to get themselves fed and watered on the double. It was to be a day of fruitless toil, with all their repairs and mending undone by fresh bomb holes, but Frank was grateful at least that there had been no casualties, not even any shrapnel wounds.

At the end of the day, they piled into the two trucks under a troubled sky streaked with torn strips of thin cloud. Frank leaned out of the lorry, staring at the watery blue.

'Worse than fucking hard labour, this,' said Green, crushing himself in between two others opposite Frank.

'Speaking from experience, eh?' said Chalky.

Green smiled with a slanting sneer. 'Some buggers get jammy postings on the beach somewhere. Imagine that, nothing to do all day but playing cards, smoking and wanking.'

Frank said nothing, but Green caught his eye as he turned around.

'I reckon Corporal Nixy here's got ambition to be in the action, ain't you, Corp?'

'Shut it, Green,' said Frank, turning away again to look at the changing sky.

'Bet your old mum's proud of you, fighting for King and country,' Green said, chuckling.

'I said belt up.'

Frank saw one of the others nudge Chalky, grin and nod towards Green. He couldn't understand why Green had picked him out as the butt of his insults, nor why he found it so irritating. It was probably because of Frank's stripe and the fact that

Green was older, a man of the world, or so he fancied. He had that ferrety look about him, ready to bite and run away.

'Belt up or what? Pulling rank, are you, sonny boy?' said Green.

Chalky kicked Green's foot. 'He could have you on a charge.'

Frank's face was burning, and the men, cramped close together in the back of the truck, body to body were watching, waiting for his next move. If they'd not been in the lorry, he'd have taken a swing at the bloke, shown he wasn't afraid to stand up for himself.

'Needs you to do it for him, eh?' said Green.

'I said fucking shut up, Green,' Frank said in a low voice, forcing himself to look into the face of his antagonist. Green wasn't the first bully he'd known. There had been a few in the home who'd made his life hell for a while and, in the end, he'd been forced to fight them. It was the only way. Even when he'd lost, he'd managed to inflict enough damage to show he was no pushover and to gain a bit of respect from the onlookers. Then the bullies had left him alone, going off in search of some other poor little sod.

'I'll meet you fair and square in the yard tonight, if that's what you want,' Frank said.

'Oooh, an officer and a gentleman, is it?' said Green in a whining treble. 'It would be my pleasure, if I was a woofter like you.'

Frank lunged at him, had his throat while he flailed with his right and half landed a punch on Green's cheekbone, but the man's knee was in his stomach, the blow winding him. He was being pulled off on each side as Green was too, in a lurching struggle. Then the truck hit something on the road and bounced, a loud crack splitting the air, hurling the men into a pile of sprawling bodies. It took some moments of untangling for them to realise what had happened. Fearing a bomb, they fought with each other to get out of the truck. Frank held back, partly through shock but also through the desire to distance himself from Green. He watched them tumble out.

'It's a fucking blow out,' someone shouted.

The lorry, now that it had stopped completely, was listing to one side, and Frank jumped down in front of the other truck that had been on their tail. Then Sergeant Campbell climbed out of the truck behind and came to inspect the damage. There was a huge slit in the tyre, which was flat and folded over as if it had melted. The driver was standing, staring and scratching his head beneath his helmet.

'Come on, you,' said the sergeant. 'Green, Cunningham, Mulholland, get it changed, then.'

Frank was heartily glad that this incident had halted his fight with Green, but he knew now, by the sergeant's manner, that he must have seen something of the fracas in the back of the truck. He offered Frank a cigarette, which he took gratefully. Sergeant Campbell lit up and moved away from the truck, nodding that Frank should come too. They walked a few yards to the side of the road as the men clattered the tools and the jack from the rear of the lorry.

'Don't let him get to you, Nixon,' said the sergeant, pushing his helmet back on his head. 'He's scum. Don't dirty your fists on him. Clever lad like you, you're worth ten of him, ignorant bastard.'

Frank drew deeply on his fag, surprised at the sergeant's warning and his praise, wondering how honest he could be with the man. Sergeant Campbell was a hard-bitten soldier, mid-thirties, Frank guessed, not given to joking, but fair and strict.

'I've got to show him, though, Sarge and the men.'

'Yeah, all right. But do you reckon you could take him?'

'Maybe,' said Frank. 'I'll give as good as I get.'

'If you have to, but just watch it.' The sergeant sighed. 'Bloody hell, there's a war on and here we are fighting with each other. It's bleeding mad.'

'Yes, I know, Sergeant.'

As he ground his cigarette butt into the dirt, Frank recognised this strip of the route. They were approaching the ridge leading to the village of Naxxar. He peered into the dusk, spying the houses on the rise of the land.

'Sarge, can I have permission to knock off now?' he said.

'Eh?'

'There's someone in the village I... I need to see.' He tried to ape the bravado of other men he'd heard boasting about women, but to his own ears, he just sounded sheepish.

The sergeant almost smiled. 'Well, well. Bit of a dark horse, aren't you, Nixon? Don't do anything I wouldn't do, and watch out for a farmer with a shotgun. Know what I mean?'

Frank blushed, glad of the failing light. 'No, it's nothing like that. I just want to say thanks to someone.'

'On your way, then, Nixon. Back in by ten-thirty, mind.'

Frank passed the truck, which was now raised on the jack, with two men squatting down and others rolling the new wheel from the back.

'See you later, lads,' he said as brightly as he could manage.

'Where you going?' said someone.

Chalky, one of the crouching men, stood up and grinned at Frank. 'Oh, I get it. This is Naxxar, isn't it? Say hello to her for me.'

'Ask if she's got any sisters,' someone said.

'Nix's got his feet under the table, has he?'

Frank didn't wait to hear any more comments, though he heard some chuckling behind him as he walked off quickly down the road. He wasn't even sure if he should call on Manwela. She might be alarmed and not open her door if he knocked. But she had been quietly welcoming and kind to him before, even with her old grandmother sitting there like a sphinx in the corner of the kitchen. She had the two little kids upstairs or playing around too, so he was hardly likely to try anything.

He knew he shouldn't think about Manwela at all in that way. She was not long widowed and looked too holy and pure for him to imagine touching her. But he wanted to go to her, to thank her for that night those months ago when Coop and the others had bought it. He wanted to see her face again, to make sure that she was real. If only he had some present to bring to her, it would give him the excuse he needed. It would have been good to give her some of his rations because he'd heard how hard it was getting for civilians.

If he hadn't the courage in the end to visit her, he could easily duck down and hide in the dark, let the trucks go past. Then his mates could think what they liked, that he'd spent the night in the bed of a pretty Maltese woman. This thought gave him a moment of exhilaration, though he quickly threw it out of his mind again. It was as daft as imagining that he'd really felt a ghost next to him in the shelter in Valletta that night or a presence in the cave with the writing. He wondered if other folk were as troubled by their imaginations in the way he was.

He walked on, through the village street now, his boots crunching on the roadway, through the square with the amazing church. Two men, in white shirts and waistcoats, came out of a house in spite of the cold evening, carrying a large frame of some sort between them. As they passed each other, he bid them a hearty 'Bonswa'—the word for good evening—and was pleased when they answered him. He'd read a little about the language in the guidebook and Lieutenant Chambers had given him a two-minute lecture on the origins and development of the Maltese language one day when he'd been crossing the yard of the barracks. There was so much interesting stuff to learn and know about and so little time. Frank wondered what it would be like to be a professor and get paid just to sit and read books.

The olive tree that hung over Manwela's wall was visible now as a darker blot ahead of him. As Frank drew near, he heard voices, a woman and a child weeping, and without realising it, he began to run. From the gate, a woman, Manwela, was hurrying out, calling back into the yard. Frank nearly collided with her in his rush but pulled back in time, knowing she had not seen him in her agitation.

'What's wrong? Is something the matter?' he said as calmly and quietly as he could, trying not to surprise her.

She jumped back, recoiling and clutching her hand to her breast, saying something in Maltese, then recognising him.

'It's Joseph. He's very sick. The doctor. I must get the doctor, but I can't leave Grandmother and David. I was going to my sister to ask her boy if he'd go to...' Her voice broke as she tried not to cry.

Frank felt helpless for a brief moment. 'I'll go for the doctor,' he said. 'You can stay here with your kid. Where's the doctor? In the village?'

'No,' she said, her voice steadying. 'We have no doctor here. It is some miles, in Balzan, two miles. Dr Agius, in the first house, near the church. Can you really go?'

'No problem,' said Frank. 'I'll run.'

She stepped up to him and clutched his arm. 'No, take the bicycle, please.'

She pulled him across the yard, calling to the small boy, David, who was standing, staring at Frank. The child scampered over to the far wall and started hauling at a bicycle that was leaning there. Frank took hold of the handlebars of the old-fashioned machine, but once he'd rolled it into the yard, he saw that it looked sound enough.

'Dr Agius, in Balzan,' said Manwela, her hand pressing against his arm again. 'It's that way. Take that road. Thank you, thank you. Be quick.'

He stepped on the pedal and swerved out of the yard and onto the road, his fatigue and doubt gone in the urgency of the moment. He'd been on this road before, a dirt track but straightish, and he built up as much speed as he could. The boy must be bad, he reckoned. These people were tough, used to a hard life and not likely malingerers or softies. Kids caught all sorts of horrible things too. He remembered an outbreak of TB in the home and three of the boys going away and never coming back. If he'd believed in praying, he'd have asked God to save the boy. Manwela had lost her husband. Her boy shouldn't be taken too. He didn't want to think about it because he knew it was quite possible.

The road was deserted, which wasn't surprising given the petrol rationing and the blackout. What he feared was a night raid, however, though these were mostly over the cities. In this black countryside, it would be hard to spot anything. He just hoped that the doctor had a car with some petrol in it. Surely they'd give a doctor an extra ration.

There was the church tower and the white house. Frank braked too quickly, skidded and toppled onto the ground. He leapt to his feet and ran to the door of the house, which opened straight onto the street. On the right of the door was a bell, and he knew that he had no choice. It clanged fit to wake the dead. A few moments later, two doors further down the street both opened and enquiring heads poked out. One man shouted something to him in Maltese.

'Dr Agius. I need Dr Agius,' Frank said. 'There's a sick child in Naxxar. Is the doctor here?'

He had not thought what he'd do if the doctor were out on another call, but the door opened, and a middle-aged man stood in front of him in his shirt sleeves and a waistcoat. He peered at Frank through round wire spectacles.

'A bomb, is it?' he said.

'No, sir. It's a sick boy. Mrs Vassallo in Naxxar, her boy Joseph. She needs you to go. It's an emergency,' said Frank.

The doctor nodded and did not enquire how Frank came to be delivering the message. 'I'll come. I have enough petrol for Naxxar and back, I hope. If not, you'll have to push me.' He spoke in the resigned, mildly jokey manner of one used to being called out, particularly in these times.

'I'll ride the bike back,' said Frank, thinking it best not to abandon Manwela's means of transport here, though he would have been grateful for a lift back in a car. His thigh muscles were still tight with the effort of his pursuit.

'As you wish. I'll see you there,' said the doctor. 'What's your name, soldier?'

Frank was sweating heavily in spite of the cool night. He'd dashed like a maniac once already, as though he were being chased by a dive bomber, and now he was careering back along the road, swerving to the side some minutes later as the doctor's car overtook him. The sight helped him to relax a little. The doctor would be there in a short while to tend to the child. He slowed down, thinking of Manwela, of her hand on his arm and how he'd like to see her again in daylight, like the time she had given him a drink of water. He remembered that her face was beautiful, with dark eyes and a full mouth. He was glad to have done this favour for her.

When he arrived at the house about half an hour later, he dismounted in the yard, finding the doctor's car there and seeing a tiny strip of light beneath the blackout of the kitchen window. Was he needed now? he wondered, wheeling the bike and leaning it against the wall again. He should be going, but he wanted to know about the boy and now, more desperately, to see Manwela.

He stood there for some minutes, undecided, the sweat-soaked shirt clinging to his skin under his tunic. He shivered.

There were voices at the door then and it opened, the doctor emerging with the child in his arms. He was talking in a steady but urgent tone to Manwela, who was holding her sick child's hand while the other boy clung to her side, moving together so that to Frank's eyes they formed a dark, moving shape. The doctor was taking the child away. To hospital? Frank stood still, watching. The doctor was opening the back door of the car and lowering the child into it, uttering some soothing words, then turning and talking again to Manwela. The car door banged shut and the engine revved to life. Frank watched the vehicle edge out through the opening of the yard, leaving Manwela and the little boy standing in the middle.

Frank stepped forward towards them and cleared his throat.

Manwela looked at him. 'You're here,' she said, her voice weak, mildly surprised.

'Your boy? Is he going to be all right? What's wrong with him?' asked Frank.

She took a step towards him and touched his arm gently, almost stroking it. He was overwhelmed with the urge to grab her in his arms, but the little lad was still clinging to her dress.

'Come inside,' she said, picking up the child. 'You must be very tired. Joseph has pneumonia. The doctor is taking him to hospital. It's best. He can have medicine there. But come in and sit by the fire. Have tea and a sandwich. I have bread.'

Frank did not try to refuse. As well as being ready to drop, he knew that she wanted him to come. The kitchen was warm, and the old woman, rocking very slightly in her chair, was sleeping.

'Sit down, please, Frank,' she said, then hesitating, 'May I call you Frank?'

His chest tightened, for he saw the shadowed features of this woman as a portrait again in the light of the small kerosene lamp, holding the child in her arms.

'Yes, that's my name,' he said, feeling idiotic.

The boy stared at him with wide black eyes.

'I must put David to bed now,' she said.

She spoke softly to the child as she carried him to a narrow stone staircase at the back of the kitchen, then disappeared up it. Frank leaned back in the chair and closed his eyes. In a moment, he would be revived. He would come to, and if he were lucky, he'd get a pot of tea and a bite of something, then be on his way. It was only five miles back, and he was feeling a bit warmer already. He was used to physical discomfort. It was part of his life. And he'd happily put up with tiredness and hunger to have time with this woman.

He heard her footsteps on the stairs and then she was back in the kitchen, pouring a little more water in the kettle and bringing a flat loaf of bread and a small lump of white cheese on a plate to the table. She sat down opposite him, and he glanced at her as she cut the bread, put it on a plate and gouged a lump of the soft white goat's cheese to place on top. She pushed it towards him.

'Thank you,' he said, feeling an overpowering hunger, tearing a piece of the bread and stuffing it into his mouth, unable to restrain himself. He swallowed an overlarge chunk. 'Will he be all right, your boy?'

'The doctor says he will recover. He is taking Joseph just to be sure. It's for the best. Tomorrow, I'll go and see him. My sister will sit with Grandmother.'

'Good,' said Frank, surprised at the relief he felt. 'He's a strong lad, I'll bet.'

Manwela looked back at him, then rose from her seat, coming round the table to him, reaching for his face, cradling his cheek in her hand. Frank hardened. It took all of his willpower not to catch hold of her, pull her to him, crush her against him. He tensed his muscles, knew that he was blushing deeply, that his cold, wet shirt was clinging to his skin. Then, her other hand was on his shoulder, she was leaning close, her hair brushing his face, and she kissed him on the lips.

CHAPTER 7

When Manwela broke away from their kiss, Frank scrambled to his feet, reaching for her again. But she pressed against his chest with the palm of her hands to prevent him from taking hold of her.

'I'm sorry,' she said, her voice breaking.

She dropped her hands, but he caught them in his. He couldn't stop himself.

'Sorry?' he said, puzzled, frantic with desire for her.

'No, I shouldn't. It's because I have no man. I have no husband.' She bowed her head, sobbing quietly.

Though Frank's heart was beating wildly and he was desperate to kiss her again, he reached around her waist and drew her to him. He held her close and stroked her hair. It seemed the right thing to do. His hunger for her was waning in this embrace, and he hoped she realised how gladly he offered her comfort.

'I miss him so much,' she said in a whisper, 'and now Joseph is ill. What will I do if he's taken from me too?'

Frank didn't know whether to say anything; he didn't want to utter empty, useless words. So he said nothing, but held her still, feeling her warmth, the slim frame of her body, her belly, her shoulders softening a little against him. Unbelieving, he realised that he had no memory of ever holding or being held by another human being in this way before. Her cheek was pressed on his chest, and he worried that he must stink of sweat, but she had stopped crying now and stayed in his arms. He hoped she wouldn't move, but of course she had to, easing herself from him in the shudder at the end of her weeping, then looking up into his face.

'You are very kind, Frank,' she said. 'Thank you for what you did today.'

His throat was too choked to respond, but he could never have put into words what he had experienced and what she had given him.

'You must eat,' she said, turning away.

He grasped her hand, wanting to keep hold of her for one more moment only, but she pulled free and moved back to her chair on the other side of the table as he sat down again. It was only then that he remembered the old woman in the chair in the corner, hoping that she hadn't woken up and seen them. Her mouth was loosely open and her head was leaning against a cushion, in a sound sleep.

The half-finished cheese and bread lay on the plate in front of him. Manwela was still looking at him, her face turned serene again, like a portrait. No wonder people kneeled and prayed to pictures if they brought on feelings like this. Men weren't supposed to get horny looking at pictures of the Virgin Mary, surely. But Manwela was a real woman he'd held in his arms and who'd kissed him. It wasn't going to go any further, he knew that. It couldn't. He looked down at the plate again, knowing that he'd been staring at her too long. He tore off another piece of bread and loaded it with cheese.

'This is very good,' he said. 'But I shouldn't be eating your food. You need all you can get for your boys.'

She smiled at him, and he wanted to return it, except that his mouth was too full of bread.

'We have enough,' she said. 'I have a good milking goat, chickens, rabbits, and the farmers here are quite generous. We are luckier in the countryside than the people in the cities. My cousins in Valletta may have to come here soon.'

'And are there lots of refugees here in Naxxar?' Frank said, gazing at her, saying anything just to hear her speak again.

'Yes, we have some families. They have moved into people's spare rooms. Some are even sleeping in outhouses and sheds, I think. They have their rations and they buy some food from us as well.'

'We're lucky too,' Frank said, 'in the army. We get enough grub, I mean food, most of the time, and rations and chocolate and stuff like that. I'll bring you some chocolate. I bet your boys like chocolate? Do you want any cigarettes? Do you smoke?'

She smiled at him again and shook her head, this time with the indulgent look she might have given an over-excited kid, and he was embarrassed to his core. He looked away, blushing, smelling the sourness of his own sweat. What did she think of him? A common, ignorant sort of bloke with no idea how to speak to a woman properly?

'Will you come again, Frank?' she said.

He looked up, pathetically grateful. 'Yes, I'd like to know how your boy goes on,' he faltered, 'and to see if there's any work needs doing round the place, you know, heavy work...'

She was staring at him, or rather at his mucky tunic, and he squirmed inwardly under her scrutiny.

'Can't get much washing done, shirts and things,' he said. 'We're meant to be neat and tidy for inspections, but it's difficult sometimes.'

'Bring me your clothes that are dirty,' she said. 'I'll wash them for you. And Grandmother is very fond of chocolate.'

Frank's happiness was a fine protective shield against the crude remarks, banter and innuendos the next morning. Even Green's skulking presence didn't trouble him. His only anxiety was to know when he could next get a day off. They never knew from day to day what they'd be doing, and with the raids so frequent now, it didn't seem likely that they'd get a leave day for some time. But he'd have to stop thinking about Manwela, or else he'd go mad. Why was he such a fool? He should have asked her where the hospital was, where the doctor had taken her son Joseph, in case it was anywhere close by where he could sneak off for an hour and perhaps meet her there. He thought with some embarrassment too of taking his washing to her, his sweaty clothes, the idea was appalling and yet she'd offered. She was a married woman after all and a mother, not some red-nailed secretary in an office who'd never seen a bit of muck. Yet she was young and so lovely, the loveliest woman he'd ever seen. She didn't look a day over twenty-five. Maltese women probably married young, he thought. She wasn't much older than him, not really. But perhaps she was just mothering him, thinking of him like another son who needed to have his washing done. That's what some mothers did, he supposed.

'In the square at six-thirty hours,' snapped Sergeant Campbell at the door. 'Need your section, Nixon, and yours, Marshall. Make it snappy, lads. We're off to the docks today.'

'Should get bloody danger money for that,' muttered Chalky.

'I thought that was the West Kents' patch,' said someone.

'They've got to go to Luqa airfield,' said Sergeant Campbell, 'it got bombed to buggery yesterday. We're going down to Senglea, the docks, to help with the unloading. That's if the poor devils manage to get the ship through.'

The merchantmen steaming through the Mediterranean into the Grand Harbour were a prime target for the enemy: German U-boats, Italian warships and, of course, the bombers. Cutting off supplies, starving the island into surrender was their best bet, they must have reckoned. The German and Italian bombers threw everything at the docks. They had flattened most of the buildings to rubble already and the cargo ships were docile prey. Frank had read in *The Times of Malta* about the fatalities, when the remnants of a recent convoy had made it through all the torpedoes, naval and air assaults. Twenty stevedores, ten merchant seamen had copped it. Then the ship had been sunk and half the cargo lost. Divers had brought up some of it, but the rest was gone forever.

Even Green was quiet in the truck on their journey south, showing no inclination to insult or torment anyone. They all smoked, complained in occasional bursts of tense talk about lice, bed bugs, their favourite beer and when they might get some leave. Nothing could distract Frank from thoughts of Manwela, however. It was terrible. He couldn't help it, going over it all again, every minute he'd been with her, doubting sometimes that she'd really kissed him. He knew it was only her lonely longing for her husband and her worry about her child that had thrown her into his arms. She couldn't really fancy him, could she? And yet, she'd asked him to visit her again and she was no whore, not a woman like that. His brain was tired with all the puzzling and doubting, so much so that he was almost grateful when their trucks came near to the harbour.

Since the last time they'd come this way, more buildings had been wrecked. A pathway through the rubble had been cleared for the passage of vehicles so that the broken stones of houses and shops now formed high piles on either side. Their line of trucks edged through to a space behind two huge stone warehouse buildings. It was still quite dark when the sergeant ordered the men in both sections, sixteen of them, quickly out of the trucks and into one of the buildings. Inside, they found a crowd of Maltese dockworkers, short sturdy men, standing in huddles, smoking. Sergeant Campbell exchanged greetings with the one in charge, and Frank noticed that Lieutenant Chambers was already there, talking to two officers in naval uniform.

It was an empty cavernous place, with a number of wooden handcarts, trolleys and crates stacked up in one corner. Through the open doors on the dock side of the warehouse, Frank could make out the skeleton of a burnt-out warship, still somehow afloat. The dockers were dragging through a number of metal, four-wheeled trolleys loaded with bulging sacks. They squeaked past the line of soldiers, out of the doors and onto the wharfside.

The figure of Lieutenant Chambers strode towards them, his gait and manner more purposeful than usual. Frank called his section to attention, and Marshall brought his alongside.

'At ease,' said the officer, though the atmosphere was charged with expectation: the muffled sounds of the dockworkers heading off to the quay, the sense that at any moment the familiar tearing engine noise might return to the sky. The air was still, as though every man were holding his breath.

'Right, this is the plan,' said Lieutenant Chambers. 'The ship's in, just docked in fact, but the enemy knows it's here, so they're going to start bombing soon. Can't do much in the dark, but it'll be light in less than half an hour. Captain Black is going to set up a smoke screen out there on the dockside on those trolleys. It's pretty thick stuff once it gets going and ought to give us good cover.'

'If it doesn't bloody choke us all first,' muttered someone behind Frank in an undertone.

"Speed is of the essence,' continued Lieutenant Chambers. 'We'll have Nixon's section first in line by the gangway, ready to carry the stuff off. The stevedores are already at work inside the vessel. Then, Marshall, you'll swap your section with Nixon's to get some time away from the thickest smoke.'

'Fucking hell,' murmured Chalky at Frank's side. 'Might be better to take our chances with the bloody bombs.'

'I don't think so,' said Frank.

'It'll be pretty awful, the smoke,' said Lieutenant Chambers. 'So, if you've got your pocket handkerchief, you might like to put it over your mouth.'

To illustrate, the officer drew out a large white, ironed hand-kerchief and fluttered it in front of his face.

'What does he think we are, a walking fucking laundry?' said Green sourly.

As the officer finished issuing his instructions, Frank could already smell smoke. A moment later, a smouldering cloud could be seen rising from the wagons that had been rolled onto the quay by the side of the waiting ship.

'Get to it, lads,' shouted Sergeant Campbell, leading them at a trot out of the warehouse, onto the quayside and into the smoke.

Some men started coughing immediately, but Frank found it bearable to begin with. He ran to the front of the gangway where some of the stevedores were already manhandling wooden crates. Up above, the arm of a small crane, now only half-visible through the smoke, swung over a hatch in the deck where the figures of two men were hooking a huge round net full of stacked boxes.

Some handcarts were lined up on the edge of the quay. Frank, Chalky and others from their section started piling up the crates to a precarious height, then heaved the carts back into the ware-house, out to the waiting men to load into the trucks. Then they plunged back into the choking fog again.

Two more journeys back and forth and they were struggling to breathe. They were starting to hear the distant buzz of aircraft engines. By now, the smoke was thick as a blanket, grey, like float-ing porridge in the air. Frank's eyes were streaming and his throat felt raw. He tried gulping the clearer air of the warehouse when they came back in, but even this was becoming dense and fouled as the whole dock was engulfed by the billowing clouds of grey. The men, ghostly shapes, moved in a random hopeless search for an escape from this hell. The sirens wailed and anti-aircraft fire from the docks burst out and cackled outside the wall of smoke.

'Nixon, get your section back into the warehouse. Marshall, come forward, at the double.' Sergeant Campbell's voice sounded stringy and weak.

The loading of the trucks offered some measure of relief, though many of the men had to stop and cough, leaning against any supporting structure to gasp their way back to normal breathing.

'Want a fag?' said some card. Though a few of the men tried to laugh, they all fell to spluttering and swearing in the end.

Something invisible beyond them exploded with a volcanic gulp and splash of water, and Frank was momentarily glad of the fog. The crackling of the ack-ack guns burst out hysterically at the unseen attackers as Frank and his section headed back out once again to the ship.

As Frank handed a box back to the man behind him by the gangway, there was a thunderous blast, and lumps of rock from the roof of the warehouse came hurtling down through the smoke. Chalky roared out on the other side of the gangway, and a moment later, Frank saw him felled, his head and shoulder disappearing over the edge between the quayside and the ship.

Frank leapt over the gangway and scrambled on his knees to grab hold of Chalky's body and tug him back from the drop into the black strip of water between ship and wharf edge. Voices yelled behind Frank as he hauled Chalky's dead weight back up, seeing a bleeding cut on his forehead. One of the Maltese stevedores was at his side. Together, they carried Chalky clear and ran with him into the warehouse, crunching over splinters and nuggets of stone.

Two other blokes came staggering back into the warehouse, but at least they were on their feet.

'*Medic*,' called Frank as they lowered Chalky to the ground. 'First aid. Over here.'

He crouched by Chalky's side and slapped his face, willing him to show some sign that he wasn't dead.

'Come on, Chalky, you bastard. Do you hear me? Come on.'

A soldier with a first aid kit came running up, and Chalky groaned as he knelt next to Frank. The Maltese dockworker stood over them.

'Grazzi haffna,' Frank said, looking up at the man, feeling his own pulse slowing with relief that Chalky was breathing.

The man nodded, then turned and ran back into the warehouse.

'You speak the lingo, then?' said the first aider, opening the box and peering at Chalky, whose eyes had snapped open suddenly.

'Oh yes, Nixy knows everything about Malta,' said Chalky in a drunken voice. 'He's my best mate, him. He's brainy. You ask him anything.'

'Shut it,' said Frank, grinning at his friend.

'Better get him to hospital,' said the first aider. 'Needs a few stitches in that head.'

'Get him in the truck,' shouted Sergeant Campbell, running over to them.

'See you later, Chalky,' said Frank, clutching his shoulder, then standing up quickly.

Again, the anti-aircraft battery burst into life, and Frank plunged back into the wall of smoke.

Six lorries had already managed to get away, loaded with supplies for storage out of the main target areas for the enemy attack. Those with armaments had left, with others ready with food for the army and air force bases around the island and the central civilian stores underground in Valletta. Frank and two others from his section climbed into the back of the last tightly loaded vehicle, cramming themselves in beside stacks of tins of corned beef. Frank felt sticky with filth and his throat was burning.

In the village of Birkirkara, the lorry slowed and crunched to a stop. Frank jumped down and found that the front of the convoy had pulled up in a line in a street near a cafe and that some of the men were climbing out. Thank God, he thought, or thank Lieutenant Chambers, who must have realised they were gagging.

'Come on,' he called back to the others in the truck, who were poking their heads out. 'Want a beer?'

They leapt out, suddenly enlivened at the prospect of a drink. Sergeant Campbell ordered a peeved-looking Marshall to watch the trucks while the rest of them made their way over to the cafe, a small single-storey building with tables and chairs outside. The owner, standing by the door in his apron, stared at the approaching crowd of around twenty filthy soldiers and called over his shoulder to someone inside. Lieutenant Chambers, leading the way, engaged the man in some talk, which brought a grin to his face. The man beckoned to them cheerily, then ducked inside the café.

The beer tasted sweeter to Frank than any he'd had in his life, but his eyes were still gritty and sore. It had been worth the pain, however, as the ship's cargo was all safely ashore.

'That was a bloody good job of work,' said Sergeant Campbell. 'Well done, boys.'

'It was only one ship though,' said one of the men. 'The rest of the convoy didn't make it. How long do you reckon we can hold out?'

'Who knows?' said the sergeant. 'The way they're rationing stuff now doesn't look good. They're even cutting down the buses. Only petrol for essential journeys.'

'You reckon the Jerries'll invade?'

'At least we could have a go at them on the ground.'

'Can we have another, Sarge?'

Frank's head was dizzy, and though his thirst was great, he refused a second beer and went to relieve himself at the back of the building. As he passed the line of trucks, he saw Marshall leaning against the first, with an empty glass in his hand, surrounded by a gaggle of chattering children. Frank returned from the other side of the café, where the last in the line of trucks was standing. He saw the open flap of the canvas at the back and the leg of a man who had just hoisted himself inside. For a second, he thought nothing of it, assuming it was one of Marshall's section, but then the idea struck him that it might be a thief. He'd best take a look.

He approached the rear of the lorry and, lifting the flap, peered in at the boxes and crates stacked inside, seeing a figure in army uniform amongst them and recognising it as Green. He was plunging his hand into a brown paper package and stuffing his trouser pockets with the contents: packets of cigarettes.

'What the fuck do you think you're doing?' said Frank.

Green twisted round quickly. 'Eh? What do *you* think?' His voice was hard and defiant, like his face. 'Only a few. No one'll miss them.'

Frank shuddered, not with fear but with anger and the consequences of what he had to do. 'Put them back, Green.'

Green didn't move. He straightened up a little and smiled, in a bogus show of friendliness. 'Come on, Corp. Take some smokes yourself. Go on. What nobody sees won't hurt them.'

'Put them back,' Frank said again. 'I'll report you. I'm not joking.'

Green hesitated for a moment, then his hand went for his trouser pockets, and he took out three packets from each, which he placed back inside the brown paper parcel. Then he pulled some more from inside his shirt. His mouth was scowling now, and he made to move towards Frank.

'Close it up again,' Frank said, surprised at his lack of feeling, fear or otherwise. It was as though the certainty of his action had knocked out all other sense. He stood back as Green jumped down from the truck.

'Fuck you, Nixon,' he said and walked away.

At least they were allowed to shower when they eventually returned to barracks. Even better, their platoon was given a day off the next day, barring last-minute emergencies. Frank lay on his bed, smoking, his book clutched to his chest, feeling almost content. He'd survived another day and done a useful job. And Chalky was going to be all right, just a bit concussed and in need of a few stitches. He'd be back in a couple of days. Then, best of all, there was the thought of seeing Manwela, if the raids weren't too bad. It was only the encounter with Green that remained the sole blot in his mind. Green was not one to climb down, to be bettered, and now his grudge would most likely grow into something bigger.

He closed his eyes and thought about Manwela and how on his day off he could go and see her after he'd visited Chalky at Imtarfa Hospital. Naxxar was near enough on the way. Perhaps the sergeant might even let him borrow a bike. He'd take her his ration of chocolate and some bits of washing. Did she really mean that she would do it for him? If he took it, he'd have to go back again and collect it. He might even go regularly. The thought that he might kiss her again started to arouse him. The clang for grub's up broke from across the yard in the canteen, ending his pleasant daydream.

Fifteen minutes later, they were tucking into a meat stew when the air-raid siren went off, and they had to leave the gravy to congeal while they ran to the shelters in the cellars of the next block. Officers and men and some civilian workers were all crammed in together. Some played cards on a small space on the floor, others chatted and joked. Frank saw Lieutenant Chambers hunched against the wall, reading a book. He sidled his way through the bodies to reach the officer.

'Ah, Nixon,' he said, peering over his book. 'Don't imagine you're having much time for reading these days.'

'No, not much, sir, but I'm on to the bit about the Great Siege in the Zammit book you lent me. I'd like to know more about it, all about the Ottomans.'

'Yes, goodness me. The Turkish empire, that's a hefty topic. The Great Siege is pretty well-documented,' said Lieutenant Chambers, his eyes lighting up, closing the book but keeping his finger in the place. 'A lot of the books are in Italian, or the contemporary accounts in Latin, but there are some translations. We'll have to wait till the end of the war to get hold of things like that. But I tell you there's a real need for a completely new look at the whole business of the siege by the Turks. If things were different, I'd get started on another book myself.'

Frank was bemused by this casual comment. 'Have you written books, sir?'

Lieutenant Chambers smiled with his teacher face again. 'Well, only a couple of school textbooks, nothing serious.'

Frank tried not to gape in amazement. He'd never met anyone who'd written a book before. 'If I get through this, I'd really like...' He stopped, feeling like a pathetic kid again, dreaming of a trainset for Christmas. He'd never had one of those and now he'd nearly confessed another unattainable ambition to the officer.

'What's that, Nixon?' said Lieutenant Chambers, frowning.

'Nothing, sir, just a stupid notion,' said Frank as the all clear sounded.

The hunger of their half-filled bellies sent them back to the canteen again to finish the cold remnants of their meal in the chilly room. They heard the sudden pounding of rain on the windows and sat waiting for a while for it to subside. Five minutes later, Frank and a couple of others ran across the yard to their quarters, diving in the open door of the bunkhouse. As soon as he was inside the door, Frank knew something was up. There was a smell of smoke.

'*Fire*,' yelled one of the men. 'There's a fucking fire in here. Get the extinguisher.'

Frank saw a column of smoke rising from somewhere near his bed.

'Christ. Haven't we had enough bleeding smoke for one day?' said someone, pushing past Frank with the metal canister.

Frank grabbed a bucket of sand, which stood outside the door, and followed him into the room. He saw, with dismay, that it was his bed on fire, smoke rising and a few flames flickering on the blackening blanket. He hurled the sand over the bed, killing the flames, while the other soldier squirted some stuff around the bed.

'At least it's not spread,' he said. 'Nice mess it's made of your bed, Corp.'

'You fucking idiot, Nixon. Left your bloody fag end burning,' said Sergeant Campbell, who had just come in behind them.

'It's OK now, Sarge. It's out,' said the helpful soldier with the extinguisher.

'What's up?' said another man, joining the small crowd around Frank's bed.

Frank stared down at the charred blanket and the smouldering book in the middle of it. *Malta: The Islands and their History*. He couldn't understand it. He'd put out his fag. He'd nipped it out and kept the rest of it for later. It was in his shirt pocket now.

CHAPTER 8

Green had done it. Frank knew. The book had a deep round burn hole in the centre of the pages where the bastard had obviously held a lit cigarette. Then he'd ignited the outer pages and used it to set fire to the bed. The chaos and interruptions of the air raid and the evacuation to the shelters had given him plenty of opportunity to get into the quarters alone. Now he was skulking around at the other side of the room, and Frank wanted to go and smash his face in. There was no way of proving that Green was guilty though, and Frank was too bothered about the ruination of the book to try and bring a case against him. There'd be little sympathy from his mates, as Frank often smoked when he was reading. So, he stuffed the burnt book under his singed mattress and went in search of another blanket from the stores even though he knew it was unlikely there'd be anybody about at this time in the evening. He just had to get outside for a bit.

As he went across the yard, he wondered how much a book like that would have cost. He'd have to offer the lieutenant some money, but he had no idea how much it should be. The officer would certainly never lend him another book now. This was the end of his pitiful effort to get more educated, he thought with some bitterness. It was a stupid idea anyway. Did he think he could be some kind of bloody historian or something? Why couldn't he just concentrate on staying alive and getting through the war?

It had stopped raining now and the night was calm and cold with a half-moon lightening the sky. There was no one about, and he discovered that of course the stores were locked up. He'd have to sleep in his clothes.

He walked on across the square towards the arched entrance gate, drawn by the sight of the inky sky speckled with stars. The lack of noise was astonishing. It calmed him. He couldn't remember when he'd last experienced anything like this precious silence. As he stood there, he imagined that in breathing the night air, he was expelling his anger. The guards, two men from the Dorsets, at the sentry posts asked him where he was going, and he offered them a smoke, joking quietly about how pointless it would be to go AWOL on this island.

'Gozo's just over there, though,' said one of the men, pointing his fag hand to the north. 'I bet it's nice and peaceful. I wouldn't say no to a little trip.'

'The sea's mined all around though,' said Frank. 'Fishing boat got blown up last week. It was in the paper.'

'Poor devils.'

Frank pointed into the darkness. 'I just want a whiff of the sea while it's quiet.'

'Don't fall in,' said the other man.

Frank walked the short distance along a pathway far enough to see the glossy blackness of the sea in the distance, its waves highlighted with slivers from the moonlight. The peace was not for long, however, and the invisible rumbling in the sky announced another imminent attack on Valletta five miles away. He peered into the dark sky and made out the shapes of about twenty aircraft, heard the drone of their engines building up. From the distance, the blurred yellow bands of searchlights striped the sky and then the distant rattle of anti-aircraft guns. Soon afterwards, he saw the fireworks—showers of yellow and red squirting into the air—and the small blots of fires burning. It would have been beautiful if it had not been war.

Frank rose early, cold because of his lack of a blanket and smelling the sour smokiness of his bed. But he had little resentment and anger left, as he had a whole free day ahead of him. What a gift. He washed and shaved quickly, anticipating his plans for the day, a visit to Chalky in the hospital and then, though he hardly dared to dwell on it too much, he'd go and see Manwela. He didn't want to contemplate the possibility that she might not be at home, that she might be visiting her son in hospital. He simply had to try and see her. He had to take every chance he could. At some point too, he'd need to speak to Lieutenant Chambers about the book, but he'd maybe leave that for a few days, till he could think how best to broach it.

Sergeant Campbell wouldn't let him borrow a bike, as they were all needed for patrols, but Frank didn't mind walking, though he knew that his journeys would take the best part of the day. He left the main road and took country paths west towards the military hospital at Imtarfa, rough stony roads alongside the low limestone walls, then up onto a ridge with a view of the sloping terraced land stretching out before him. He greeted two men digging in a small field and another repairing the gate of his yard, which contained two thin goats. From the sky, any Jerry pilot could look down and think him a farmer too. Leftover bombs were dropped on the countryside quite often. The raids were designed to destroy the will and morale of the people as well as wrecking the airfields, docks and ammunition stores. People held their breath when planes passed overhead, glad but guilty, knowing that some other poor sod somewhere else was probably going to cop it.

He reached the hospital, on higher land beyond Ta Qali airfield, at about ten o'clock. The matron pursed her lips when he asked if he could see Lance Corporal White of the Second Battalion of the Devonshires, but she pointed the way, telling him he could only stay for half an hour. He passed a man on crutches with a bandaged stump of a leg and a nurse pushing a slumped patient in a wheelchair. The stone floors of the corridor were scrubbed clean and smelt of carbolic. Frank reached Ward C and pushed open the door, finding a long room with rows of iron beds on either side. Some men were sitting in bed, others smoking in groups, a few reading the paper in chairs at their bedsides. Chalky, a bandage round his head, was lying propped up on pillows, staring at the ceiling, slack-mouthed and glum.

His face lit up when he spotted Frank. 'Hey, Nixy. Good to see you, mate.'

Frank shook his friend's hand, grasping his arm, gladder than he'd imagined to see Chalky nearly himself again, his restless blue eyes darting around.

'Got to get out of this place, Nix,' he said. 'It's full of the bloody sick and injured. You could pick up anything in here, TB, polio, all sorts, and it's boring as hell. Doc says he'll discharge me once he knows I'm not barmy in the head.' He rolled his eyes.

Frank laughed, looking around at the other patients.

Chalky continued, 'Some blokes like it, the skivers, that is. But if it weren't for the nurses, I'd be off my head. It's enough to make you take up reading. Here, you got any of your books on you?'

'That's a bit of a sore point,' said Frank. 'But haven't they got any in here? I thought there was a trolley or something came round hospitals.'

'Might have, but I haven't seen any.'

'I'll go and find out,' said Frank. 'Have you got enough smokes?'

'Yes,' said Chalky, 'but if you find me a stray nurse, bring her back, eh?'

Frank went out of the ward and spotted a nurse, a pleasant round-faced Maltese girl, coming out of a doorway on the corridor.

'We're only allowed to take books round after two o'clock, Matron's orders,' she said in response to Frank's question. 'So your friend will have to wait.'

'Really?' Frank smiled at her. 'You couldn't just let me choose one for him now?'

The nurse cast a quick glance over her shoulder, then looked back at Frank. 'Well, all right, just for you.'

Frank saw, to his surprise, that she was blushing.

'This way. The books are in here,' she said, indicating a door a few yards to her right. She led the way, opening the door of a deep cupboard in which was a trolley on wheels loaded with books. 'Take one for your friend. Write in here his name and the name of the book.' She handed him a small, tattered notebook.

'Thanks very much,' he said.

'It's a pleasure,' she said, blushing again. 'I've got to go. Shut the door behind you. Come back any time you want.'

Frank watched the nurse retreating down the corridor, realising that, for a change, he'd not been the bashful one.

At the sight of the books, he had a sudden inspiration that he might find a history book, perhaps even buy it from the hospital store, to give to Lieutenant Chambers as part compensation for the ruin of his other. However, one look at the collection showed him his error. *The Mystery of Dr F-Manchu, Murder at the Vicarage, Fallen Angel, King Kong.* They were thick, with shabby lurid covers, but he found *Of Mice and Men* by John Steinbeck, which was quite short. On reading the blurb on the back, he wished he could borrow it himself. He carefully wrote the details in the notebook and went back to the ward.

An hour later, he was on the road again, with a growing sense of excitement as he made his way towards Naxxar. He stopped in Mosta for a bite to eat in a cafe as the Rediffusion loudspeaker in the village square crackled out the latest news about the bombing. 'The enemy has struck again at the heart of the cities of Senglea and Vittorioso... Water mains damaged... Houses in Triq il-Mina I-Kbira have been destroyed...'

The announcement was soon overwhelmed, however, by the scream of an air-raid warning siren, and everyone in the cafe started shifting, grumbling and making their way out to the nearest shelter. It was in a basement under a two-storey house and was a tight fit for all the folk who'd been on the street. There was no panic, only a quiet resignation on the faces of the people as they filed into the damp darkness. Going into shelters was routine for everyone now, an inconvenient necessity most times, more frightening when the ground shook and bits of stone crumbled on you inside. He'd been spooked too underground on those two occasions when his imagination had got the better of him. Standing wedged in with the other people, this time he was just impatient for the all-clear, as the time was going on and his desire to see Manwela was growing stronger and more desperate the more he was delayed.

An hour later, he edged his way out with the others and was back on the road to Naxxar. He'd brought two bars of chocolate and a small bundle of his dirty washing in his haversack, but it embarrassed him to think about it. If she didn't ask him for it, he wouldn't say anything. He quickened his stride as he approached the village. Two old women, standing on their doorsteps, paused in their gossip to stare as he went by. He greeted them with a hearty 'Bonġu', at which they smiled and exchanged a few comments, chuckling to each other.

By the time he reached Manwela's yard, his heart was pulsing furiously. Her four white chickens pecked in their pen in the yard and the tethered goat bleated at him as he went to the door and knocked. There was no answer, and his heart sank. She must be out at the hospital. But what about her grandmother and her other boy? He wondered whether to knock again just as the door opened slowly and a stocky woman with a fuzz of black hair stood there. Her shapeless face took Frank by surprise in place of the pretty one he'd expected to see, and he started.

'Ex-excuse me,' he stuttered, 'I'm looking for –'

'My sister is not here,' she said in a heavy Maltese accent accompanied by a hard stare.

'When is she coming back?' said Frank, struggling to see any resemblance between this woman and Manwela.

The woman's face did not change. 'Hospital,' she said.

'Her son? Is he...?'

She shrugged.

Frank had no idea what to do now. This woman clearly disliked him on sight, or perhaps it was soldiers or foreigners she distrusted. She was certainly not going to be drawn into further conversation and he had little confidence in his power to persuade her to tell him more. If only he could leave Manwela a message, find out about Joseph, tell her he'd called. He stood facing the woman, wretchedly searching for something to say and knowing at any point that the woman was liable to shut the door in his face. Then he remembered the chocolate in his haversack and swung it from his shoulder, fumbling with the buckles and straps. The woman folded her arms and watched him, her wordless scrutiny making his search for the chocolate more desperate and clumsy. The bars had worked their way to the bottom, under his dirty washing, and in his attempts to reach them, a pair of dirty underpants and a shirt spilled out on the doorstep.

It was then that Frank saw the small boy, David, standing just behind the woman's legs, staring at the sight of him grovelling in the bag. But Frank felt the chocolate bars and pulled them out, holding them towards the woman.

'Mrs Vassallo's grandmother likes chocolate, I think.'

'I want, I want,' said the little boy, propelling himself in the air in a series of eager jumps.

To Frank's surprise, the woman's face cracked into a laugh.

'Grazzi,' she said, snatching the two bars of chocolate, handing one to the little boy with some kind of stern instruction that caused his face to fall. Then she turned back to Frank with a brisk 'Sahha' and slammed the door.

He bent down to stuff his dirty clothes back in the bag, disappointment seeping into him, sickening his stomach.

It was early afternoon as Frank made his way, in a dispirited mood, along the last leg of his journey back to the barracks. He'd been stupid to expect Manwela to be at home waiting for him to arrive. He needed to get a grip of himself and not be such drip, such a bloody soft twerp. As he walked, he struggled to salvage some optimism and not let disappointment sour this precious free day, the last he might have for some time. He didn't want to go back yet, but he was tired with all the trekking he'd done, halfway over the island, and he needed to have a drink of water and get rid of his bag of dirty clothes. Perhaps he could just go back for a quick kip or learn a few more words of Maltese. If only he'd had more history to read, he'd have been quite happy. Perhaps some of the damaged book might still be readable, though he doubted it. This reminded him of the difficult duty he had yet to do: tell Lieutenant Chambers about it.

On his approach to the main entrance of the barracks, he saw a motorcycle and rider coming out hesitantly, revving too much and weaving over the road, a novice with limited control of the machine, by the look of him. The engine sputtered to a stop, and the rider, an officer, put his feet down. The two men on guard watched this spectacle and exchanged a few words, though neither went to assist the rider. Frank saw now that the incompetent motorcyclist was in fact his platoon commander, Lieutenant

Chambers. He had dismounted and was wheeling the machine to the side of the road, to let a squad of the Dorsets march out. As Frank came nearer, the lanky, awkward figure of the officer peered at the machine in puzzlement. Frank was no expert himself, but he'd had a few rides when training and had helped his first motorcycle-mad corporal in the repair shop sometimes. There was no avoiding the officer now. Perhaps, Frank thought, he might be better able to confess about the book if he could be of some help to the lieutenant first.

Lieutenant Chambers looked up and saw Frank approaching, then straightened up, with a pained expression on his face.

'Nixon, do you happen to know anything about these wretched things? Can't seem to keep the damn thing going. It's a swine to start too. Any ideas?'

Frank approached, swinging his haversack off his shoulder. 'Don't know, sir, but I'll have a look.'

The motorbike was a normal Norton 16H, pretty beaten up with balding tyres, but Frank immediately found the problem.

'It's the choke, sir. Once you've started up, you need to release it as quick as possible or it'll flood the engine. I think that's what happened. You'll have to leave it a bit to dry out.'

'Damn,' said the lieutenant, 'how long will that take? I need to get to Valletta before five.'

'Well, we could try it again in about five minutes,' said Frank.

The officer scratched his neck. 'I need to get to the bookshop. The chap that owns it closed up when the bombing started, but he's just started opening on Tuesday afternoons for a couple of hours, so Captain Miller told me. He's got the best collection of new and second-hand books on the island. You'd be interested in getting a look too, wouldn't you, Nixon?'

'Sir,' said Frank, swallowing like a small boy about to be caned, 'I need to tell you something.'

'What? You've not discovered another cave, have you?' said the officer with a smile.

Frank told him quickly about the fate of his book, though he didn't say anything about his suspicions of Green's act of vandalism. There was little point. It wouldn't restore the ruined book.

'I'm sorry, sir. It was an accident. If you tell me how much, I'll pay. I owe you. I'm sorry.' He glanced up at Lieutenant Chambers, who was frowning at him.

The officer sighed, his face stern, and Frank wouldn't have been surprised if he'd got a sharp clip round the ear. 'That's a pity,' he said. 'Not sure I'll be able to get another copy. It's out of print, you see.'

'I'm sorry, sir,' said Frank, wishing the officer had shown more anger and wanting to run away now he knew that the book could not be replaced.

There was an awkward silence. Frank stared at the dusty ground, not daring to look up.

'I tell you what, Nixon, if you want to atone for your misdeed in some way, why not give me a ride into Valletta on this? You can ride one of these wretched things, can't you, if I ride pillion?'

Frank felt himself redden in the face. 'Yes, I suppose so, sir.'

He remembered the late Corporal Myles's warning remarks about Lieutenant Chambers being a queer.

'Come on, then, get it started up,' said the lieutenant.

Frank mounted the bike, kicked down hard on the starter pedal and the engine coughed into life. The officer climbed up clumsily behind him.

'Best hold on, sir,' shouted Frank and pulled away.

They were a mile down the road towards Valletta, and Frank found himself enjoying the thrill of the air, the countryside rushing past and the precarious speed of the machine. Then he remembered that he'd left his haversack of dirty washing behind on the road. But he didn't care. On their left was the sea, a dark and sparkling blue, stretched out unblemished before them, and Frank wished that it might always be like that. Concrete pillboxes and gun emplacements stood at regular intervals along the coastal edges and fences of barbed wire disfigured every small sandy strip or stony beach.

'Steady on,' called the lieutenant to Frank as they slewed dangerously round a corner taken too fast, the tyres skidding on the gritty road.

They were soon approaching the road that skirted the creeks on the approach to Floriana. Manoel Island and its old fever hospital, now the base for the submariners, lay on their left. Frank coaxed the labouring machine up the slope to Floriana, the pleasant suburb of Valletta with its own fortified wall around, through the Portes des Bombes. There was less bomb damage here, though some of the elegant stone houses had lost their front elevations and stood like people discovered naked, their clothes rudely ripped from them. Piles of stone testified to other buildings that had been completely obliterated. Some women were clambering over the stones of a recently wrecked house, tugging at things in the rubble. There were few vehicles on the straight Triq Sant'Anna leading to the city gates of Valletta, only some donkey carts, a number of carozzi, bicycles and many pedestrians going about their daily lives, defying the constant and wearying onslaught of bombing.

In a small square in the city centre, Frank drew the motorcycle to a halt.

'Well, that was very exhilarating. Thanks, Nixon,' said the officer. He climbed off a little unsteadily and loosened his cap, which he had pulled down over his brows, making him look more like a village idiot than an army officer.

'I think we're in need of some refreshment. What do you say? There's a cafe near to Mr Falson's bookshop. I'm sure you could do with a beer.'

'Yes, sir,' Frank said, embarrassed but grateful.

It was odd for a soldier to be in the company of an officer like this, on a kind of social footing, but most people would probably think he was the lieutenant's batman, if they thought anything of it. It was wartime after all, and the city was full of armed forces personnel up to all sorts of tricks.

'Let me get them, sir,' said Frank when they reached the cafe, a rundown little place with crumbling paintwork on the windows, rickety tables and chairs and a fat man behind the bar.

'Well, that's very generous, Nixon,' said the officer. 'Look, you don't need to keep paying me back in kind for that book, you know.'

Frank nodded and wondered if in another life, if he'd been born into different circumstances, a different class, he and this amiable, eccentric officer might have been friends. Frank bought two glasses of pale, watery-looking beer and set them down on a table in the corner. Lieutenant Chambers started stuffing his pipe with tobacco.

'So, tell me, Nixon, what sparked your interest in history?'

Frank told him about his few experiences of visiting historic sites and his paltry collection of guidebooks. 'I'd really like to know and understand more, sir,' he said, feeling more at ease with the aid of the beer and the officer's air of relaxed carelessness. 'It's because of history we're in this state today.'

'How true. But you left school as soon as you could, I suppose?' said the officer, lighting his pipe.

'Had to, sir. And I wasn't much cop, I mean, very clever. I should have tried harder, I suppose. One lad got a scholarship, and he went on and did his school certificate. I joined up as a junior soldier.'

'Hmm, and you'd like to take up studying, would you?'

'Yes, sir, but I've missed the boat now, I reckon, even if I get home in one piece.'

The lieutenant puffed on his pipe. 'I wouldn't say that, Nixon. Haven't you ever heard of night school, the Mechanics' Institutes or the WEA?'

'No, sir,' said Frank.

'My wife is a great advocate of that sort of thing, you know, education for the working man, and woman, of course.'

'Your wife, sir?' Frank tried not to sound too surprised.

'Yes, Millicent,' said the officer. 'Damn clever woman, my wife, and a splendid looker. Don't know how she ended up with me.'

Lieutenant Chambers stared out towards the street, as though he expected to see his attractive wife arriving at any moment. 'Read classics at Oxford, much brainier than me. She's doing war work now, you know, communications. We're not meant to know about it, very hush-hush. But before the war, she used to teach at Birkbeck College and for the WEA. She said she wanted to teach people who were really eager to learn and had never had the chance. She's never been one for darning socks.'

Frank was amazed at these revelations and hoped he wasn't gawping too much at the officer as he spoke.

'Have you got any kids, sir?'

The lieutenant shook his head and knocked out the remnants of his ash into a tin ashtray on the table. 'Sadly, no,' he said. 'Millicent couldn't carry any beyond a month or so. Lost four of them. It wasn't right to keep trying.'

Frank was sorry he'd asked, shocked at his tactless question. He shifted his feet, wondered whether it was right to offer con-dolences, but stayed quiet in case he committed another gaffe.

'Well, at least there'll be no fatherless children if I don't make it back,' said Lieutenant Chambers, taking a swift drink of his beer and swiping a finger along the bottom of his moustache. 'Let's talk books, unless you prefer soldiering.'

'I know a bit about the second and nothing about the first,' said Frank.

'Well, in that case, let's be on our way to Mr Falson's shop.'

The bookshop was in a narrow lane just off Triq Il-Merkanti, and the shop was a thin, three-storey building, but it looked dead and closed up from the outside. The door was locked. At first, Frank thought the lieutenant must have been misinformed about the fact that it would be open at all that day. Lieutenant Chambers rapped on the door several times, and the door was finally opened by a priestly-looking man, black-coated with a close-cropped head and thick spectacles.

'Bongu, Sinjur Falson,' said Lieutenant Chambers, then continued in a few bursts of Maltese at which the man smiled and nodded, answering eagerly and standing aside for them with his hand extended to welcome them in.

'That's the extent of my Maltese, I'm afraid,' said Lieutenant Chambers, introducing himself. 'And this is Corporal Nixon from my platoon, Second Battalion the Devonshire Regiment. I only wish we were visiting your shop at a happier and more peaceful time.'

'Delighted, gentlemen,' the bookseller replied with a yellow-toothed smile, 'but it is a good distraction, reading, even in time of war, is it not? Now, what interests you in particular? What language do you prefer? I have texts in French, German, Arabic, Russian—'

'I think we'd best stick to English,' said the officer, 'and we're particularly interested in the history of the Maltese islands and the Mediterranean, isn't that right, Nixon?'

Frank nodded, beginning to feel as if he'd somehow stepped into someone else's life by mistake. He'd never seen a place like this, nor been addressed as a gentleman. The shop had bookshelves from floor to ceiling down both walls. In the middle, more shelves formed a wide partition, leaving only narrow passages to squeeze by on either side. The spines of books were jammed together on the shelves in all colours: dull brown leather, faded black, reds and blues. It was like an over-stuffed library from which no one ever borrowed any books.

'Quite a collection, isn't it?' said the lieutenant to Frank.

'This way,' said the bookseller, beckoning with his finger that they should follow him.

They squeezed their way through to the end of the shop, where a metal spiral staircase led to an upper floor. Here was a similar sight, a room crammed with shelves, this time with books in stacks on the floor as well.

'Here is the Maltese history collection,' said the bookseller. 'English here, from this shelf to the one below. Then there are memoirs, diaries and other older records, none I believe in English. I must check through them all one of these days and take the most valuable to the museum, I think. But in the meantime, gentlemen, help yourselves. Call me if you have need of assistance.'

Frank contemplated the row in front of him, daunted and doubtful about where and how to start. Lieutenant Chambers had moved into the next aisle, so Frank was able to dither without embarrassment, scanning the titles and authors on the spines. He took off the shelf *A History of Malta during the Period of the French and British Occupations 1798 – 1815* by William Hardman and within a few paragraphs was drawn in, recognising some facts and information he'd already come across.

Some time later, Frank had selected four books he would like to buy, though he couldn't find any indication of the price on them. They'd probably be far too pricey for him. He wondered whether to ask Lieutenant Chambers, but the officer was now sitting on the floor, leaning against a shelf, deeply absorbed in reading a small, leather-bound book. The pages appeared, as far as Frank could make out, to be written in handwriting, not print.

'Fascinating, absolutely fascinating,' the officer said, looking up. 'I think this is one of the books that belongs in the museum.' Lieutenant Chambers hauled himself to his feet, holding the small dingy-looking volume in one hand.

'What is it, sir?'

'It's a diary, a diary from 1798, written during the French occupation of Malta.' The officer held out the book to Frank. It was written in a tiny, neat script in some foreign language.

'This is the journal of one Lieutenant Pierre-Auguste Bourgault, a French officer in Napoleon Bonaparte's army.'

'Was this before the British took over?' said Frank, peering at the book, wishing he could read a foreign language too.

'Yes, Napoleon had his sights set on Egypt, and Malta was a good jumping off point. The Maltese were not very keen on the Knights who were ruling them at that time, so they welcomed the French. Napoleon kicked out the Knights and then set to, reorganising things,'

'How did the British take over, then?' asked Frank.

'Well, Napoleon, with all his reforming zeal and territorial ambition, soon made himself very unpopular with the Maltese. He ordered the dismantling of the rule of the church. Lots of the Maltese churches and religious institutions were plundered. He purloined anything valuable from churches, closed monasteries to pay for his army and navy. Very silly thing to do.'

Lieutenant Chambers was slowly turning over the pages of the diary as he spoke.

'So, the Maltese had had enough. They rose in rebellion against the French, killed a couple of thousand of them too and then attacked Valletta where the rest of the French army was holed up. The Maltese had the help of the British, of course, good old Lord Nelson, who was always happy to take a pot at the French.

But there was a long siege, two years in fact, before the French surrendered to the British.'

'Another siege?' said Frank. 'And this is the actual diary of a bloke, I mean an officer, who was here at the time?'

'Yes, and I must have it, providing it's not too madly expensive,' said the officer, as excited as a small child in a sweet shop. 'What about you? Have you found anything of—'

The air-raid warning sounded, cutting off the lieutenant's last words, and now it was growing in volume and urgency to its full wolf-like howl.

'Damnation,' said Lieutenant Chambers, closing the book and grabbing two others he had set aside.

Downstairs, the bookseller was in an extreme state of agitation, urging them to hurry out so that he could close up and protect the shop.

'Oh dear God in heaven, why can't they leave us in peace? I've got to put the shutters up,' he said. 'I can't leave until the shutters are up.'

'I'll do it, sir. Tell me where they are,' said Frank.

The shopkeeper looked startled but grateful and pointed to a small office off the main shop where several large wooden boards were leaning against the wall. Frank reluctantly set down his books and lifted up the first panel, running out into the street and placing it against one window. The lieutenant followed and started fastening it in place with the metal brackets while Frank ran back in for the next.

The siren howled and wardens were shouting to hurry people to the shelters. People rushed by at the end of the street. Mr Falson stood in the alley, fidgeting back and forth on his feet and wringing his hands.

'I'll do this last one,' said Frank. 'You lock the door, sir, and both get on your way.'

'Good man,' said Lieutenant Chambers as he ushered the bookseller away quickly up the alley to the street where others were rushing to the nearest shelter.

Frank had to force the last metal rod into the bracket of the window shutter, but managed it in a few minutes, leaning against it to ensure that it was properly closed.

A loud explosion sounded from somewhere beyond the alley, and he ran up the way the other two had gone. Then came a hideous banshee whistling noise, like some maniac dog on the loose, and a rumbling, a quaking in the ground, then the heavy crashing of masonry. There was no one else on the street when he came out from the alley, sidling along by the buildings, not daring to look up. He scrambled over a pile of rubble, seeing a greater mountain of what had once been a building ahead, in the middle of the roadway. He didn't know whether to go on or go back to the alley again.

The air went quiet, the dust floating slowly down. Frank stood, taut and immobile, looking at the pile of stones. Wondering if there was a way through, he noticed, at the foot of the tumbled wreckage some ten yards ahead of him, an object, a small brown book. It lay like a dead rat, and he stumbled over the rubble to grab it, discovering to his alarm that it was the diary Lieutenant Chambers had found in the shop. He searched the hill of broken stone blocks with his eyes, clutching the book, his heart pounding. The cover felt strangely warm in his hand, as though it had been held next to the heat of someone's body, then from the thing itself, but it couldn't be, came a groan, deep in the throat of someone in terrible agony.

CHAPTER 9

CITTA NOTABILE, MALTA, SEPTEMBER 1798

It was a sign of the times that one such as he, Pierre-Auguste Bourgault, should be entertained in a palazzo. In preparation for the soirée, he took more pains with his hair, trimmed his moustache and put on his newly brushed uniform. A small surge of pride assailed him as he stood in front of his looking glass, the son of a Breton bootmaker in the uniform of Lieutenant of the Seventh Light Infantry in the Army of the Republic. He was not often given to such vanities, however, being a true child of the Revolution, with a clear vision of his duty.

Here on this rocky island, peopled by an ignorant, superstitious peasantry and an idle nobility, there was much work to be done. This invitation to his commanding officer and himself, to the house of the wealthy notary Bezzini was just the beginning. It would surely prove to be an important step in overcoming certain difficulties with the Maltese. These people did not fully appreciate, nor indeed understand, the new liberties and rights that the Republic of France was bestowing so generously upon them.

Pierre-Auguste quitted the garret room, which he shared with two fellow officers, descended the stone staircase and found the commander of the garrison, Capitaine Rodolphe Masson, standing by the fireplace in the wide hallway. Their billet, this grand house, had been the home of some aged noble who had been shuffled off somewhere when the Seventh Light needed suitable officers' quarters. At the sound of Pierre-Auguste's footsteps, the capitaine turned. Pierre-Auguste stood to attention and saluted.

'Come,' said the capitaine with a smile. 'We may forget rank this evening, for we are at leisure, are we not?'

Pierre-Auguste's shoulders slackened, grateful to Masson for this invitation of friendship. He did not know the commander well, having only served under him since the departure of the Seventh Light Infantry from Marseilles a month ago, but from what he had surmised so far, the capitaine was a competent soldier of affable disposition.

'Let us hope that Senjur Bezzini has some pretty daughters at least,' said Capitaine Masson, 'otherwise it may be hard toil enduring the complaints from the petty nobles and miserable priests. Dear God, let's hope there are no priests. This island is infested with them, like black rats. And churches too. Have you ever seen so many churches?'

Pierre-Auguste laughed out of courtesy to his commander, though he experienced some secret discomfort at these irreverent comments. His mother, who had been inclined to piety, had instilled in him a lasting, though irrational respect for the church. He trusted that his commander, when face-to-face with his hosts, would display the necessary diplomacy and tact. Both would be needed to calm the ripples that were evident in the attitudes of some of the populace against them.

The two walked together towards the gateway leading out of the grounds of the mansion turned barracks. Two soldiers were posted at the gate and saluted as the officers passed through, on to a main thoroughfare of white grit, like most of the roads on the island. Pierre-Auguste had never seen landscape of such aridity when he had first arrived, though there were pockets of colour and fruitfulness, where the ingenuity of the farmers and gardeners, coupled with Nature's bounties, even in this climate, created fecundity.

The suburb, Rabat, through which they now walked lay outside the tall walls of the fortified town of Citta Notabile, the ancient Mdina of the Arabs. They passed one or two elegant palazzos, for this was the area where the majority of the aristocracy had their houses, away from the harbours and coasts around Valletta. The nobles knew well how to keep themselves secure, immured in their fortresses, far from the ravages of the corsairs, which had afflicted their less fortunate Maltese brethren. Between the grander houses were smaller dwellings, many low stone walls forming terraced gardens and some humble hovels belonging to the poorer sort. Goats bleated from small enclosures and a few barefoot children came by bearing flagons of water.

'It is to be welcomed, this invitation, is it not?' said Pierre-Auguste. 'It shows a willingness on the part of the Maltese to become more familiar with the principles and values of our great Republic.'

Capitaine Masson laughed lightly. 'Yes, of course, my friend, it does, no doubt. What better aim could we have but to turn them all into Frenchmen?'

Pierre-Auguste felt his face flush, aware that the capitaine was mocking him and worse that he had witnessed his discomfiture. Masson laughed again and clapped Pierre-Auguste on the back with relaxed bonhomie.

'No, my friend, I am jesting only. We will never turn these people into Frenchmen. They are half Arab, half Italian after all. The common people are harmless enough and docile, ruled as they are by their priests. The nobles, now stripped of their titles, are powerless. The proud and dissolute Knights of the Order of St John were the real rulers of this island, and they, as you know, have been expelled. So, it is a rudderless ship we have boarded. We must steer it our way now.'

Pierre-Auguste did not like the swagger of his commanding officer's certainty, nor his belittling of the populace upon whose island they found themselves not wholly welcome guests. They were nearing the golden yellow stone fortress walls of the Citta Notabile and directed their steps towards the main portal, guarded by some of their own men from the garrison.

'There is a greater enemy,' Capitaine Masson continued, 'the British. Now there is a force we must overcome. But General Bonaparte is their equal, have no doubt about that, and he shall have a great victory in Egypt.'

They crossed through the gateway into the narrow streets of the fortress town, with tall houses on either side, all constructed of blocks of the same gold-white stone. Some had elaborate carvings adorning their front elevations, others with huge ornate door handles. In the shade of these alleys, up a slight incline, Pierre-Auguste felt contained, imprisoned almost by the many-storeyed buildings in this tiny, compact city.

Shutters hung open now as the evening cooled the air, and linen bedding hung like empty shrouds from some windows. A woman leaned out from one of the windows ahead. Pierre-Auguste saw her bare arms brandishing a chamber pot. Something in her attitude, the tilt of her head, the sharpness of her eyes, betrayed her intent.

Pierre-Auguste caught Masson's arm to halt him from his progress up the street just as the woman hurled the slops from her pot to splash and spurt upon the cobbles in their path. The woman's head disappeared from view while the capitaine, unperturbed, remarked on the pleasant warmth of the evening.

The palazzo was an elegant two-storey mansion with an arched entrance. Here, a servant admitted them and led them through to a marble hallway of grand but not magnificent proportions and thence into an open courtyard where many guests, swathed in a hum of conversation, were assembled. Lanterns hung about the walls and upon the balustrade of a stone staircase that led to a gallery above.

The guests appeared to be Maltese of the better sort, though a number of the men wore no coats, only silk shirts and waist-coats, just as the peasants of the island did, though these guests were clearly of greatly superior quality. Their costumes had the look of traditional dress, but Pierre-Auguste noted that they all wore tricolour cockades of France, as they were obliged by law to do. There were ladies, most becomingly attired, with pretty dresses of vivid coloured silk and fringed shawls in the manner of Italians, their hair arranged attractively in the style of ancient Roman women. These people were not tall, but were sturdy of stature, dark-haired and brown-eyed. Pierre-Auguste and Cap-itaine Masson stood out starkly in their uniforms as the only Frenchmen.

Pierre-Auguste was aware of a slight feeling of malaise in his gut. Was it unease or hunger? He was not sure. Masson, however, smiled and was clearly gratified by the civilised and cultivated de-meanour of the party thus assembled. The notary Sinjur Bezzini greeted them in French, with the appropriate courtesies.

'Welcome, gentlemen,' he said. 'I am so glad you could attend our soirée. Capitaine Masson and Lieutenant Bourgault, allow me to present to you my wife.'

The lady was short and plumpish, wearing an extravagant necklace of jade stones set in silver about her fleshy neck. She smiled pleasantly.

'Enchanté, madame,' said Pierre-Auguste, bowing in his turn, to which she returned him a broad smile and said something quietly to her husband in Maltese.

A servant appeared with a tray of glasses of wine.

'Messieurs, you must taste my wine,' said Sinjur Bezzini. 'It is from one of our own vineyards. We cannot hope, of course, on our poor small island to equal your great French wine growers, but I think you will find it very pleasing.'

The wine was very good, and Pierre-Auguste was pleased to accept a generous refilling of his glass. He felt his face flush and wished that he, like the shirt-sleeved guests, had the liberty of their cooler attire.

A number of other men soon joined their group, clustering around Pierre-Auguste and Masson. They were introduced to most of these, but Pierre-Auguste, his brain a little fuzzy with the effects of the wine, remembered only one. He was a small gentleman with piercing black eyes, who spoke deliberate, heavily accented French: Sinjur Lorenzo Bugeja. He seemed keen to talk of military affairs, to know the strength of the garrisons at Rabat and in Valletta and pursued with great persistence his desire for knowledge of this with Capitaine Masson.

'It is the English, you know, who want to attack, I think,' Sinjur Bugeja said. 'Have you powder enough and canon to stop them?'

Masson laughed. 'The English, we are ready for them, of course. We have above four thousand men on the island, most in Valletta. And it is the strongest fortress I have ever seen. Nor have two hundred years weakened it since it withstood the might of the Turks. The English are nothing to them. We have a good stock of armaments at the palace of St Antonio too. No, we need have no fear of the English, my friend.'

Sinjur Bugeja seemed satisfied with this show of confidence and smiled while the servant replenished their glasses once more. As talk of the island's fortifications and General Bonaparte's campaigns continued, Pierre-Auguste's eye had been caught by a very alluring young lady on the other side of the courtyard. She stood alone, fingering the leaves of a lemon tree, plucking one and holding it delicately to her nose.

He was tired of listening to the talk of military strategy. Feeling an almost uncontrollable tug of attraction to this dark-haired beauty who lacked any visible companion, he managed to slip away from the edge of the group. As Pierre-Auguste approached her, he saw, to his delight, that she had withdrawn a little and was half-shielded by one of the pillars supporting the upper gallery. What harm to engage a charming young lady in polite conversation in such a gathering? At that moment, she looked up, and he was struck by her deep brown, penetrating eyes. Her face was unsmiling, fine-featured, proud. He was a little afraid, but dosed with courage from the wine, he approached and bowed to her.

'Madame, may I intrude upon you and presume to present myself?' he said.

She looked at him without a flicker of acknowledgement, but neither was it of displeasure, he thought. Perhaps she was unfamiliar with French, in which case he recognised that the conversation would be short, as he knew no other tongue. But to his surprise, she spoke, and in his language.

'Well, monsieur, you may, I suppose.'

'You do me a great honour.'

He announced his name and rank, watched for her reaction and was disappointed to see no change in her unsmiling face. 'And may I know your name?' he said, knowing that he was flushing but hoping that the evening light obscured this from her.

'Monsieur, I am Florencia Bugeja, and that gentleman with whom you were talking is my father.'

Her voice was soft but clear and confident, her French fluent, with a charming Italian accent. However, her eyes were unsmiling and fixed on him in a manner that made him quake before her. Had she been a Frenchwoman, he would have felt inadequate, but as a foreigner with different manners and customs, she was terrifying to him. He struggled to regain the power of speech.

'I hope you are gratified,' he said after what seemed like an interminable interval of silence, 'by the new liberties and rights that your people have been granted.'

She said nothing, giving no hint that she had even understood him. He wished now that he had not made this foolish approach to her and that he was safely back in the company of the capitaine and the others talking about ordnance. But he could not retreat now.

'General Bonaparte and his commissioners are great reformers,' he said, clearing his throat. 'They seek to bring justice to the oppressed, dismantle those instruments and institutions that hold people in thrall. This is the grand plan for Malta.'

She suddenly moved a step closer to him, her eyes black and piercing. He knew that he had recoiled from her, for he felt his heel strike against the marble pillar behind him.

'You hypocrites. Justice for the oppressed?' Her voice was a hard whisper, the hiss of a cat. 'General Bonaparte merely invents new instruments of oppression and falsely claims to offer us freedom and equality. He comes here, as other marauders, corsairs, emperors have done for centuries, to make us slaves. It is our fate and our misery, on these small islands, that we must always be beholden to the powerful.'

Back against the pillar, Pierre-Auguste struggled for some kind of defence against this attack.

'But, madame, what can you mean?' he said in a voice that sounded feeble and timorous, while she, like a stalking beast, moved on him again.

'It is for money, that's all. You fleece us to pay for your wars and your armies. Your wicked government levies taxes on us, plunders our churches and palaces for silver and gold to melt down for your army chests. You steal land from us, you cheat and thieve and make such things lawful by your evil articles and statutes. My father has told me all.'

'Madame, please. I beg you to...' Pierre-Auguste faltered, searching in panic for a response that might stay her. 'It is a time of change, of transition to a better system. The new laws will serve you well. If you have grievances, I'm sure—'

'God rot the souls of all Frenchmen,' she said, so close to him that he could feel her hot breath in his face.

'Your systems and laws have stolen leases from hundreds of people, forcing them into poverty. You have stopped pensions and alms for the poor and your laws steal from our sacred places, monasteries. You strangle the sanctity of our priests.'

'Madame, this is unjust,' he said, desperate, horrified at this harpy's attack. 'You do not understand. There is a larger picture than the small consequences that you describe. It is the vision of, of the Revolution.'

Pierre-Auguste's voice had become a strangled plea, but she stepped away from him again, her breast rising and falling rapidly, her eyes blacker than bog water. She plucked the tricolour emblem from her gown and threw it on the stone-flagged floor, grinding it with her foot.

'I spit on all Frenchmen. I curse your devil Bonaparte. I will laugh to see you perish in the sea or drown in your own blood at the end of a sword.' She turned swiftly and was gone, slipping through the chattering, laughing people and then through a doorway into the house.

Pierre-Auguste felt himself shaking and, with difficulty, straightened himself up from the position he had adopted, a cringing stoop.

He glanced around praying that no one had witnessed the scene. The young woman had spoken in a bitter whisper and they had been for the most part in the shadow of the pillar, well-obscured. He was relieved to hear the buzz of conversation, still loud and amiable, with no sound of menace. But on the other side of the courtyard, he saw that Capitaine Masson was slumped in a chair, his tunic half undone, dead drunk, with a servant standing over him, fanning him with a napkin. Filled with an urgency to escape the place, Pierre-Auguste rushed to the side of his commanding officer and shook him by the arm, managing to rouse him sufficiently to stand.

'Sir, we must go,' Pierre-Auguste whispered.

'No, no, mon brave. Courage, the wine is good and the company too.'

Pierre-Auguste nodded to the servant in an entreaty to help him with the drunken officer.

'Please give our apologies to Monsieur Bezzini,' said Pierre-Auguste as he hoisted Masson up and half-carried him past the smiling faces of some of the guests to the hallway. Neither their host nor his wife were to be seen, but Pierre-Auguste decided firmly against going to seek him out.

Two days later, Pierre-Auguste, still shaken from his experience at the soirée, took up his journal, in which he had written nothing since that event. It had been his intent to record all of his life as a soldier and servant of the Republic, for posterity. Now he wrote with a fevered urgency all that he could recall of the young woman's accusations, outrageous though he had judged them to be. But in so doing, he felt a wave of doubt and disgust. These had been more than the hysterical outpourings of a suggestible girl voicing the complaints of a few disgruntled Maltese noblemen who had had their livery and escutcheons stripped from their mansions. He had heard about other protests in Valletta of merchants and shopkeepers, crowds of the poor too, who had gathered demanding grain at affordable prices.

He had told Capitaine Masson about the young woman's outburst, begged him to investigate the causes of discontent and hardship of the Maltese, to send a plea to the civil authorities, to the commissioner himself to hear the islanders' complaints. But Masson had, with characteristic disdain, dismissed them as falsehoods and exaggerations.

Pierre-Auguste had to break off from his writing, however, when he heard a trumpet outside, demanding his presence at the inspection of the garrison troops. He closed his journal, wrapped it in a handkerchief and replaced it in his box under the bed, then took up his sword and belt and ran down to the yard where Capitaine Masson was already preparing to inspect the ranks of their men.

Pierre-Auguste, while crossing the yard, saw a man, a civilian, at the gate, gasping with the haste of running, demanding to be let in, which the two guards permitted on hearing his business. He made for Pierre-Auguste and burst forth his news in fragmented French.

'Trouble... Citta Notabile... the church. Come,' the man managed to utter.

'What kind of trouble?' asked Pierre-Auguste.

The man, uncomprehending, shook his head and pointed at Masson. 'He come. Tell him.'

Pierre-Auguste approached Capitaine Masson swiftly.

'Merde,' he said, thrusting his sword back into its sheath, 'we must delay inspection. Come. Let's see what mischief is afoot.'

'Sir, should we not take a platoon with us? There may be a crowd,' said Pierre-Auguste.

The officer shook his head. 'There is no need. It is petty fracas, dispelled by the sight of a sword, you will see.'

As Pierre-Auguste and Capitaine Masson approached the church of Our Lady of Mount Carmel within the walls of the Citta Notabile, they saw a small crowd clustered outside the door. Angry voices arose from the gathering, in the centre of which was a horse-drawn cart, the beasts whinnying at the press of the people, the driver flailing ineffectually at them with his whip. Two men in dark coats, with the look of officials, notaries or clerks, Pierre-Auguste thought, stood a little apart from the crowd, gesticulating and talking with a priest and two men in monks' habits. The two officials looked up at the sight of the commander of the garrison and Pierre-Auguste. They approached, accompanied by a rude hissing from the crowd.

One of the officials, a red-faced, blustering individual called out, 'Capitaine, you must assist us, please. These people will not let us go about our business.'

His voice was all but drowned out by the gabbling of the crowd, so he raised it to a shout. 'We have orders to uplift these items from the church and take them to Valletta for auction. We have the instructions and the signed orders from the commissioner himself. These foolish people do not seem to understand the rule of law.'

A stone flew from somewhere in the crowd and struck the official on the head, knocking his hat to the ground and giving rise to a wave of scornful laughter.

'Capitaine, it is your duty. You must enforce this and clear these obstructions from our way,' said the official while his companion, a small Maltese, flailed his arm at the crowd and squealed out a translation to them in their own tongue.

Masson turned and surveyed the crowd, then drew his sword.

'Allez-vous-en!' he called to the people, then turned to the Maltese official. 'Tell them in their language too, in case they do not understand.'

Pierre-Auguste drew his sword too and found to his dismay that one of his legs was quivering and his mouth was dry as dust. The crowd did not move, continuing their hissing and booing, but suddenly from above their heads, the church bell clanged once, twice, then mounted in volume to a manic tempo that obliterated all other sounds. From an alley at the side of the church, a band of common men emerged, armed with clubs and pitchforks, pausing only twenty paces short of the gathering. With every hideous peal of the bell, a few more men appeared from doorways and from the ends of alleys.

'Messieurs,' said Capitaine Masson in an undertone. 'We need a place of safety, I think.'

'This way,' said the Maltese official. 'I know a gentleman who will give us refuge.' He was pointing to the opposite side of the small square, from which led a narrow upward sloping street.

They set off towards the incline, led by the officials and Masson, with Pierre-Auguste taking the rear, sword drawn and ready, glancing behind, so charged with fear and agitation that he would have sliced apart even a passing cat or dog. They ran through the tunnel of tall houses to another small open square in which stood two large villas with arched doorways and over-hanging covered balconies of the type favoured in these parts.

The officials ran to the door of one of the houses and hammered furiously upon it, calling the while in urgent voices. In response to this frantic knocking, a servant opened the door and, without awaiting further invitation, the fugitives pushed inside, Pierre-Auguste leaping in last. The fat-faced official gasped at the servant, ordering him to secure the door. The man swiftly slid the metal bar in place, and the group stood panting, listening to the noise outside, the pounding feet of the mob and their guttural shouts.

A middle-aged man in a silk dressing gown appeared on the stairs, frowning with alarm and puzzlement at the sight of the four panting fugitives.

The red-faced official launched into an explanation, in Italian, which caused the owner's frown to deepen, his eyes to betray his fear.

'Monsieur,' said Capitaine Masson. 'Forgive us for bursting in upon you so rudely, but we seek shelter and respite from the wild townspeople outside. They have worked themselves into a frenzy about some government business. We seek your protection until they calm themselves.'

The proprietor's face blanched as a terrible crunching, splitting sound sent Pierre-Auguste and the others leaping away from the door into the hallway. A hatchet had splintered the wood, its blade embedded in the centre of the door.

'Upstairs, we must go upstairs,' said Masson, rushing for the staircase, where the officials had already started a scrambling ascent.

The owner, clutching the edges of his gown in a white hand, flattened himself against the curving wall as they passed. Pierre-Auguste gestured that the gentleman should follow after the retreating officials, while he remained the last to retreat up to the landing. Another blow landed on the door, and a cheer blew through the ragged hole.

Upon the landing, the owner ushered them into a large room overlooking the street, in which a lady and a maid were standing, white-faced and terrified, by the fireplace. The red-faced official blurted his explanation while the owner mopped his face with a handkerchief, his wife hanging on to his arm.

'You must calm them, Capitaine,' said the terrified owner of the house. 'It is you they wish to blame, you and your army and your commission, for the ills that have come upon us. You must go to them and make them leave peacefully. You bring danger here.'

Capitaine Masson's face had by now lost all colour, his assurance had vanished, his proud bearing replaced by the crouching stance of an animal at bay. His sword blade quivered. Pierre-Auguste was shocked at this transformation, though his own terror manifested itself in a different way, by a momentary paralysis. He managed to utter some words, however, the only possible course of action.

'Sir, we must reason with them,' he said in a voice as steady as he could summon. 'They have grievances, and we must listen. We must promise to take them to the authorities. We must give assurances.'

Pierre-Auguste's words seemed to stir the capitaine to a stronger hold upon himself, and he stood up, cleared his throat and resumed something of his familiar martial bearing. 'You are right, Lieutenant. We must parley. That is the way of civilised people. They must see the power of reason over force. Please let them in. I will speak to them.'

'Not here, Capitaine, I beg of you,' said the proprietor in a feeble voice. 'My wife cannot witness violence. Please leave our home. Meet them in the street below, will you not?'

The red-faced official stepped towards the man, gesturing angrily with a document and waving it in his face. Another loud crash came from below, and all in the upper chamber knew that the front door was gone. Then came the thundering of feet on the stairs. The wife squealed and grabbed her husband's arm, the couple shrinking back with their servant and maid into the corner of the room. Capitaine Masson stepped forward in front of the officials. Pierre-Auguste moved to his side, sword drawn, the blade shivering.

The door of the parlour was kicked, thumped and then swung open to admit the vanguard of the mob, six sturdy townsmen in working clothes, one wielding a long knife, curved like an Arab scimitar, others with wooden stakes, chisels and clubs. Behind them, others pressed in a mass. For a moment, there was a pause.

Masson breathed deeply, then he spoke, glancing aside to the Maltese official first. 'Monsieur, will you be so good as to translate my words, to make sure they are heard and understood?'

Pierre-Auguste did not hear whether the man answered or not. Masson raised his sword and threw it upon the floor, nodding that Pierre-Auguste should do likewise.

'I declare that no harm will come to you if you withdraw now and go peacefully to your homes,' said the capitaine. 'Neither the commission nor the Army of the Republic will seek to punish any of you for this affray.'

Pierre-Auguste's chest tightened as he dropped his sword upon the floor. The sweat upon his brow turned cold. This was not right. Would the capitaine say no more?

The short pause was broken. The six men at the front leapt forward and seized the capitaine, lifting him bodily, charging towards the balcony window. With a wild howl, they hurled him through the splintering glass and out onto the street below. Pierre-Auguste fell to his knees and bowed his head, which exploded into blackness a second later.

CHAPTER 10

MALTA, JULY 1941

M anwela's boy, Joseph, was sickly pale, but he was smiling.
His younger brother sat at his feet, like a vassal adoring
his king, this kitchen his palace. Frank took off his helmet and
handed it to Joseph, half of his face disappearing beneath it, leaving only a grinning mouth. Manwela stood looking on, hands on
hips, shaking her head in amusement, though Frank wondered if
there was a hint of disapproval too.

'Good to see you back,' said Frank to the boy.

Then he looked at Manwela, and she smiled. She'd smiled at
him many times now, but each one gave him the same joy and
disbelief as the first.

'He'll have to take it easy for a bit, I suppose,' Frank said.

'Yes,' Manwela replied. 'The doctor said he must not be tired or
play too long. And he must have good food. That is very difficult
these days.'

The old woman, who had been watching these proceedings
from her chair in the corner of the room, lifted a finger and
pointed at Frank, saying something in Maltese, in a tone that
sounded to him like an accusation. Manwela replied, her voice
smooth, soothing, her enunciation slow. Frank heard her say his
name and say he was British and was here to fight the Germans.

129

He wasn't sure what else, as his knowledge of the language was still extremely limited.

'She's asking who you are again. Her memory is getting worse every day. She doesn't recognise you, though she has seen you many times,' said Manwela.

Frank nodded, glancing at the old woman, who had settled back in her chair and now watched her great-grandsons as they argued about the helmet.

'She says that the boys must not be soldiers when they're grown,' said Manwela.

'She's right,' said Frank. 'Anything but that.'

Manwela nodded but said nothing. He wondered what choices these children would have in this world where they were growing up. They were witnessing their country being blasted and destroyed all around them in a war that they might lose. History showed that after war comes peace, but when and at what cost?

'Will you stay for supper with us?' said Manwela.

'I'd like to, Manwela,' he said, savouring her name, still thrilled that she had invited him to use it. 'But I've got to get back for an exercise in an hour, so I'll have to be on my way. Anyway, it'll leave more for you.'

He wished he could have taken her hand, could have touched her; instead, he stepped over to the boys, reclaiming his helmet from Joseph with a smile.

'I want hat,' said David, jumping up. 'Frank hat.'

'I want Frank's hat,' Joseph corrected with a smug look.

Frank laughed. 'Next time, I promise, you'll have it. Now, here's a bit of something for you all,' he said, handing David half a bar of chocolate, 'but you'll have to split it in four. One piece for your mother, one for your great-grandma, one for Joseph and one for you.'

The boy took it with a solemn expression, as though weighed down by this responsibility.

'Say thank you, boys,' said Manwela, at which they grinned and pronounced the words clearly to Frank with shy pride at their English.

'I am glad my sister is not here,' said Manwela. 'She would like some too.'

Frank laughed, recalling the forbidding woman who had scared him more than a Stuka dive bomber when he'd called on Manwela and found her out that day all those months ago. He moved to the door, bidding the boys goodbye, watched by the old woman. Manwela came with him into the yard, where the bicycle was propped up against the wall. She let him use it regularly to return to the barracks when he was in a hurry. This he relished because it meant that he would have to return it each time.

She was close to him, standing at his shoulder as he took hold of the bike's handlebars. He wanted so badly to tell her what he felt. It pained him, afflicted him.

'Bring your washing next time, Frank,' she said.

'If you don't mind,' he replied, not looking at her. He knew if he did, he'd have to catch hold of her and kiss her.

He wheeled the bike away, leaving her standing in the yard.

Pedalling hard and careering over the rough road helped Frank release some of his frustration and longing. He loved Manwela desperately, but it was hopeless because there was no point to it, no future in it. Even if he could have her, in a field, in a barn or somewhere, not in her house, that was for certain, it wouldn't be right. Other men and women in this shattered place lived and loved for the moment, which he understood, but a woman like Manwela, with children, couldn't just do as she pleased. She had to think about the future. But would sleeping with her ruin her future or her children's? He didn't know. She liked him; he knew that. She laughed in his company, invited him to be with her and her family. She thanked him warmly for the few bits of rations he brought her. She ironed his shirts, his coarse army issue, so perfectly that they were transformed unrecognisably. She had kissed him once in her need. Did she long for closeness and pleasure too? If only he knew. He could hardly ask her. The Maltese were very religious, and he knew that Manwela went to Mass every week. But the tarts in Strait Street in Valletta were catholic too, and this didn't hold them back in their business.

He was tired of thinking of these possibilities and uncertainties, angry with himself that he didn't know how to behave. He was almost glad to see the barracks ahead and the prospect of some exhausting field exercises to occupy his mind and body.

There had been a lull in the bombing. The Luftwaffe had, so they'd heard, withdrawn from their base in Sicily, leaving the Italians to continue their nuisance raids. The Devonshires were never idle, though they were sometimes bored: patrolling the coasts, doing gun drills, artillery training and the endless repairs to potholes in the airfields. They had activities laid on from time to time to keep the men out of mischief, to provide some distraction from the heat, the tension of waiting for a raid and the fear engendered during the bombing. Concert parties visited various villages where troops were based, and they were due to perform at St Andrew's Barracks sometime soon. That evening too, they had been informed that the education officer, Captain Fitzmaurice, had organised a lecture after their evening meal, on an unspecified topic. Frank knew that Lieutenant Chambers would be there and looked forward to a chance to speak to him.

He'd have been heartily sorry if Lieutenant Chambers had been under the pile of rubble in the street in Valletta, as Frank had thought him to be that day. It had been a huge relief to discover that his platoon commander was alive and well in the shelter, along with the nervous bookseller, Mr Falson. After rescuing the abandoned diary, Frank had picked his way over the rubble and gained entry to the old railway tunnel, which was the nearest shelter, with the lieutenant's book in his pocket. He'd dismissed the ridiculous notions he'd had about the diary when he'd felt it twitch in his hand. It was the trauma of the air raid, the noise, the heat that had made him imagine things. It was the bloody twentieth century after all and he wasn't superstitious.

He had found the officer and Mr Falson crouched down by one of the walls, amidst the packed crowd in the shelter.

'*Nixon*,' the lieutenant had said, scrambling to his feet. 'Thank God you're safe. Mr Falson and I feared the worst. So glad you made it, old chap.'

Frank was gratified and a little embarrassed by this show of feeling from the officer. The luck of not being blown to bits could turn the most reticent person into a gabbling idiot. That's how it affected him sometimes, and Lieutenant Chambers too, it seemed. The officer was even more excited when Frank pulled out the book from his shirt.

'Good God, the journal, the soldier's journal,' said the lieutenant, his hand shaking as he took it from Frank. 'Look, Mr Falson, Nixon has saved the book, the journal of the Napoleonic officer.'

Their other close companions in the shelter stared, as though they were surrounded by madmen, raving over a small, dingy book as though it were some priceless treasure.

'I dropped it in all the rush,' said Lieutenant Chambers, 'I could hardly go back for it once the street had started caving in'.

He carefully turned to the first page.

'Look at the dates. Here's the first entry, November 1795. It starts three years before the French occupation of the island,' he said, holding it almost to his nose to scrutinise it. 'Oh dear, my French is a bit ropey and the writing will be quite a difficulty.'

Mr Falson, who had risen to his feet considerably recovered, was peering at the close-written script on the open pages. 'A most interesting find. I had forgotten it was there. I could get someone to translate it for you, if you wish,' he said. 'I know several people who are familiar with the language.'

The officer pursed his lips. 'That's kind of you, but I think in the circumstances, I'd prefer to have a go at it myself, if you don't mind. But I promise to hand it over to the museum if they want it.'

Frank stared at the diary. 'I'd like to know what he wrote too.'

'Yes, of course, Nixon,' said the lieutenant. 'I'll get to work on it as soon as I have the chance.'

But since that day, months ago, there hadn't been an opportunity to speak to Lieutenant Chambers. So now, Frank reflected, as with the writing in the cave, it was most probable that he would never discover anything about those voices from the past.

After another day of training in loading and aiming mortars, then instructions on arming Hurricanes, Frank's platoon, led by Sergeant Campbell, returned to barracks starving and tired. Over the past weeks, the quality and variety of the food had taken a turn for the worse.

'Not bloody corned beef again,' said someone.

'*Hoi*, call that a portion?'

'It's fucking rationing,' said one of the servers irritably, in response to the men's complaints that evening in the canteen.

They were finishing their meal amidst such grumbling when Sergeant Campbell stood up to make an announcement

'Right, lads, listen. The good news is Captain Fitzmaurice has gone down with "Malta Dog" and can't deliver the lecture tonight.'

There was a subdued cheer out of respect for the sufferings of the education officer. Several of the men had been afflicted by this particularly unpleasant form of dysentery.

'And the bad news is,' continued the sergeant, 'Lieutenant Chambers is taking over and will give a talk tonight on the ancient history of Malta, or something like that. Same time, same place. I want to see every man of you there.'

'Fucking hell,' muttered someone at the far end of the room. 'Not him.'

'Do we have to go, Sarge?'

'Shut up,' said Sergeant Campbell. 'It's to improve your minds and, by God, do they need improving.'

'Couldn't we just have a chat with Nix here? He knows lots of that stuff about Malta. Wouldn't that do?' It was Chalky, who was grinning at Frank.

The sergeant shook his head in amused weariness rather than anger. 'You're like a bunch of bloody kids, you lot. Be there, right?'

Frank pitied the unfortunate Lieutenant Chambers for having to face such an unwilling and unruly crowd. He'd discovered that the officer was in fact a teacher, as he had suspected, though he'd taught in a prep school—small posh boys with only about eight in a class. He remembered his own primary class of around forty, though they sat most of the time in silent terror of the teacher whose cane was an extension of his arm. Lieutenant Chambers, however, seemed oblivious and untroubled by the frequent facetious remarks at his expense, which he must surely have overheard from the men.

In spite of his platoon commander's unsoldierly ways, Frank liked the man, found his enthusiasm inspiring, appreciated the respect with which his questions were answered, the way they extended into discussions beyond the mundane and the superficial. His attitude and the books he had lent had opened Frank's eyes and his mind to worlds that he could half understand and explore, that could be the subject of serious study, even by someone like him. His discovery of the striking evidence of past lives and events all around him had reignited a curiosity that he had

135

always had and which he now knew would have to be satisfied somehow.

After they'd eaten, Sergeant Campbell rallied the men again and gradually, mostly reluctantly, they started filing out of the canteen, along the corridor that led to a large empty meeting room. Only a small clutch of men stood outside the door, smoking and talking, hanging about, waiting to absent themselves as soon as the sergeant was out of sight.

Frank, at the front of the line, entered the room first, where he found Lieutenant Chambers dragging a table into a central position in the room. On the floor stood a black tin contraption, like a huge camera with a long lens, which he lifted onto the table. A flex dangled from the back, and Frank wondered how he was going to power it up, but didn't want to show his ignorance.

'He's got a magic lantern, boys,' sniggered one of the men behind him.

'Can I help, sir?' said Frank.

'Yes, thank you, Nixon,' said the officer, looking up. 'Get these chaps to arrange the chairs in rows, please. Leave a channel down the middle though.'

Frank enlisted Chalky's help and, with some others, created rows for the audience, amidst many muttered jokes about going to the pictures and hoping it was going to be Dorothy Lamour or Jane Russell. Lieutenant Chambers was fiddling with the machine and asked one of the men to climb up and plug the flex into the light socket, which dangled from the fitting above.

'Nixon, would you operate this when we need it?' said the officer to Frank.

'Teacher's pet,' muttered someone.

If Captain Fitzmaurice, a rugby front row forward, had been conducting this event, it would have been a much less chaotic affair, Frank reflected. Sergeant Campbell, who would obviously have rather been somewhere else, was standing smoking and talking to some of the men in the corner.

'Lift this flap here,' said Lieutenant Chambers to Frank, unperturbed, it seemed, by the restless buzz around him. 'And put the pictures in when I tell you. It projects the image onto the wall in front. The light source is inside.'

Frank nodded doubtfully, feeling the heat of the bulb on the top of the machine. He looked at the images, which were excellent photographs of some of the ancient temples that stood in various parts of the island and on Gozo. He wished he'd had a chance to visit them and looked forward to this introduction, willing the others to shut up and let Lieutenant Chambers get started.

He did, and surprisingly, managed to call them all to order. With a sheaf of closely written papers flapping in his hand, Lieutenant Chambers stood at the front and cleared his throat.

'So, here we all are, defending these Maltese islands from attack and doing our best to beat off our enemies. Countless other soldiers have, over the ages, done what we do now. And through these years, merchants, pirates, explorers, slavers, empire builders have recognised the strategic importance of Malta. It has been invaded, settled, conquered, besieged, with each wave of people leaving their mark on these small rocky islands. They have left us a rich and varied legacy of monuments, artefacts and language, which reveal to us something of their lives and cultures.'

So far so good, thought Frank gratefully. The men were almost silent, and Lieutenant Chambers' pleasant voice and well-paced delivery had caught their attention.

'In this lecture, I shall start at the earliest known evidence of man's exploits on these islands so that you can appreciate the astonishing relics of past ages that surround you.'

The room was dim already with the blackout blinds, but there was a light just outside in the corridor that shed a glow into the space. Lieutenant Chambers asked Chalky to switch this off and signalled to Frank to place the first picture on the slide.

'You'll see, in this first photograph—'

'Bugger all,' someone said, laughing as Chalky flicked the switch and the machine lost power too.

'Try the other switch, White,' called Lieutenant Chambers.

'Done it, sir,' came Chalky's voice from the corridor.

'Oh dear,' said Lieutenant Chambers in the darkness, 'can someone help me with my epidiascope?'

'Not bloody likely, sir,' snorted someone.

'Oooh, you are saucy. I wouldn't dare touch your epidiascope,' shrieked another in a high-pitched voice.

'Put the light on again, Chalky, so we can see,' called Frank as the lieutenant made his way to the machine, amidst the laughter.

'Pipe down, you lot,' said Sergeant Campbell without conviction.

'Damnable thing,' murmured Lieutenant Chambers to Frank as he fumbled with the side of the machine. 'It opens up here somewhere.'

Frank saw a small catch, which he pushed back to free the casing and open the machine. 'The bulb's gone, has it, sir?'

'*Why are we wait–ing? Why–eye are we wait–ing?*' sang a group of the men in the front row.

'I'm not sure that this is going to be an unqualified success, Nixon,' said the officer in a sorrowful tone.

'Couldn't you do the lecture without the pictures, sir?' said Frank.

'I could,' he said with a frown, 'but it would be much duller without and I'm not sure I'd have any audience left by the end of it.'

Frank did not want to agree too speedily. 'Isn't there a spare bulb, sir?'

The officer looked at him, as though the suggestion had itself lit a fresh bulb in his head. 'Of course, in the officers' mess. Would you just run round there now and ask anyone to look in the box under my bed? I'm sure there's a spare.'

'Yes, sir,' said Frank, making off, seeing Sergeant Campbell rise from his seat again with a sigh amidst the dying chorus of the men's singing.

'Shut up, you lot. We'll get it going again in a while. Nixon's on the job.'

'He would be,' shouted someone.

Frank ran down the corridor, through the canteen and out across the dark yard. There was no moon visible, few stars and thankfully no aircraft. It was unusually calm, with the lighter shadows of clouds in the deep blue hanging there. He rounded the block and headed for the officers' quarters, reckoning that it would take him at least ten minutes by the time he'd asked an officer to look for the spare bulb.

The lane that led from their block and sleeping quarters ran alongside the perimeter fence. Up ahead, Frank saw something moving, several dark figures near the building, one of them seeming to pass through the fence to the other side. Thieves, bloody burglars, he thought in astonishment, wondering what the best action to take was. There was no time to go back and bring men to catch them at it. The only course was to raise the alarm. He wished he had his whistle on him. He'd have to make a hell of a noise and hope that the officers in their mess would hear and come to investigate. He might at least manage to shock the intruders sufficiently to drop whatever they were stealing in order to make their escape.

Two of the figures were carrying heavy bags or sacks and were squeezing their way through the fence. He yelled as loudly as he could, 'Stop, thieves.' He almost laughed at himself for using such a ridiculous cry, like someone in bloody *Oliver Twist*. 'Hoi, you buggers. Stop. Drop it.'

He ran at full speed towards the men, shouting as raucously as he could, finding his voice strangled with the effort. Two more men followed the others through, though one had become ensnared in the wire of the fence. He was pulling and struggling in the wire but broke free a moment later. Where was the fifth man? Frank was sure he'd seen five of them.

He reached the hole in the fence, saw the rough pliered cuts and ducked through the gap himself, shouting back once again towards the officers' mess. There was no sign that anyone had heard, however. He had no choice but to go after them. Perhaps he'd catch up with the last one, whose back he could just make out. But he only managed to move forward a few yards before he felt a heavy, agonising blow on the back of his head, then nothing.

CHAPTER 11

F rank was being carried. His body was suspended on something, swinging, a support that swayed and made the inside of his head crackle with pain.

'It's all right, Corp,' a voice was saying.

'Hoi, Nix, can you hear me?'

'Hope they get the fucking bastards.'

He couldn't see much except for a dark sky when he blinked, then the shape of a man's back, and he could hear heavy breathing near his head. He was on a stretcher. Had there been a bomb? Were all his bits still there? The barracks must have taken a hit. No, that wasn't right.

He closed his eyes for a while, and the churning in his head eased a little, then he remembered squeezing through wire. Why had he squeezed through a wire fence, for Christ's sake?

He reached his hand to the back of his head and found a cloth there, damp and spongy with wet. Fuck, it was his blood. 'What happened?'

Chalky was above him, looking down. 'You were trying to play the hero again, Nix. Got a crack on the head. Wanted all the glory for yourself, did you?'

As Frank looked at Chalky's grinning face, he started to remember.

'What did they take?' asked Frank. 'Did you get them? Who were they?'

'Best shut up with your questions for now, mate.' It was Sergeant Campbell's voice. 'Let's get you back and get your head seen to.'

'I missed the lecture,' said Frank, knowing it was a stupid thing to say as soon as he uttered it. His head hurt. He couldn't think properly.

'Yeah, you did. What a pity,' said someone, chuckling.

There was more laughter behind him.

'It's not too bad,' said the medic who'd patched him up in the sickroom, 'but you'd best see the doc in the morning. You might be concussed. How many fingers am I holding up?'

'None, you prick,' said Frank. The man was leaning back against a cupboard with his arms folded. 'But have you got anything for a headache?'

'Couple of aspirin. That's all I can give you, mate. Best get to bed and sleep for a bit. Kip down here if you like. It's quieter here than that pigpen down there in the bunkhouse.'

Frank swallowed the pills, lay down on a hospital trolley next to the wall in the sickroom, and the medic threw a blanket over him.

'Thanks,' said Frank as the man left, leaving the door ajar.

He couldn't sleep, however. Though he was glad to be lying down flat, the bump on the back of his head throbbed. His head pressed on the thick pad, held in place by a huge bandage, which made him feel like a mummy. He turned on his side, but he was too tense to drop off. He was angry that his attempt to raise the alarm and apprehend the thieves had failed. He closed his eyes, but was still alert, uncomfortable, in pain and edgy. The smell of disinfectant and carbolic sharpened the air, and he wondered if he should go back to the bunkhouse after all. He twisted round and faced the wall.

'Nixon.'

The voice was unmistakable as Lieutenant Chambers', and when Frank turned over, the officer was standing in the doorway, his face obscure in the dim light.

'Got on the end of some villains, I hear,' said the officer, moving into the room. 'I thought you'd run off in disgust.'

'No, sir, not at all,' said Frank, shifting on the couch, wondering whether he should try to stand up. 'Did you manage to finish the lecture?'

'Stay where you are. Best keep lying down, I should think,' said the lieutenant, sounding a bit like a nurse. 'As it happened, most of the men left after you'd gone. Claimed they were short on sleep, which might possibly have been true. A few of them stayed behind and asked me to tell them some more about the temples. So, we looked at the photographs and had a good chat about them. Lance Corporal White was quite interested, in fact.'

Frank smiled, grateful for Chalky's loyalty.

'That's good, sir. Sorry about the bulb. I'd like to see the temples for myself one day.'

'Yes, Hagar Qim and Mnajdra temples are the most impressive, though the ones in Gozo are pretty interesting too, I believe. Little chance of getting over there, however. And we've still got to find that cave of yours, haven't we?'

Frank wished he could have sat up, but his head was still throbbing horribly.

'By the way,' said the officer, 'I met a chap from the Maltese archaeological society the other day, just by chance at army HQ in Valletta. He told me he'd never heard of any caves or burial chambers in the area around Madliena. So, just think, Nixon, you could have made a unique discovery.'

After the officer had left, Frank felt vaguely pleased but puzzled about what was real and what was delusional. He wasn't in the best of states to think at all. At the moment, he could hardly separate the experience in the cave from his recent peculiar half-dreaming state after the blow to his head. At times, he doubted that he'd really been in the cave at all; however, he certainly remembered the strong sense of an invisible presence in the place, just as he had felt the clammy shoulder of a man who wasn't there in the air-raid shelter in Valletta. Then there was the weird feeling when he'd handled the journal of the eighteenth century infantry officer. Was he going seriously mad or just suffering from an overactive imagination?

When he was a kid, he'd liked imagining he was a Roman centurion, leading his men into battle against the Goths or Erik the Viking, a warlord leaping ashore on the coast of England and burning down churches. He thought he really knew what it would have been like, churning through the waves in a Viking longship, with the stinging salt spray in your face, scanning the horizon for a sliver of land in the vast stretch of the ocean. But this was probably pretty normal for kids. Some just preferred cowboys and Indians. He closed his eyes, trying to will himself to sleep. It was quiet now, no noise from outside or anywhere.

Some time later, Frank awoke in the pitch black. His headache was duller now, but his bladder was full. He swung his legs off the couch and got up, feeling reasonably steady on his feet, fumbling his way to the door, to reach the light switch. It was a low wattage bulb, but it lit the room to a dull greyness. By this feeble light, he made his way along the corridor towards the urinals in the wash block. The stone floor was cool and gritty under his feet, and he guessed it might be around two or three o'clock in the morning. A glow from the low-powered night light leaked from above the partition wall that separated the toilets from the corridor. He heard trickling water. Was there someone in there, or was it the creaky plumbing of the old building?

He entered the area, lit vaguely blue with the night light, the porcelain urinals shadowed in relief like a long line of gravestones. The lavatory cubicles were at the far end. He squinted along the length of the row of stalls. Near the last one, he saw a place where the greyness thickened, forming the figure of a man, tall, thin and upright, as though on parade. Frank blinked, screwed his eyes up and looked again, but the shape was still there, moving. Then came a sound, a swishing, a slash of something metal swiping the air once, twice. Was that the glint of a blade?

Frank's body was suddenly cold, though he felt sweat gathering on his brow. 'Who's there?' His voice sounded pathetic and reedy. Why hadn't he just peed in the basin in the sickroom?

'Your aunt Fanny,' came a guttural comment from one of the cubicles. 'Can't a bloke have a crap in peace?'

Frank, choked with embarrassment, turned swiftly to one of the urinals and relieved himself. He glanced back at the end of the line, and the shadow, to his relief, was gone. Then the door of one of the cubicles swung open, and a soldier came out, still in his khakis. As the man came closer to Frank, he saw that it was Green.

'Night,' he said, brushing past without looking at Frank or making any comment.

Frank made his way back along the corridor to the sickroom, not daring to look behind him, wishing above all to avoid another encounter with Green. What was he doing still wandering around dressed at this hour?

When Frank got back, he found that he was shaking all over. He climbed onto the trolley and pulled the blanket over his head, as he had done in the home when he'd wanted to shut things out and not think or imagine. What the hell was wrong with him? He must be hallucinating as a result of concussion. He'd ask the doctor about it tomorrow. It would be all right in the morning. It couldn't be long to wait.

Still wakeful and sweating, he lay there, knowing that Green wasn't a hallucination, nor a ghost. He was as real, unfortunately, as always. There was something odd about finding him there though. Green had not indulged in his usual aggressive talk, nor ridicule, which was surprising. Surprising that he hadn't been to bed, but then Frank remembered that he'd been wandering around in his underpants and shirt himself. God, if he could only go to sleep and switch off his brain for a while.

A cheerful whistling rendition of 'We'll Meet Again' woke Frank from a shallow doze, and he knew at once where he was. The small sprightly figure of the doctor flitted past him then disappeared into a cupboard, which seemed to be some kind of office or storeroom. He was back a moment later as Frank pulled himself up on his elbows.

'Morning,' the doctor said. 'Don't usually have men waiting overnight. What happened to you, then?'

Frank told him a brief version of his encounter with the thieves.

'Nasty,' said the doctor, 'but I see someone's been patching you up. That's some bandage. Should really have seen you last night if it was head. You could have a fractured skull or brain damage.'

Frank assured him that he felt all right, but the pad had stuck to his hair and skin. When the doctor removed it, there was a warm trickle down his neck.

'Damn it,' said the doctor. 'Need a nurse here for this messy stuff. Never mind. Doesn't look too bad.'

Frank felt the doctor wiping at the blood on his neck and dabbing at the wound.

'It'll need a stitch or two. Hang on a mo while I get the equipment. Come and sit on the chair so I can get at you properly.'

Frank slid off the trolley, pulled on his shorts and sat down while the doctor clattered about in the tall tin cupboard in the corner, knocking over packages and boxes as he did so.

'All fingers and thumbs today, but don't worry, my needle finger's pretty steady.' He held up a violently trembling hand and burst out laughing. 'Ah, here we are.'

Assembling a spool of black thread, a tin dish, cotton wool and a small brown bottle, he moved near to Frank, as Frank got ready to grit his teeth.

'This'll hurt a bit. But I'll be quick,' said the doctor. 'You're not one of those chaps that passes out, are you?' He dabbed something cold and stinging on the wound.

'Do you think I've got concussion?' said Frank, as a partly diversionary tactic.

'Haven't a clue,' said the doctor cheerily, squinting as he threaded the needle. 'Why, are you seeing double?'

'Not exactly,' said Frank, 'but what are the symptoms?'

'Headache, nausea, loss of memory, seeing double or flashes, that sort of thing.'

'Hallucinations?' said Frank.

The doctor waved the threaded needle in the air. 'Hallucinations? You've been seeing visions? Here, in the barracks? Could be, I suppose. On the other hand, could be ghosts.'

He laughed loudly, and Frank felt a sharp stab in his head that made his eyes water.

'Wouldn't be at all surprised in this ramshackle old place. Spooks me a bit,' the doctor continued, making another stab. 'It was built by us Brits in the nineteenth century as a barracks. I think this block was used as a hospital in the Crimean War.'

Frank ground his teeth together, wondering if they might crack with the pressure as he tried not to yell out.

'Hmm, that's quite neat,' said the doctor after several very long painful moments, 'although I say it myself.'

He paused to admire his handiwork, which allowed Frank to breathe again and prepare himself for the next stab. He'd think about Manwela. That would distract him. He'd imagine the moment when he would tell her he loved her and how she would confess that she felt the same. Then they could be married. They could get married quarters here at the barracks and—

'There we are. All done,' said the doctor, chuckling, as if he'd just enjoyed a tasty supper. 'Very good. You'll have a bit of a bald patch at the back there, but I shouldn't worry too much about that. I don't imagine it'll keep the girls away, Corporal.'

Frank felt his body slacken, but his brow was dripping. 'Thanks very much, sir,' he said.

'It's my pleasure. Hang on a mo. I've got to put a dressing on it. Come back in a week or two and I'll take the stitches out, and if you have any more visions of course.'

Lieutenant Chambers gave Frank the day off and told him to rest up. Frank asked permission to leave the barracks.

'Are you sure you're up to it, Nixon? Where are you going? Not to Valletta, I hope?'

'I'm fine, sir. It's just that... there's a... family I visit in Naxxar sometimes. The little lad's been sick with pneumonia and his mother—'

'Ah, I see,' said the officer, and Frank found himself blushing under his gaze. Lieutenant Chambers' eyes retained a vaguely puzzled look.

'And I borrowed their bicycle, so I need to take it back,' Frank said.

'Good, well, yes, right, but mind how you go, Nixon. At least it's a bit quieter these days. But word is that the Germans are moving more bombers and fighters back to Sicily sometime soon. Then it'll be a different story.'

Lieutenant Chambers sighed, taking his pipe out of his pocket. 'So, it looks like it'll be a while before we get a chance for any exploring. But I'm keen to get a bit of a party up for some sight-seeing as soon as we get the chance. Would you be interested?'

'Yes, sir, certainly would.'

Frank's head only pulsed dully now, but he felt surprisingly light on his feet and energetic considering his lack of sleep. He went back to the bunkhouse and was greeted with welcoming shouts and the usual banter. Green was still lying in bed even though he should have been up and ready for work. Frank was glad it did not fall to him this morning to chivvy him up, the lazy sod.

'I'm off duty today, platoon commander's orders,' Frank said. 'Sorry to dump this on you, Chalky.'

Chalky was grinning. 'You skiver,' he said. 'You look perfectly good to me. What have you got under that bandage anyway?'

'I'm going to have a bloody bald patch,' Frank complained, though this fact didn't trouble him much. 'All because of those bastards. What did they get, anyway?'

'Tidy little stash of whisky, fags, soap and razor blades. No chance of finding the culprits. The CO's going to tell the police, but they'll never see the stuff again. You did your best, Nixy.' Chalky patted him on the back gently, as though aware Frank could be too delicate for a firmer gesture. 'Anyway, I'm sure the officers can manage. It'll do them good to go without a few of their luxuries, like the rest of us. See how the other half live. Let's have a look at your bald patch, then.'

Frank ducked out of Chalky's reach and went for a wash and shave. The toilet block was bright with sunlight and the stink of its reality. He wondered how he could have imagined that he'd seen some vision or ghost in here. Hallucinations, ghosts and visions were the stuff of kids and madmen, and he felt perfectly sane this morning. His head was clear, but he noticed to his dismay that Green was there shaving. Frank kept his distance, his eyes trained ahead on the mirror, hearing Green running the water at his basin.

'Got a good crack on the head, didn't you, Corp?' Green said, and Frank glanced at him quickly, just enough to see him withdraw his razor from a small leather case. It was a cut-throat razor with a white ivory or bone handle. 'You want to watch out,' he continued.

Frank felt his breathing quicken as he realised, without any doubt, that Green had been involved in the robbery. He had a criminal record. Corporal Myles had warned him that Green was one to avoid, just like Sergeant Campbell had, and Frank had found him in an act of theft already. He'd also been wandering about fully dressed in the small hours of the morning. It was a bit more than suspicious. What had he been doing? Sneaking back from stashing the stuff away somewhere with his accomplices?

'You'd better watch out too,' Frank said, trying to hold his voice steady, drying his face quickly.

'Oh yeah?' said Green, soaping his face with casual strokes of a brush. 'What are you going to do, pretty boy?'

'Put you on report for a start,' Frank said, his throat so constricted that his voice came out as a bleat.

Green flashed his razor open and looked at Frank without a word.

Frank gathered his stuff and left the place as quickly as he could. If only he could give back his Corporal's stripe, go back to just minding his own business and letting blokes get on with whatever they did. He hated being responsible for the behaviour of others. Perhaps he was a coward. He didn't think he was when it came to being under fire or being bombed. He was able to keep his nerve and focus on the job, loading the guns, firing rifles, hauling out the injured, though the sight of casualties turned his stomach sometimes and bothered him in his dreams. He could cope with all that, but not with confronting men like Green, who had no morals, no guilt and looked after their own backs before anyone else's. Frank had never had any authority in his life, and he didn't want it now. Some men craved it, for whatever reason, to pay back old scores, to have the power to punish, to instil obedience in others, but not him.

Perhaps he could speak to Lieutenant Chambers about being demoted. He'd possibly understand, though he'd be unlikely to offer any good advice about how Frank might become a better leader of men. He was hardly an exemplary officer himself. Sergeant Campbell could handle Green, but Frank couldn't go to him with his problem. He'd be too ashamed to admit to his weakness. He badly wanted to report his suspicions of Green to one of his superiors, but they could do nothing without proof and there were only his suspicions and the circumstantial evidence. All accusations were pointless. He was a feeble NCO. He'd always been at the bottom of the pile and was better off there, for himself and for the good of his mates. Someone had to do something about blokes like Green.

The pleasant anticipation of his day off was soured now by this mood until he thought of Manwela and immediately felt happier. Deciding to dismiss all thoughts of Green, he set off to see her, nervous but full of hope. The morning was balmy and warm, though he knew it would soon be stifling again. As he was getting the bicycle out of the shed, the air-raid alert sounded, so he was delayed by an hour in setting out, which further stoked up his eagerness.

He put on his helmet and pedalled off, up the slight incline on the way to Naxxar, hoping that today there would be the chance of a few moments alone with Manwela. Today, he'd do it. He'd tell Manwela of his feelings for her. This way, he'd know if his love was returned. If she was shocked or offended, he'd have to stop going to her. That would at least be an end to it, being tormented by his desire for her. He wouldn't be a coward in this at least.

Approaching the outskirts of the village, he spied the olive tree bending over from Manwela's yard and heard voices, lots of them. He dismounted and pushed the bike the last few yards to the gate and, looking in, saw the place full of people. There were children, about eight of them of various ages, cavorting about. Joseph and David were among them, sitting in the middle of a circle of the others, who chanted and sang as they ran around in some kind of game. At the door stood Manwela and two other women, both older than her. Though it was a happy sight, he knew that this visitation meant that there would be little hope of talking to Manwela on her own. His earlier resolve trickled away like water down a drain. He was on the point of turning round and leaving, but knew that he must deliver the bicycle back and not sneak off, abandoning it by the wall. So, he opened the gate.

Manwela looked up and saw him, turned to the two women with whom she exchanged a few words and then, smiling, picked her way through the children. They paused at this interruption, all eyes on him, and the activity halted.

'Frank,' shouted Joseph, waving his hands in the air, and David came trotting after his mother.

'You've got company,' Frank said. 'I don't want to interrupt. I just brought the bike back.'

Manwela seemed prettier than ever today, her colour high, her mouth and eyes smiling at him. 'Come in. Have some tea with us,' she said.

'No, it doesn't matter,' he said, feeling wretched.

'*Frank, Frank, chocolate,*' squealed David.

'Sssh,' said Manwela, catching hold of the child and pulling him back in an embrace. 'Don't be cheeky.'

'Sheeky?' he said, looking up at his mother.

Frank couldn't help laughing, opened the gate and wheeled the bike across the yard, the eyes of all upon him.

'These are my cousins, Lucia and Marija,' said Manwela, 'and their children.' She pointed, reeling off their names. 'Mario, Paola, Rikkardo, Luca and little Florencia. They are coming to live here. Their houses were bombed. They have nowhere else to go.'

The kitchen was a hubbub until Manwela and her cousins calmed the children and Manwela handed round small pieces of a hard cake that the visitors had brought. The old grandmother sat smiling but looked bemused while the women and children chattered. Frank sat, watching while incomprehensible streams of talk flowed around him, feeling increasingly like an alien and an irrelevant presence in the room. The curiosity about his bandage had not lasted long. He caught Manwela's eye once or twice, and her expression was difficult to read. Then the door opened, and the fat, fuzz-haired sister and a smaller replica of herself about ten years old entered to a round of greetings.

The sister, seeing Frank, acknowledged him with a dismissive glance and spoke at length to the cousins, as though complaining about this interloper in their midst. At least this is what Frank imagined, having grasped some snippets of her talk: 'soldier', 'eating the food', 'riding a bicycle'.

He rose and said, 'grazzi hafna' and 'sahha' as graciously as he could in his state of desolation. He went out into the yard, not looking back.

Frank struggled hard with his disappointment as he walked up the road and away from the village, feeling the sun beating down on his head. The metal helmet heated up like a furnace, and his head had started to pound again. He took the helmet off for a moment and felt the scorch of the sun on his face. The water in his canteen was gone, as he'd forgotten to fill it in his haste to leave. He was a fool. And he would never get close to Manwela now, not with this houseful of women and children. There would be no peace and privacy at all.

He watched the dust fly up from his boots, which were now powdered white with the stuff, and was overwhelmed with depression and failure. He was failing in his duty, his job and in his courtship, if he could even call it that. He was a useless wet, a charity boy, born to be ignored, to be a nobody.

The temperature had risen to a baking level, with the air pressing in all around, and he looked ahead for some kind of shelter. There was nothing immediately visible in the open countryside ahead, although he knew there was a hamlet on this road, where they sometimes had makeshift shops and stalls selling vegetables. At least, they had before the food shortages. Perhaps these would be there today and he'd be able to get a drink.

A man driving a donkey cart passed him from that direction. A woman was sitting on his cart with a basket half full of something covered with a cloth. Supplies were running miserably low in some places, though the country folk at least had access to more of their own produce from their gardens and fields. A girl of around fourteen came by too, holding the hands of two barefoot toddling children. They greeted him with broad smiles. The girl was carrying a cloth bag with something bulging in it slung over her shoulder. Signs of food and drink nearby, maybe.

The hamlet was a small cluster of flat-roofed houses with rough walled gardens behind. Ahead, at the side of the road, there were a number of people at a faded red-canopied stall. An old man wearing a straw hat, sitting on a wicker chair, looked up as he approached. The stall was a couple of planks holding a few large underripe melons.

'Bonġu,' said Frank, deciding to try out some of his Maltese. 'Ghandek xi ilma?'

The old man responded in English, with a gummy smile. 'Very good, very good, soldier. My wife come. You thirsty?'

He turned and shouted into the house that stood immediately behind the stall. An elderly woman appeared some moments later with a glass jug full of cloudy-looking stuff. At the sight of this, Frank's throat ached with thirst. The woman dumped the jug on the stall and then filled a glass for Frank and one for her husband. Frank drank the lemonade, trying not to gulp, and its bitterness was delicious to the point of pain. The old man sipped at his drink.

'Good, good,' he said, holding up his glass as though offering a toast.

'Yes, cheers,' said Frank, looking around him.

Down a passage between two houses, there were a few other tables from which people seemed to be selling more foodstuffs and other items.

'Is this the market today?' he asked the old man.

His empty mouth gaped open in a laugh. 'Market, yes, market, but not good things to buy.'

'How much for the drink?' said Frank.

The man told him, and he handed over a few coins. Feeling a little refreshed, he went around to the back of the stall, into the lane behind, to look at the other merchandise, undeterred by the old man's comment. It struck him that he might buy something for Manwela and her expanded household. She'd have all those mouths to feed, although the cousins would bring their rations with them, he supposed. He longed to be able to give her something, to buy her affection. She'd be grateful for anything extra, he thought. If he were well off, or even on better pay, she would perhaps think him someone more significant, more worthy. Gifts and money could lure with an irresistible power, he knew, remembering a time when he was a little kid in St Augustine's.

That time, when Frank was seven years old, a Mr and Mrs Richardson, rich and childless, had come to the home, looking for a boy to take home and be their son. Mrs Richardson had a fur coat, which made her look like a grizzly bear, and her husband didn't smile as the two of them inspected the line of suitable boys. They had all been scrubbed clean and even given better shirts and jerseys to put on. Mr and Mrs Richardson were so rich they'd given everyone sweets and brought a huge box of used dinky cars for them to play with. Mr and Mrs Richardson talked to most of the boys and watched them play for a while.

Frank had lain awake that night, thinking of how, if he were chosen, he'd probably have a box of cars all to himself and a bedroom of his own. These imaginings had created an ache of longing in him for all the delights that would be his: picture books and even a trainset. But Mr and Mrs Richardson didn't take anyone in the end. Matron said it was because they wanted a baby, not a boy of seven. But he wasn't seven years old now; he was a grown man and needed to bloody pull himself together.

It was cooler in the lane, shaded from the sun by the houses. A few tired flowers straggled in pots outside some of the front doors along the street. There wasn't much on the two tables—some wrinkled potatoes, melons and rusted tins of fruit and corned beef—excess supplies from someone's ration, no doubt. There was a strong smell of goat from a small lump of cheese wrapped in muslin. A boy of about twelve or thirteen sat hunched behind one of these tables. This table was draped over with a checked tablecloth, and Frank noticed the corner of a cardboard box beneath it. He paused by the table, then took a step back for a clearer sight of what was below. What was the kid hiding? Black market stuff?

The youth behind the stall looked up at him, and his eyes flickered uneasily. He glanced along the alley, as though he wanted to scarper.

'What's under there?' said Frank, lifting the edge of the cloth with his toe.

The boy shook his head. 'Ma nitkellimx bil-Ingliz.'

Frank wasn't convinced. Most Maltese people spoke at least a bit of English.

'X'hemm taħt?' said Frank, hoping he'd used the right words. By the look of panic in his eyes, the boy had clearly got the message. He scrambled to his feet, looking pretty desperate.

'Sir, dan mhux tieghi,' he said, and Frank wasn't exactly sure what this meant.

'Show me,' Frank said, lifting the edge of the tablecloth.

The boy reached under the table and brought out a bottle sheepishly, like a magician revealing a rabbit that had died in the middle of a trick. It was a bottle of Johnnie Walker Black Label.

Frank tried to keep his face expressionless. 'Cigarettes?'

The boy produced two packets of Capstan from the hiding place.

'Do you know where these came from?' said Frank.

The boy shook his head, his face pale. 'I not know.'

'I thought you didn't speak English,' said Frank.

'I not know,' said the boy again.

'I hope you don't, son,' said Frank. 'Now, let's see the rest of it.'

The boy's eyes flashed with fear again, but this time at a man who had appeared beside Frank. He was a short, burly farmer type. He looked at Frank with small, hard eyes from a face crinkled and dark as leather. Another man was coming along the alley too and rushed to stand beside the boy. Frank had only a second to think, an uncomfortable second, but he knew what to do. He tugged at the tablecloth, which came half away from the table. There were quite a number of boxes: two or three of whisky and a load of packages that looked like cigarettes.

'This is stolen stuff,' Frank said, surprised at his steady tone. 'It was taken last night from the officers' mess at St Andrew's Barracks. The police are looking for it.'

The stocky man said something to the others, but Frank couldn't catch any of it. The boy grasped the arm of the man beside him who, Frank realised, was probably his father.

'Dak jitkellem bil-Malti,' the boy said, and his father's face fell. Frank recognised the phrase, 'He speaks Maltese'. He was struck for a moment that they were really panicked by this discovery and the consequences for them.

'Please, no police. No trouble,' said the father. 'We not thieves. A man gave us.'

'Well, I'll have to report this to my commanding officer and to the police. They'll want to know where you got it.'

'No, sir,' said the stocky man, and Frank noticed that some of the other people had crept around and that he was hemmed in on all sides.

Frank's heart was thumping hard, and he felt sweat burst in his armpits into his already sodden shirt. But he found, to his surprise, that his alarm was subsiding as he took in the situation. These people were hardly going to kick his head in for a few bottles of whisky, some cigarettes and candles.

'Look, I tell you what,' Frank said in a moment of inspiration, 'let me take this stuff back, and we'll say no more. I'll tell my commanding officer that you gave it back and you didn't steal it in the first place.'

The three at the table exchanged glances, then there followed some quick exchanges between the two men and mutterings among the small crowd, with much pointing and gesticulation. The old man with the straw hat came along, leading a donkey and cart with squeaking wheels. There was some further angry talk between the burly man and the boy's father, with a few others joining in. Frank stood back and watched, mildly amused, but not wishing to show it.

'You take back. No police,' said the boy's father. 'Guilio go with you. Good boy. No police, Sinjur.'

'No police,' said Frank.

Frank realised there were more boxes than he had thought as he helped load them onto the cart. No wonder they'd needed a

158

band of thieves to nick all this stuff. The boy climbed up onto the seat of the cart, and Frank hoisted himself up beside him. His father raised his hand in a gesture of farewell, his face still tense and anxious. The boy, however, seemed pretty relaxed now and shook the reins to make the donkey plod forward, pulling the creaking cart.

Frank's only concern was that Captain Miller might wish to pursue the matter with the police, but Frank had already decided to go to Lieutenant Chambers for his help in preventing this. The officers would get their stuff back. That was surely all that mattered. Frank watched the donkey's dusty rump moving slowly, felt the creak and rock of the cart and the sun beating down and was content with the outcome of this unexpected adventure.

The boy kept glancing at Frank, as though he was expecting a blow to the head or a sharp telling off.

'How many English planes?' he said.

'I don't know exactly,' said Frank, 'I'm in the infantry, not the air force, but I reckon we've got about fifty Hurricanes. You've seen them, haven't you?'

The boy nodded, and his face lit up in a smile. 'I like Hurricanes, Messerschmidts better, but Speetfires the best.'

Frank smiled at the boy, glad that the tension had passed into easy chat.

'You an officer?' said the boy, looking at Frank's stripe. 'An army captain?'

Frank laughed and shook his head as he caught a distant view of the barracks ahead.

CHAPTER 12

FEBRUARY – MARCH 1942

As soon as they'd scrambled out of the slit trench, ready to start shovelling away the rubble, the droning and another stream of bombers came again. Frank dared himself to glance up at the sky. The last times, there had been fifty of them; this time, it looked more like a hundred. It was right what people said: the Luftwaffe meant to neutralise the island by flattening every square inch of it.

'*Get back*,' Frank shouted to his section.

Chalky and the others turned and threw themselves flat on the churned-up ground, too far from the slit trench to make it in. The ground was sludge, a quagmire from the last days of heavy winter rain.

The nearest Bofors gun post, about twenty yards from the trench, went quiet for a moment while the bombardiers re-sighted the barrels and the gun commander shouted instructions. Two of the crew were feeding the rounds in when a streak of bullets from a murderous low-flying aircraft ripped up the ground in a line, like a knife slicing through cloth, and struck them both, sending one flying up in the air and removing the face of the other. The gun bucked like a mad horse, but the bombardiers clung on to it. The two remaining gunners staggered to their feet and grappled with the machine to help the others right it again. With a scream, another Stuka came diving in, straight for the position. Frank didn't dare watch, ducking his head as the gunfire missed its target but raked up fountains of mud and rock. The remaining four men were still there, thank Christ. Frank didn't wait for the next attack. They needed ammunition loaders, or they were finished.

'Come on, Chalky, come on,' he yelled, leaping up quickly and running towards the sandbagged position.

Much of the sandbag wall had been knocked awry, and the two gunners' bodies lay only a few yards behind it. The gun commander shouted for Frank and Chalky to feed in the next rounds.

'We'll get the fucker the next time.'

The plane screamed, came low, a bull charging straight at them, and the gunners let go. Frank felt no fear anymore. His hands moved like a speeded-up film reel. His head was filled with noise and the stink of cordite, as though these had replaced his brain. Above them, the aircraft shrieked, like a dying animal, slewed away, streaking smoke behind it, then dived to earth. As it turned into a fireball, the gunners cheered and Chalky punched Frank in the arm. But there were more on the way, four abreast, swinging in low again as Frank and Chalky focused and, lightning swift, fed in the shells again and again. The bombardiers swung the barrels steadily, peering through their sights. Frank lost count of time. All he knew was that he must keep on loading, on and on, until he was taken out or it was over. He didn't think about it ending.

Then there was a gap, a lull, which none of them could believe. The sky was empty except for a few dark blots of smoke. On the ground, the burning carcasses of aircraft were scattered, fire crews spurting water on some and a peculiar and eerie silence taking over. None of them could speak. Frank's ears buzzed, his brain numb. One of the gunners slumped down from his position and buried his face in his arm. The commander and the lance bombardier wiped their sweating and filthy faces with their sleeves. Frank looked at Chalky, who was struck dumb too and could only nod back.

Sergeant Campbell came running up from the trench behind the position. 'Bloody good work, lads.'

'Yeah, thanks,' said the gun commander, turning to Frank and Chalky.

The sergeant looked back at the bodies. 'Come on, we'll need to see to them.'

The commander nodded solemnly in thanks as Frank and Chalky climbed out of the wrecked pit of the gun position to where the two bodies lay. An ambulance was lurching its way across the littered airstrip towards them.

Frank stared so that his eyes lost their focus, as a way of not seeing, while he helped lift the dead men's bodies onto the canvas sheet provided by the ambulance crew. The other members of the gun crew watched with blank faces. Frank's ears were still ringing as he and Chalky followed the rest of the men from his platoon, trailing their way across the airfield to the assembly point, where he could see Lieutenant Chambers standing, watching them approach.

The next month was a relentless, draining routine of long shifts, between which men slept and rose like the undead each day.

'A hundred fucking raids last week,' said someone in the canteen. 'More raids here in seven days than in the whole of the ruddy London blitz, so the paper says.'

'God only knows what Valletta's like now and the docks. There'll be nothing left soon.'

'Going to blast the blessed island into the sea.'

Frank thought of all the places he'd seen and admired in Valletta and how many of them were now only hummocks of broken stone. Mr Falson's bookshop was right in the centre and was probably wrecked, like many of the other buildings around it. He supposed it might have been even worse if the stone hadn't been so strong and solid. The old fortifications were still there. The Royal Opera House had been flattened, but the cathedral had survived, for the moment.

There was always talk of invasion, even of surrender, and Frank wondered vaguely what life would be like as a prisoner of war. What was the point of thinking about any kind of future in all this? And yet Frank could not give up all hope, could not deny nor ignore his thoughts about Manwela.

For one of their spells of duty, most of his platoon had been sent to help build a new runway at Qrendi, where they'd had to sleep in an old henhouse and didn't manage to wash for two weeks. But before they'd gone, he'd managed to visit Manwela. It was this memory that stayed warm and sweet with him, consoled him when his pessimism threatened to swamp him. He'd decided to brave Manwela's crowded household, to brazen out the chance of not being welcome, just to see her, to be with her in the same room. She had welcomed him, had smiled and seemed pleased to see him. She was cooking something she told him was 'Soppa Tal-Armla', Widow's soup.

'Very suitable for me, the soup of poor widows,' she said with a weak laugh. 'It is so difficult now with the terrible prices. I can't even buy eggs.'

The chatter spilled around them at the table.

'People have started slaughtering their goats. We can't kill Margarita. We'll have no milk or cheese,' Manwela said.

Frank was desperate to help. 'I'll see what I can get hold of. I can do a bit of bargaining,' Frank said, deciding that he'd use his ration of cigarettes and chocolate to barter for any food he could pick up from the NAAFI or from other men more desperate for tobacco than him.

'You are kind, Frank,' Manwela said, holding his gaze for a moment.

When he left Manwela and the others in the kitchen, to make his way back to the barracks, she ran after him into the road. He turned at the sound of her steps, and she came close to him, grasping his arm, looking into his face, her eyes dark, intense, full of what she wanted to tell him.

'Frank, I'm sorry we have no time, no place to talk.'

He bent to kiss her, knowing that she wanted it too, but a child's voice squealed behind them, 'Mama', and David burst out of the yard. Manwela grasped Frank's hand briefly, then turned from him to watch her small son running up the road.

Recalling this encounter lent Frank both frustration and delight. The hope kept him going through all the bleak days when there was no chance of seeing her.

Their work on airfield defences and bomb damage repair alternated with tedious days away from the barracks manning coastal positions, kipping down in the pillboxes and eating disgusting food half cooked on midget kerosene stoves. On one such occasion, Chalky offered Frank a smoke, which he refused, in his efforts to conserve his supplies for bartering.

'Not seen your lovely widow for a bit, then?' said Chalky, yawning, knowing the answer but clearly wanting a chat.

'No,' said Frank, 'not been much chance, has there? She's got her hands full too, with her house full of people, all her relatives and their kids.'

Chalky yawned again. 'It's good, though, to have a family, I mean. I've got a big family, twenty cousins. My mum and dad had four brothers and sisters apiece and they went forth and multiplied.' He laughed. 'Just like Maltese folk. Some of them've got loads of kiddies, but then they're Catholics. Are you a Catholic?'

Frank smiled at his friend's prattle. 'No, I'm not anything. When I was in the home, the vicar kept coming round all the

THE DUST OF MELITA

time, trying to tell us that God loves us. "Does he really?" this little lad says to him once. "Yes, of course he does," says the vicar. "He is your Father. You are all his children." And the little lad pipes up, "Well, why doesn't he come and play football with us, then?"'

'You never had a family, not at all?' said Chalky.

'Just my mum,' said Frank, 'but I can't remember her much, only vaguely.'

'Pity,' said Chalky, glancing at Frank. 'Still, the army's your family now. Better than nothing, I suppose. At least you've got us.'

'Yeah,' said Frank, laughing and not inclined at that moment to disagree.

Chalky didn't say any more, but Frank wouldn't have minded telling him about his fantasy, about getting married and having kids and a proper house one day. It would have been good to talk about it.

They were only back at St Andrew's for a day or two before they were ordered out again to help build some more gun positions on the north-eastern coast, to strengthen the defences.

'Only a day this time, lads,' said Sergeant Campbell. 'Shouldn't be too bad, unless the Jerries decide to invade, of course.'

They left the barracks at eight and marched up the coast road. Lieutenant Chambers and Sergeant Campbell had gone on ahead in a jeep to get instructions from the Royal Engineers. It was a warm spring day, with the sea and sky an impossible blue. Frank gazed at the sight beyond the barbed wire fences, thinking how extraordinary it would be to be here as a visitor, a person with the time to ramble and explore and sit on the beach. There were pockets of colour, flowers in clumps scattered over the white rocky land. Some of the men of the Dorsets were manning posts on the coastal edges and hailed them as they passed. Small rocky promontories pointed into the sea and the road swung round a narrow bay before they reached the village of Bugibba and the wider more impressive St. Paul's Bay.

Frank had read the story about the Apostle Paul being shipwrecked here. It was even mentioned in the New Testament. He performed miracle cures and converted the Maltese, which made them amongst the earliest Christians, and so the people always felt their islands to be blessed. The folk did seem to have pretty solid faith in God, Jesus, Mary and all the saints. And they'd certainly need all the strength of that faith to endure all this punishment for much longer.

At the site, on the north side of St. Paul's Bay, they rested briefly before the sections were instructed by the RE officer about the moving and piling up of the blocks of white limestone into neat walls. It was heavy work but was finished quite quickly, as it had been decided that only one position was needed after all. Sergeant Campbell told them to take a breather, so the men found places to sit and smoke under olive trees and behind a low stone wall. Frank wondered whether this was Lieutenant Chambers' way of getting his platoon a bit of respite from the toil and tension of the last month. Here, they seemed far away from the destruction that was happening on other parts of the island even though it was only a few miles away. There were signs of the hostilities, however: the defences on the headland, the sinister sparkling in the sky far in the distance. Like a flock of tiny silver birds, a whole squadron of them by the look of it, out to the east, enemy planes were heading for the docks or the airfields.

'Pity we didn't have one of those great big coastal guns like the navy's got down at Sliema,' said one of the men. 'That'd blast the bastards out of the sky.'

'Too far away, even for them,' said someone else.

Some of the men, including Sergeant Campbell, were dozing off. Frank stared at the sky, feeling his eyelids droop. Their moments of peace didn't last long, however, as Lieutenant Chambers and the RE officer drove up in the jeep and they knew they'd be on the move again.

Sergeant Campbell scrambled to his feet. 'Right, Nix's section, back to barracks. Marshall's, take over here and we'll relieve you at eighteen hours.'

Frank set off with his men back down into St. Paul's Bay. From halfway down the descending road, they could see a group of airmen sitting on the beach. It was a rest camp for the fighter pilots, one of the few quiet places on the island.

'All right for some, isn't it?' said one of the men.

'Can we have an ice cream, Corp?' called another.

'Wish we could,' said Frank.

Bad as it was for the infantry, stuck on the ground under fire, being bombed, and squashed like ants underfoot, Frank always thought it would have been a worse fate to be up in the air. Hurtling through the sky in one of those flimsy little metal boxes and being shot at would have been, to his mind, beyond terror. Fighter pilots didn't have long-term prospects. He didn't begrudge the RAF blokes their relaxation.

As Frank and his section reached the flat road by the beach, a jeep shot past them, swerving, erratic, careering along, as though the steering or brakes had failed and the driver had lost control.

'Bloody hell,' said Chalky, 'that's Chambers.'

'Who does he think he is, fucking Batman?' said one of the men.

Frank watched, alarmed, as the vehicle slewed and bumped its way ahead of them. Some of the airmen on the beach stood up and watched too. Luckily, there was nothing in the way of it on the road. Inside the jeep, the officer's body looked loose, like a doll or a dummy, and Frank was seized with the thought that he might be dead. But how? There hadn't been any raids. A heart attack?

'Come on, better get down there,' said Frank, dashing off after the vehicle, his boots pounding on the dusty road ahead of the others. The jeep hit a rock on the edge of the road and leapt across to the other side. It appeared that the driver had managed to brake and get some kind of control, as the vehicle stopped with a squeal and a jolt. Frank sprinted up to find the officer sitting dazed and motionless behind the wheel in a flurry of dust. Lieutenant Chambers' face was red and sweating, his eyes bloodshot.

'Sir, are you all right?' said Frank, gasping with the effort of his run.

The officer shook his head slowly, as though he were trying to think of the answer. 'Good Lord, that was a bit hair-raising,' he said.

'What happened, sir? Is there a fault with the jeep?'

'No, it's not that. I'm not feeling quite myself, I'm afraid. I think I must have a touch of the flu,' he said.

'Malta Dog perhaps?'

'Maybe,' said Lieutenant Chambers. 'It just came over me. Head went woozy for a minute, and I couldn't... well, never mind. I've been luckier than most chaps so far.'

Frank turned and saw Chalky and the others slowing their pace to a gentle trot.

'I don't think I'd better drive this thing back,' said the officer. 'Would you oblige, please, Nixon?'

'Hang on, sir,' he said, 'I'll put Chalky, Lance Corporal White, in charge.'

Frank rejoined his men, who were hanging around a few yards behind the jeep.

'Is he OK?' said Chalky.

'Yes, I think so, but I've got to drive him.'

'Oi, can you give us a lift too, Corp?' One of the men laughed. 'I'm coming over all funny.'

Someone muttered, 'Best watch out, Corp, if he's got the trots.'

Frank returned to the jeep to find that Lieutenant Chambers had moved into the passenger seat. His face was a bad colour, grey and sticky with sweat, but he managed to smile feebly at Frank.

'Thanks, Nixon. I'm sure I'll be fine when I get my head down.'

They were soon on the top of the south side of the bay, a beautiful curve with the blue sea trapped in a sparkling pocket between the slopes. Frank found the movement of air as they sped along exhilarating, and Lieutenant Chambers, appearing to have recovered a little, was gazing at the view.

'Lovely place,' he murmured. 'God knows what will become of it.'

Frank said nothing as the road swung out along the coast. They passed two machine-gun posts on the top of the cliff, enclosures of stone, where some gunners were standing in a group, smoking. The next post was the stone sangar, the one that Frank and others in his section, including his dead comrades, had built.

'It was just along here, that cave,' said Frank, pointing to his right.

'Really?' said Lieutenant Chambers, sitting up in his seat. 'Where, exactly?'

'On a ridge, only about four hundred or five hundred yards along from here, just up there beyond that wall,' said Frank, recognising the lie of the land quite well now that he saw it again.

'Let's take a look, shall we?'

'Sir?' said Frank, wide-eyed at the officer.

'Come on, Nixon. You said you'd show me.'

'But, sir, you're not well. It's a sort of tunnel. You've got to crawl...'

The officer looked at him, his eyes fixed and determined. 'Look, we might never get another chance.'

Frank stared back at him, ready to attempt another protest.

'I could order you, if that would make you feel better, Nixon,' said the officer with a grin. 'Drive up as close as you can.'

Frank discovered that he was as excited as Lieutenant Chambers at the prospect of going into the cave. It was true, there might be no other opportunity to discover the secrets it held. No one knew what was going to happen in this war. They might both be dead next week. If they could just get in and have a look at the carvings, copy down the writing, they would at least have a record. If someone could translate it too, it might tell them... God knows what. His excitement grew. But did they have any light? Matches were no good. Pen and paper? Lieutenant Chambers' mind was clearly working along the same lines.

'There's a torch in the box in the back,' said the officer, 'and I never go anywhere without a notebook, Nixon. Don't worry. We're as prepared as we could be. I only wish I had a camera with a flashlamp.'

Frank bumped the vehicle over the rocky ground as far as he could, alongside the wall where he had relieved himself that day, past the bomb craters. And there they came upon it: the small, black opening in the rockface.

Lieutenant Chambers was not too steady on his feet to begin with, but he assured Frank that he could manage and pushed ahead stubbornly. Frank followed, feeling a mix of exhilaration and fear. They stood for a moment inspecting the entrance, Lieutenant Chambers stooping over and shining the torch into the hole, illuminating the walls of the narrow tunnel.

'Take the torch, Nixon. You lead the way.'

'Are you sure you want to go in, sir?'

'Yes, yes, for goodness' sake, stop fussing. You're worse than my mother-in-law,' the lieutenant replied.

Frank crouched down and, with the torch in one hand, elbowed himself in as before, hearing the officer shuffling behind him. By the dancing light of the torch, he could see the texture of the tunnel walls clearly and also that it widened and deepened more rapidly than he'd thought. They reached the sloping part where Frank had begun to slide down and where the ledge at the end led to the cavern-like room with the writings.

'There's a bit of a drop down here, sir,' he said, turning his head and hearing the officer wheezing behind him.

They both shuffled around to sit up. Frank circled the beam of the torchlight around the substantial space beyond where they sat, revealing quite clearly the smooth surface of the wall used by the scribe and the dense pattern of the writing.

'Good Lord, Nixon,' whispered Lieutenant Chambers. 'What have we here? I can't believe what I'm seeing. Could be a burial chamber of some sort. There are some Roman catacombs near Citta Vecchia, that's Mdina, or Citta Notabile, as it was also known at one time. This is very crude though and perhaps unfinished. I don't know. Let's take a closer look.'

Frank stared at the writings too, feeling no alarm at revisiting the place that had scared him so badly, where he'd felt, and thought he'd heard, the peculiar presence beside him. Now, with a companion, there was less scope for the erratic roving of his imagination.

They both slid down to the edge, and Frank jumped the remaining four feet to the cave floor, hoping that Lieutenant Chambers could manage it. The officer followed with a thump and keeled over. Frank helped him up, his hands feeling the soaking khaki of the officer's shirt. He had a burning fever and shouldn't be doing this. Lieutenant Chambers took out his handkerchief and mopped his face, breathing heavily. Frank turned the torchlight full on the writing.

'My God,' said Lieutenant Chambers, 'it's Greek. Goodness gracious. What have you found, Nixon? I'll have to get this down. By God, I'll have to get it. And the archaeological chaps from the museum must see this. Damn war. If only we could have it properly examined.'

He pulled out his notebook and pencil and stepped close to the wall. 'Hold the torch close, up there, at the top first. That's it.'

Frank wondered how long the torch battery would last and worried that it might be dimming a bit. The lieutenant kept writing, looking, dropping his head down and breathing with increasing difficulty, it seemed. He halted, muttering inaudibly sometimes. Frank wanted to ask what implement the writer might have used, but he knew he shouldn't interrupt the officer's concentration. At his feet, he felt loose stones or chippings, and when Lieutenant Chambers paused again, he lowered the torch for a moment and shone it on several pieces of flint and a spiked bit of what looked like metal.

'Would these have been what they wrote with, sir, do you think?'

The officer peered at the pieces in Frank's hand, breathing heavily and turning the page of his notebook. 'Yes, Nixon. Bring them with you, could you?'

Frank pocketed the pieces and resumed his duty of holding the light, halfway down the wall now. But Lieutenant Chambers only managed another few minutes of copying before the pencil fell from his hand and he collapsed suddenly to his knees.

Frank grabbed him by the shoulders to steady him, but the officer had lost consciousness, his head lolling, his body falling in a dead weight. Frank laid him down, then slapped his cheeks to try for a response. He cursed himself, suppressing the feeling of panic that he had done something seriously foolish in telling Lieutenant Chambers about the cave.

'Sir, wake up. We'd better be going now,' he said, wondering if he should try and find a pulse.

Although the sick man was his major concern, Frank had lost sight of the notebook. The officer would never forgive him if he didn't find it and bring it away. He shone the torch around the officer's body and saw the white page of the book on the ground. Frank stretched to pick it up and stuffed it into his shirt pocket.

'Sir, sir, wake up,' he said again, knowing it was hopeless. He'd have to get him up and out of here. He could be seriously ill. Frank certainly couldn't leave him here in the dark. 'Fucking hell and bloody Nora,' he swore aloud to expel some of his tension and alarm.

Breathing deeply, Frank put the torch up on the ledge and encircled the body of his commanding officer with his arms. He hauled him upright, against the wall of rock where the ledge jutted out. If he could just get him up there, to the slope, he could drag him along and out of the tunnel. But the task was impossible. It was four feet up and the unconscious lieutenant was an unwieldy weight to raise up on his own.

There was no other way but to push him up, inch by inch if necessary, until he was over the edge, then climb up after him. Frank bent again, in the darkness, gripped the lieutenant's lower body and yanked upwards, straining. But the ledge was too high, and the head and shoulders flopped over heavily. It was no good. Frank, with panic sickening his stomach, gulped a lungful of hot, moist air. The man would be bloody dead before he could get him out.

Then there was a waft of breath, a soft stroking of his face, just like before, a silk smooth movement near him, a whisper in his ear, as though someone stood at his shoulder, coaxing, soothing.

Frank gasped, calling out in a mad screech of a voice, 'Well, fucking help me, then!'

Then the lieutenant's body was moving up, with his head and shoulders reaching over the ledge. Frank was still pushing the legs, but he found them going from his grip, up to the shelf above. His feet scrambled for a hold on the rock, and he thrust himself up after the officer, crawling beside the unconscious body, onto the sloping tunnel floor. Lieutenant Chambers was not dead.

'Thank you, Jesus, God,' Frank whispered.

The officer was breathing, or someone was breathing close to him, but Frank kept his cheek pressed to the hard rock and lay still. He wouldn't let himself think or imagine what was around him in the darkness, nor what lay ahead.

He started again, grasping hold of Lieutenant Chambers, turning him over and clamping him around the chest, then shuffling slowly and painfully on his rear. After many slow and agonising minutes, Frank had hauled him into the tunnel in sight of the hole of light at the end. Here he lay again for some moments, staring at the opening of sunlight at the end, exhausted. Light-headed, he thought of the sayings, 'light at the end of the tunnel' and 'writing on the wall'. He would have laughed at his ludicrous position if he'd had the strength and not thought that his platoon commander might be dead. He dragged the body on and out into the light.

Lieutenant Chambers groaned, and Frank's heart leapt.

'Did we get it all down, Nixon?' he mumbled. 'All of it?'

'Yes, sir,' said Frank.

The nearest hospital, St. Luke's, was only about four miles away. Thank God for a small island, thought Frank as he steered the jeep to the front entrance and rushed in to get help. Five minutes later, he watched as Lieutenant Chambers was stretchered into the building.

'He was taken ill up beyond St. Paul's Bay,' Frank told the sister in charge.

'I was going to take him back to barracks, but he got too bad and collapsed.'

'Any vomiting, diarrhoea, fever? Was he complaining about pain anywhere?'

Frank told her about the high fever, but he was certainly not going to admit that he'd taken the officer potholing. When he thought about it again, he felt ridiculous, then guilty that he should have let the sick man go down into that dark, damp hole.

'Are you going to wait?' said the sister.

'Yes, I'd better. I should take word back to the CO if he's going to be out of action for a bit. What do you reckon it is?'

The nurse shrugged. 'I wouldn't like to say. But you did right to bring him in.'

'Any chance of a glass of water?' Frank asked, his mouth as dry as sawdust.

She smiled. 'Of course, Corporal. I'm sorry. You look done in. Take a seat. I might even be able to get you a cup of tea and a biscuit if you're really lucky.'

Frank slumped into a chair against the wall and rested his head. His muscles ached but were easing off a bit now. After two glasses of water, a cup of tea and a stale biscuit, he was a little restored. In his shirt pocket, he felt the notebook and took it out. He also had the small hard pieces of the flint and the fragments of the metal scribing tool, if that's what it was. The notebook was dirty and some of the pages were crumpled. He turned them carefully one by one, seeing Lieutenant Chambers' neat little pencil sketches, his reflections about the island, a few poems and then, at the end, the copied Greek writing from the cave.

The officer had done a very good job, considering that he was close to collapse, though the last page was erratic, sloping and barely legible. Frank knew that he had only managed to copy about half of the writing. This was one step further towards discovering what those people from the past had recorded there in the underground tomb. But he doubted now that he would ever know it all.

CHAPTER 13

MALTA, 870 AD

Loukia's father wasn't frightened of anything. He was happy to plunge in among the bees, even let them crawl into his ears and over his mouth. She would stay away from the stone hive, with its many little windows where the bees flew in and out. She would wait for her father up here on her usual sitting stone until he had collected all the honeycombs. She loved honey and could feast for ever on the shining globules that Avina dropped onto her flat bread.

'Are you nearly finished, Father?' she called to him in a sing-song voice, just to remind him that she was there.

This was a good place for the bees to have a home, up here on the hill. They could see it easily and find their way back even if their flowers were on the other side of the island. Her sitting stone made her even higher; she could see far out to sea. Her father and brother and Evoric would come here often to look at the sea. Sometimes they were not happy with what they saw, and once, only a short time ago, they'd seen wicked men coming in their galleys. Father had made them all stay indoors while he went and spoke to the enemies. He'd tended to some who were wounded and then they were gone again.

Loukia stood on her stone to shake away the memory of that time when her mother had cried and held on to her so tightly that she couldn't breathe. There were no galleys today, but there was one little boat. It had a red sail and was coming in to the beach, which lay right at the bottom of the cliff. Snaky, steep paths led up from the beach to their house and even up here.

'*Father*,' she called, and her voice was louder this time, for she wanted him to see the boat before it disappeared from her view.

She heard her father's soft voice from inside the bees' stone cave. 'Have patience, child.'

She stared hard at the boat to see how many people were on it. They were only black dots, maybe three of them, and one was pulling down the sail, then rowing the boat to shore. They were probably fishermen. Sometimes fishermen came from Gozo with baskets of fish to sell. Now a man from the boat had jumped into the sea and was pulling it ashore.

'Father, come. There's a boat,' she called, thinking that this would surely bring him quickly.

It did. He came out of the doorway, stooping with his head that looked huge in his hat, carrying the clumps of honeycombs in both hands. The bees dotted around him.

'A boat?' he said.

'Only a little one, blue with a red sail. But I can't see it anymore.'

Loukia's father placed the honeycombs carefully in the wheelbarrow and, pulling his hat off, put it on top of them. Some bees were still crawling over his hairy arm, then took off, twirled a little in the air and were gone.

'And how many people did you see in the boat, my child?' he said, coming to her, reaching up to lift her down from her stone. He flew her down from her stone like a bird, and her face swooped near to his. She saw the trickles of sweat in the lines of his face and his blue eyes that matched the sky.

'There were only two or three maybe. They looked like little ants,' she said, thinking that these people might be climbing up the path by now.

'Come, we must go and welcome them,' said Father, gripping the handles of the barrow and steering it round, ready to go down the hill.

He did not speak any more as they went down the stony path to their villa. He was not angry, though. Loukia knew this. He was just thinking, because his brow was creased and he was always thinking. Loukia hoped that Avina had made some lemonade because she was very thirsty. Before they had even reached the gateway to the yard, Avina came running. This was odd because she was most usually in the kitchen in the morning. Her face was crumpled with worry and she was panting.

'Master,' she said, 'some people have come from Gozo. They tell of something terrible. Come quick and hear them.'

'Who are they, Avina?'

'A fisherman and his wife and children. They're half-dead, Master.'

Father wheeled the barrow quickly into the yard, and Loukia had to trot to keep up with him.

Loukia had never seen a man cry. Her brother Constans had cried once when he was stung by a jellyfish, but he did not cry now because he was eleven years old and nearly a man. But the fisherman wept with so many tears that his face was wet. His wife cried only a little and held on to her baby. There was another bigger boy, though he was much smaller than Loukia. Avina poured more of her lemonade into cups for them, and Loukia watched the small boy, whose head only reached to the table, guzzle down the drink.

The fisherman told them his story of how they'd had to run away from their village on the island and taken to their boat to escape. It had started one night, when a great fleet of galleys had crept up on the north side of the island. At first everyone had thought they were corsairs and just hid away their valuable things and got ready. But these were not pirates; they were soldiers, Arab warriors, thousands of them. They had come ashore and rampaged over the whole island. They had swept the countryside, killing all the men and the old people, taking the women and children in chains and putting others in cages of wood.

Loukia crept close to her mother, frightened by the fisherman's eyes as he told the horrible story.

'Some of our people ran to the citadel and closed the gates,' he said, 'but the Muslims shot burning arrows in, scaled the walls and broke down the gates. They slaughtered anyone who stood against them, captured the young and healthy for slaves. They stole the treasure from our churches, then burned them down, pulled down the houses—'

'Were you there to witness this?' said Father.

Loukia found her mother's hand. Then Constans and Evoric came into the kitchen, and the fisherman's body jolted with shock and he wept again. Loukia felt her own eyes hurt. She had caught the man's fear and seen the pictures in her mind as he'd spoke.

'What has happened?' said Constans.

'Sssh, listen to this man's story,' said Father.

The fisherman shuddered and wiped his face upon his sleeve. 'Two men told us of this. They escaped from the town. They had been working in the fields below the walls of the citadel and had run away when they saw the army. They ran all night to the south and brought the news to our village. So, we left our homes with nothing except our lives.'

'How long ago? How long ago did you sail from the island?' said Father.

'A day only. We saw the army coming over the hill. We had no time. Some people had no boats. They had no time to flee. We heard them screaming, but we could do nothing, and the wind was in our sails.'

'How many of you escaped?'

'Four boats only, just those who fish the seas. But we lost them in a storm, or the Arab galleys have taken them. I do not know.'

He paused. The room was silent for a brief moment as Loukia and her family stared at the fugitives.

'Bring cheese and bread and olives and milk too, Avina,' said Mother.

Loukia followed her mother to the store cupboard and helped Avina carry the platters to the table. The small boy tried to grab the cheese, but his mother caught his hand and spoke to him in a sharp whisper. Loukia's father pulled up a stool to the table, and Constans did likewise.

'And you say it was an army of thousands?' said Father.

The fisherman nodded weakly. 'That's what the men said. And we could even hear them from our village—the drums and the sound of pipes. We saw the flames and smoke of fires burning everywhere, the citadel and the houses. The men said that the army was coming like locusts devouring the land. They spoke of four hundred galleys anchored off the shore.'

'Let them eat now,' said Mother, laying a hand on Father's arm.

The family ate like starving dogs, even the woman, who tore at the bread with her teeth.

'Will they come here, Father?' said Constans.

Loukia wanted her father's reply, but nothing came. Instead, he stood up and went out of the kitchen, leaving them to stare at each other and the starving fisherman and his family. Soon, the food had gone.

The fisherman wiped his mouth. 'God bless you, mistress,' he said.

Loukia's mother nodded at him. 'Let us pray for the souls of all those who have perished and for our own deliverance.'

They all knelt before Mother Mary's kind face in the picture on the wall.

Loukia wished her father would come back. It was he who usually spoke the prayers. God would listen to him because he was a man and the head of their family and never afraid, even of infidels and enemies. He was wise too and a doctor and knew about everything in the world. They bowed their heads and prayed, and Loukia heard her father come back in quietly and felt him kneel at her side.

'Mary, Mother of God, look down upon your children. Protect and guide us, as we humble ourselves before you,' said Mother.

When they rose to their feet, Father spoke.

'We must go to the fortress at Melite. We cannot stay here,' he said in a voice as heavy as a stone.

'Leave here?' said Mother. 'You have always said, through all our troubles, that we would never go from here. It is our home, our life.'

He nodded at her. 'Yes, you are right. I promised this. I love this place, our comfortable home and fertile garden, the sea, the beauty that brings us close to God. But I must break my word. This danger is too great. I have prayed for guidance, and I believe God wants us to save ourselves from the evil that threatens us. We must act with wisdom and with courage. The rest is in God's hands.'

'Courage? You say we should run away?' said Constans, his lip trembling.

'My boy, we cannot fight this force, thousands of men. This time, money bribes or binding a few infidels' wounds will not save us, as they have in the past. This is no pirates' raid, but an invasion. Our best chance is in the fortified city. We must pack up food and water, warm cloaks for the night, tools and implements for our journey, and we must leave tonight.'

No one said another word against Father's declaration. Loukia wanted to weep, but her mother and Avina had already gone to the store cupboard to gather up food.

Father looked at the fisherman and his family. 'You are most welcome to journey with us,' he said. 'It is the only course left to you, I think.'

Their two donkey carts were loaded high with baskets of cheese, fruit and bread, several large amphorae with oil, wine and water and pots of last year's honey. One of the goats was tied behind a cart, the rest released to roam upon the land. Loukia cried secretly for all that was left behind, their pretty vases and picture, rugs and tapestries. Constans said that the wicked soldiers would ruin everything when they came. Loukia thought of them stamping through the cool passages of their house, breaking the lemon trees, smashing the fountain in the courtyard, burning the chairs and tables and Father's library. Evoric saw her crying and put his heavy, crusty hand upon her shoulder as they went out into the yard for the last time.

Father led the way. There was no talk. The fisherman carried his little boy upon his back, his wife had the baby strapped to her body with a shawl. The family had no belongings at all but walked almost as slowly as Loukia, who did her best and had to skip fast sometimes to keep up. Evoric carried the two biggest amphorae strung by a harness on his shoulders, like an ox. He was very strong because he had been a galley slave once, so Father said.

The road was bumpy in the dark, but Father was in front with his staff. Mother followed, with Avina and Constans leading the donkeys. They left the sea behind them, and when dawn came, it had gone, and they were in the middle of an empty stretch of stony countryside. Some small enclosures hemmed in by low stone walls were planted with tall, dry grasses or with the white fluffballs of cotton and clumps of prickly pear and olive trees. A small white square ahead was a peasant's house. He was working in a field, hacking at the soil with a hooked stick as they came by on the track. Father stopped and spoke to him, told him of the danger.

'I'll not shift,' said the peasant man. 'I'll not flee from any Arabs. This is my land, and I'll die on it.'

Loukia thought the man was very brave, but her father was brave too and he had made them flee.

They camped that night, sheltering behind a wall, and made a little fire in a ring of stones. Amina heated a milky gruel that they could all eat, even the fisherman's baby, though it squealed when its mother put the stuff to its lips. Loukia heard the woman singing to it in the evening and it was quiet then. Mother covered Loukia and Constans with a thick cloak. Loukia watched the stars that were sprinkled all across the sky, hearing her mother and father talking in low voices and a donkey snorting now and then.

The next day, Loukia woke stiff, missing her comfortable straw bed at home, but the day was warm, her mother cheerful and they breakfasted well, sitting in a circle like a large family, with Avina and Evoric too. The fisherman smiled at her, and Loukia showed his little boy her doll made from white driftwood. Evoric had carved it with a pretty face for her.

They set off again, and Loukia wondered how far it was to the city of Melite, where they would be safe.

'Why is it safe in the city, Father?' she asked, running to catch up with him as he strode ahead.

'Because it has high walls, built very thick by the Romans long ago. And there are guards and soldiers, the emperor's soldiers, with weapons to fight against the Arabs. We will go inside the walls, and the gates will be closed to keep the enemy out.'

This seemed like a fine idea to Loukia, though she wanted to ask if there would be room for all the people who needed to be safe. Something about her father's way of talking, his solemn face and his hand upon her head made her keep her silence, however. Then the sea appeared again, a bay with high cliffs circling it.

'We will go this way along the top there to keep sight of the sea until we have to head inland,' said Father.

The sea was huge and empty, with only little waves that sparkled. Constans smiled when he saw it, as though he knew some secret. Mother embraced Loukia too, suddenly, and Loukia did not so much mind this strange journey that was taking her away from her home. Avina was carrying the fisherman's baby now and talking with its mother as they went along. Soon, they turned to take a winding track leading away, with the sea at their backs. When the track dipped down by a crumbling wall, they stopped for a rest and to eat.

Loukia needed to find a place to make her water and so she walked a little distance along by a rocky wall to find a place. The wall suddenly became a solid white rock with a round black hole in it that looked like a big burrow for an animal or a tunnel to a cave. She had seen many caves before. On the beach, the sea made holes and arches in the rock and caves in many places. She and Constans had sometimes gone into the caves, though, upon finding out, it had angered Father, who'd said that when the sea was wild it would rush in and drown them. But this was not a watery cave, this one up here in the country land. She peed quickly behind a rock, then poked her head a little way into the hole. It was a very long tunnel, as far as she could see. She heard her mother calling her and ran back to the others over the bumpy stones.

'Where is Evoric?' Loukia said, noticing that he was not in their circle as they ate.

'He is coming behind,' said Father. 'Do not worry. We'll keep him food to eat.'

Sometimes Evoric stayed a little behind them, but he always came to eat. She wanted him there. She loved him, though he was their slave. He was a big, quiet man. Father said he did not speak much because he knew only a little of their Greek language and had had a hole burned in his tongue when he was captured by the emperor's army. She loved Avina, with her kind, wrinkled face, her strong arms and gentle hands.

'Look, here comes Evoric,' said Constans, looking up to where the hefty figure was charging down towards them.

'Why is he running?' said Loukia.

Mother stood up suddenly and the fisherman hoisted up his little boy, who was rambling over some rocks. Evoric came closer, and Loukia's stomach felt watery inside when she saw the look on his face.

'Master,' he called when still twenty paces from them, gasping, his body glistening with sweat, 'ships. They come.'

'How many, Evoric?'

He stopped, gasping and gulping, as though the words were lumps of bread choking him. He held up both of his hands, his fingers spread, then opened and closed them many times.

'On beach,' he said. 'Run, Master. Go.'

'Mary Mother of God, protect us,' said Loukia's mother.

Father stood still as a stone. 'We cannot run, Evoric. We will be caught. We must accept our fate and pray for strength.'

'*No,*' Mother was shrieking, clasping Loukia to her.

The fisherman's wife started weeping, making horrible snorting sobs.

'We could hide,' said Loukia, suddenly remembering the tunnel that she had come upon.

No one heard her, as her mouth was muffled by her mother's embrace and the weeping that swelled around her.

Loukia struggled free. 'We could hide,' she said again, pulling at her mother's arm. 'I found a place.'

'Oh, child,' said her mother, her voice shredding into sobs.

But Father stepped to her, crouched down and grasped her by the shoulders. 'Where, child? Show us.'

Loukia turned round and pointed back towards the place along the wall where the black hole went into the rock. All eyes followed her hand, and a moment later, she was leading them, stumbling over the stones, towards the place.

Constans ran ahead and peered into it. 'You stupid little fool,' he said, his face twisted in anger. 'It's only a narrow tunnel.

'No, wait,' said Father, 'there may be something beyond it. There are many caverns beneath the earth, made by water underground. In some parts, people use them for stores or for laying their dead. I'll go in.'

One of the donkeys brayed loudly at them, and Evoric ran to calm the animal. They watched as Father disappeared inside the tunnel, head, shoulders, body, feet, and Loukia prayed to God to bring him out again. What if he should fall into a hole or meet some monster lurking in its lair? But his head soon came out, and he was smiling.

'There is a cave, a big one. The tunnel leads to it. God has shown us, through this child, a place of safety. Come. Hurry.'

He scrambled quickly to his feet. 'Everyone, unload the food, bring all the baskets here and the water, oil, everything. We must take it all in here. Evoric, bring the carts. When they are unloaded, drag them away. Let the donkeys free, the goat also. Chase them from this place.'

Loukia and Constans ran backwards and forwards with the smaller baskets and bundles while Father dragged the biggest amphorae of oil and water into the hole. Evoric, having drawn the carts away and loosed the animals, returned and speeded their moving of the provisions into the tunnel and the cave beyond, which none but Father had seen.

'It's dark. Father needs a light,' said Constans, scrambling back from the opening. Avina found a fire striker and a stump of candle and handed these to him.

'Come in, all of you now,' called Father from the depths.

The fisherman's boy cried as he watched his mother's legs disappearing first into the hole, but his father lifted him and pushed him after her. Then it was Loukia's turn. The tunnel was quite wide for her to go on her hands and knees, and though it was dark, she could see a flickering glow ahead of her and heard the little boy squeal. His mother, with the baby strapped to her belly, sat on a slope from which the roof rose higher, making itself into a cavern. They sat on a ledge, and beyond this was a lower place where Father and Constans were standing. The candle was flickering in a little hollow in the wall. Their stores and belongings lay strewn across the floor of the cave.

'Come. Come quickly now,' said Father to Loukia, lifting her down, then the fisherman's boy and the woman herself. Mother, Avina and the fisherman came next.

'Evoric, make good the entrance,' called Father up to him, and as they crowded together, they heard the grating of heavy moving stones at the tunnel's end.

He appeared some moments later and slid down from the ledge to join them all. 'No one see now, Master,' he said.

Inside, the cave smelt damp and musty. Loukia did not like the feel of the gritty stone floor, though it was better once their cloaks had been spread upon it. Avina found a little oil lamp, and once it was lit, it seemed more like a proper room. Evoric piled up the provisions and supplies in the corner to make more space in the middle for them to sit. He then took up a hammer and chisel and started digging and hacking in the darkest corner. At first, Loukia thought he might be trying to tunnel out, but then realised he was making a latrine.

'Rock, Master. No earth to soak,' he said.

'I know,' said Father. 'We must manage as best we can.'

Evoric resumed his digging, small stones and grit flying up, with steady banging and scraping sounds.

'No one can hear us from above, can they?' said Constans.

'Nor can we hear them,' said Mother. 'How long must we stay down here?'

Her voice quivered a little, and Father did not answer for a moment. But he rose and placed his hand upon Mother's head, then on Loukia's and her brother's. He blessed the others too in this way, even Avina and Evoric.

'Come, Evoric,' he said. 'Leave your labours. Let us all pray. I think this cave might once have been a place of worship. See how this wall is carved smooth, as though people meant to fashion it into a tomb or holy place? We must give thanks to God for this sanctuary, for his loving mercy.'

Loukia woke many times, blind in the thick blackness but grateful for the feel of her mother's body at her side. She gripped her mother's robe, clutching her doll in her other hand. There were other sounds, of breathing and snoring in the steamy darkness. She thought she heard the baby whimpering once or twice. How would they know it was morning when they couldn't see the sun? she wondered. How would they know when the wicked enemies had gone away? When would it be safe to go out again?

They awakened one by one, each person yawning or moving.

Her mother rose and tried to feel her way to the corner of the cave. 'Husband, some light,' she murmured.

Sparks came and then a glow from the lamp lit the chamber, which revealed the bodies all around and their faces to each other. The stink from the latrine hole filled the place with a sickening vapour, but Avina found some sweet-smelling herbs to strew on a mat, which she laid over it.

They broke their fast on bread and cheese, bringing back a little of the good feeling Loukia remembered from their campfire in the open.

'We must talk about what to do next,' said Father. 'How long to stay. Soon, I must go and move a stone to look out and see if the day has passed.'

'Someone could go out at night,' said the fisherman, 'to find out if there is still danger.'

'That might be wise because the night would hide us, but it might hide the infidel army too,' Father said. 'A large army will take time to pass by. I think we should wait for another day before anyone ventures out.'

No one disagreed.

'Meantime, we should occupy ourselves to pass the time.'

'I dig,' said Evoric, picking up his implement again.

'We will sort through the food and supplies,' said Mother.

Father looked at the fisherman and his family. 'You, my friend, must tend your little ones.' He frowned as he contemplated the mother, who still held the baby bound to her body. 'Is your baby sick? He is very quiet. Shall I look at him? I am a doctor.'

The woman unwrapped the shawl from her body, and Father stooped over the infant. Even from where she stood, Loukia could see that the baby was not moving. Its little legs and arms were hanging loose and its eyes were closed. Father laid his hand on its chest and stroked its face.

'Is he feeding from the breast?' he said.

The woman shook her head. 'He will not suck.'

'Try a little honey on his lips,' said Father. 'Avina, please bring a pot. We will pray for him,' he continued, 'this innocent child and ourselves.'

Each person did some small things. Constans played with the little boy, lifting him up and down until both were tired. They talked and told some stories of their lives. Avina pounded some

189

of the grain between two stones. None spoke of the fortress city where they were going. No one spoke of what they hoped.

Father stood up and ran his hand over the smooth surface of the wall. 'I will write here, for the rock is soft enough, with a sharp implement. See how Evoric has carved us two good holes?' He rummaged in a bag of tools and brought out some pieces of flint and an iron gouge and picked up the hammer Evoric had been working with.

'What will you write, Father?' asked Loukia, standing at his side.

The little boy, Constans and the fisherman too crowded around and watched as her father made the first marks.

'First, I will praise God, then I will write our story,' he said, taking up the gouge and scoring a deep mark into the stone.

'The story will be here when we are gone,' said the fisherman.

CHAPTER 14

They watered the wine to slake their thirst the next day, and Mother said they could have no more for a while. The air was stifling. Loukia found that if she lay very still, she could bear it. The little boy had cried himself to exhaustion in his father's arms and the mother, with the shape of her baby still bound to her, lay asleep. Mother and Constans too. Only Evoric, Avina and Loukia watched Father as he scored lines, straight or sloping in curves, with the gouge, then, with the flint and hammer, chipped and cracked to make these into hollow grooves. Loukia wished that she could read.

Evoric stared. 'Holy words,' he muttered to himself.

When his hand started to bleed, Father stopped and sat with the others. Mother and Avina passed round the cheese, though the bread was all gone. They had honey, though, and dipped their fingers into the pot, licking the grit and dirt off with the sweetness.

'How is your child?' Father asked the fisherman's wife.

'He has taken the breast,' the mother replied quietly, though she folded her arms close around her bundle and would not let Father see inside it.

Father nodded. 'Good, good.' He glanced around at the others. 'Tomorrow, we must choose someone to go out.'

'How will you choose?' said the fisherman.

'I go,' said Evoric suddenly.

All were silent, though Loukia secretly wished he had not spoken.

'Let us go first to the tunnel mouth, move some of the stones and spy out,' said Father. 'Then we can go one by one to the opening, very quietly, for there will be fresh air to breathe. I will go first to make a hole.'

Evoric helped Father hoist himself back upon the ledge, and they all watched as he crouched, then dropped to his knees to crawl back along to the tunnel entrance. Some time later, he came shuffling back.

'I could see no sign of anyone there, but we must be cautious.'

Each of them in turn, apart from the fisherman's boy and his mother, with the baby, crawled along the tunnel to put their eyes and noses to the hole. When it was Loukia's turn, she breathed in the cooler air, spying only a clump of prickly pears, rocks and a small patch of dry ground beyond the hole.

Later, Father rose. 'Come, Evoric, let us make an exit for you.' He took Evoric by the hand, then hugged him as though he were a brother and not a slave.

'God go with you, Evoric,' said Mother.

The others murmured their blessings to him as he hoisted himself onto the ledge and readied himself for crawling out. Loukia thought she heard Avina sobbing, but when she turned to the slave woman, her grey head was bowed and her hands clasped in prayer.

All day, Father chipped on and on with his carvings on the wall. Each hour, the shapes slowly spread across the space, then down.

'Read what you have written,' said the fisherman.

Father stepped back a little and looked at his handiwork. 'I, Theodorus, doctor of the island of Gaudomelete, set down my testimony, in the sight of God, in praise of His Almighty power and humbly to beg for His Mercy. Though we are hidden from the world, He sees our plight and hears our prayers.'

They ate the pounded dry grain that night, bound with honey, and there were groans as they lay in the darkness. Loukia's belly was tender and swollen, but she was sicker in her heart that Evoric had not returned.

'He must have roamed far in all directions for a sight of the enemy,' said Father.

'He is a slave,' said the fisherman. 'Why should he return to you when he could be a free man?'

Loukia did not like the voice that the fisherman used. His boy squealed and squirmed, and his mother tried to calm him.

Father frowned and shook his head. 'Evoric will not be free if he meets the invaders.'

'That's true,' said the fisherman, 'if he is a true Christian man.'

'He has served me loyally for more than fifteen years,' said Father, 'since before the birth of our son Constans here. I would trust him with my life.'

'But is he a true Christian? He has a look about him of an infidel.'

'He was a Muslim by birth and had his tongue cut for praying to the infidel god. But he is a baptised Christian,' said Mother.

The fisherman stared back at Mother, then spat into the dust. 'It was a foolish thing to send him. He'll find his own kind out there. They'll seek us out and cut our throats as they did my neighbours in our village.'

Avina cried out. 'No. He is a good man. He prayed to Allah, like we all did in our tribe, but now he prays to Jesus and the Holy Mother Mary. He is faithful. He will come back.'

'You are an infidel also,' said the fisherman, glaring. 'You do not belong with us.'

Loukia buried her face in her mother's side.

'My friend, these you call infidels, our good and faithful servants, fed you and served you in your need,' came Loukia's father's soft voice.

'Only on your orders,' said the fisherman, his voice dark and low.

Father said nothing more and took up his tools again to continue with his writing. The only sound was the chip and scrape upon the stone. The hot air was sour and suffocating.

Father checked the passage of another day and night and then another, through the small chinks between the entrance stones. They drank the last of the water and had only half of one amphora of wine remaining. The cave stank vilely now, and though they had become used to the foulness of their own dirt, there was another different stink.

Father finished his carving for the day, and the fisherman crawled to the tunnel spyhole, which they had taken to leaving open in the hope of letting in some cleaner air. He returned, fidgeting, cursing and scratching at his skin. Loukia felt very filthy too, and one day when she was dozing, she imagined herself to be swimming in the sea, then rinsing her body with the shocking cold of fresh water, which made her skin tingle as she gasped and awoke. But she found herself still sticky, hot and aching in the head.

'I must go out before it is dark today,' said Father, then kneeling before the fisherman's wife, he continued in a gentle voice, 'and I must take your child too and bury him.'

'*No*,' screamed the woman, hugging the bundle to her chest.

Loukia watched the fisherman struggle with his wife, press his hand to her screaming mouth, hold her down while Father and Mother undid her shawl and lifted the baby from her breast. The stench made Loukia's stomach lurch, her throat choke and gag. Avina held the little boy in her arms, his face turned towards the wall.

'Let us pray for the poor child,' said Father. 'He is with God now and the Holy Mother Mary. Come pray for him.'

At last, the woman was quieted, and Mother wrapped the bundle of the baby in a thick shawl. Father placed this above him on the ledge, then, with the fisherman's aid, he hauled his body along the passage with his elbow, towing the bundle behind him. They that were left sank into silence.

Loukia stared at her father's writings on the wall and prayed again and again that he would come back. Mother lay at her side, silent too, with no words of comfort to offer. Constans crouched in the corner, as though he would make himself part of the stone. The fisherman sat with his head bowed, and his wife lay with her face to the wall. Only Avina moved, walking backwards and forwards with the little boy asleep in her arms.

The lamp sputtered, and Mother rose to drip more oil into it, then again a long time later. At last, there was a shuffling sound, the stones at the mouth of the tunnel shifting.

'It's Father. He's back.' Constans said, his voice cracking. He scrambled to the ledge.

'Jesus Lord, we thank you,' said Mother, slowly rising to her feet.

Loukia felt her eyes stinging as she peered for the first sight of her father, and Avina, slumped against the wall, raised her head, the child still asleep in her arms.

'God bless him,' murmured the fisherman.

Father was there, crouching on the ledge, dragging some branches of prickly pear after him.

'Husband,' said Mother, holding out her arms to him.

He came down among them like an angel from heaven, though his face was not shining with a happy message. 'Have we a little wine left?' he asked, sitting down.

Avina brought the nearly empty amphora into the middle of the circle. Loukia watched as she poured some into each cup, wondering why Father was not speaking, what he was not telling them. He drank his cup in one gulp, then turned to the fisherman and his wife.

'I buried your child in a safe sanctuary where his body will not be defiled,' he said. 'It is a little tomb of stone outside the cave.'

The fisherman's wife looked at Father with blank eyes and nodded.

'Evoric? Did you find Evoric?' said Loukia.

'You little fool,' said Constans, who said cruel things to her since they had fled from their home. 'He's not here, is he?'

'Yes, I found him,' said Father, bowing his head. 'God rest his soul. I found what remained of his earthly body.'

Mother gasped, and Loukia felt a sudden stab in her chest.

'They have put his head upon a stake at the edge of their camp,' he said.

'Their camp?' said the fisherman. 'The Arab army?'

'Where?' Constans stood up and grasped his father's arm, as though to shake the answer from him.

'About five hundred paces from here, upon the rise of the hill,' Father said. 'I hid behind a stone in the hollow so they did not see me.'

Avina stepped forward, her eyes fixed on the fisherman. 'Evoric was brave and faithful to us. He died for us.'

'Let us pray for his soul,' said Mother.

Loukia wept, her mother stroking her hair.

'They do not know we are here, so we are safe,' she said. 'Evoric kept us safe.'

Constans sneered. 'But we have no water left.'

'Sit down, my son,' said Father. 'We can mash up the prickly pears, which have some moisture in them. This will serve us for a day or so. Then I will go out again to look for a spring or well. Now we should drink the rest of the wine, eat what food we have and sleep. We will decide tomorrow what's best, with the coming of a new day.'

On that new day, the fisherman said that he and his family were going out.

'Better to live as slaves than to perish here,' he said. 'We will leave at night and go back towards the sea again. Perhaps the Arabs will not see us, and we might beg food of the farmer on our way. We will find our boat upon the beach.'

'God go with you, my friend,' said Father. 'I am sorry that I could not lead you and your family to safety.'

'If they take you, you must not betray us,' said Constans bitterly.

The fisherman turned to him. 'I swear I will say nothing, boy.'

The fisherman went first, and Father lifted the little boy after him, then the mother. Loukia sat hugging her arms around herself and staring at the floor, listening to the shuffling as they crawled along the tunnel, the clattering of the stones being removed and then, at last, Father replacing them.

Mother and Avina pounded the prickly pears into a mush, which was foul to taste but filled their bellies. Loukia lay down as her father poured more oil into the small lamp and set about his carving again. He worked on and on, and Loukia heard her mother whisper to him.

'Have you come to the end of our story, Husband?'

He did not reply, but put down the flint and stone, lay down upon the floor and blew out the lamp.

Loukia was not sure when Avina left them. Mother said she had gone to look for water and did not come back.

'Perhaps we should return to the sea, like the fisherman,' said Constans. His voice was dull and quiet, his mouth crusted with white stuff.

Loukia's throat was tight and sore.

'Maybe,' Father said, 'tomorrow.'

They drank some of the oil but were all sick and lay down for a long, long time. Loukia dozed, hearing Father chipping at the rock. Then Loukia could not hear any sound at all and there was only blackness. She reached for her mother, and her hand touched a cold thing in her mother's gown. She cried out in the darkness for Father, but he didn't answer.

'Constans, Constans,' she called again and again, but there was no reply.

They must be all asleep. Loukia was tired too and very thirsty. She would get water. There must be water outside, then they could all drink and be well again. She must save them. She stumbled in the dark and found the wall, but the ledge was too high for her. If she pulled some things and piled them up, she could climb and reach. She fell over many times, tripped over Constans, who wouldn't wake up. Her legs were shaking under her, and she only wanted to fall down and sleep, but all the time she told herself about the water. She must be brave like Evoric and Avina. She dragged the cloaks, the empty amphora, the bag of tools and made a wobbly step to climb upon.

Her belly scraped on the hard ground, her hands and knees were raw and the grit stung and pricked her as she crawled. She was in the tunnel then and had to lie still for a moment, close her eyes, sleep just for a little while. Then she saw the specks of light between the stones at the end of the tunnel, tiny pretty little sparkles, like stars in a black sky. They would light her way out to the water. She would reach them in a moment.

CHAPTER 15

MALTA, JUNE 1942

'We're only the little people, Nixon,' said Lieutenant Chambers. 'Our stories are not significant, nor are we as individuals. We are unknown instances in a bigger narrative.'

'But surely the stories of individuals can tell us a lot about their times, their circumstances, the societies they lived in, can't they?' said Frank. 'Take this journal by the French officer, for example.'

Lieutenant Chambers smiled drowsily and lifted a stiff hand, as though it were not part of him, dropping it back on the bed again. 'Yes, that's true to an extent,' he said. 'There's some interesting stuff, as far as I can make out.'

Frank eyed the battered volume he'd pulled from the bomb rubble, which was lying on the officer's bed. 'So, do you think history is just about great men, like Julius Caesar or Napoleon, then?'

'Now that is a very interesting question, Nixon. Some historians see the study of history as the biographies of great men, despotic or noble. However, these great men are not operating in a vacuum, are they?'

'You mean they need people to follow them?' said Frank.

'Exactly, and the conditions of great need or turmoil. They are not solely responsible for all the things that happen, like wars.'

'Even Hitler?' said Frank.

'Ah, well, that's another good question.' He sighed heavily and closed his eyes. 'Dear God, when this is all over, what will historians make of it?'

'It'll depend on who writes the history, won't it? The Germans'll write a different version from us, won't they?'

Lieutenant Chambers' eyes flicked open again. 'Goodness me, Nixon. I suppose you'll be asking me whose side God's on next. You really must take this further. I mean your education, when you get back home.'

'I'd like to, sir,' said Frank.

'Well, get in touch with Millicent, as I said. She'll be very glad to steer you in the right direction.'

Lieutenant Chambers sighed again and picked up the small book from the bedcovers. 'I'm so damnably tired,' he said. 'It's all this stuff they're giving me. I've only managed to translate about a quarter of it, if that. And I need a decent French dictionary to do it. My French is simply not up to it.'

'Could I get you one, sir,' Frank said, 'if I went to the bookshop in Valletta?'

The officer laughed weakly. 'Well, that would be marvellous, but do you think Mr Falson's shop is still standing? The whole area must be in pretty bad shape by now, from what we hear on the radio. Not much open at all. Most people are more concerned with where their next meal's coming from than reading books, I should imagine.'

'Wouldn't do any harm to try,' Frank said, fired by even this slim possibility of going to the shop again.

'You're not going to let me rest, Nixon, till I've done this, are you?'

Frank blushed. 'No, sir, it's not that. It's just with you being here and...'

He shifted on the chair by the officer's bed, wishing that he hadn't started making this suggestion. A nurse glided past the end of the beds, and someone coughed. What do you say to someone with polio, the paralytic type, a man who was likely to have to spend the rest of his life in a wheelchair?

'Just for something to do,' Frank floundered.

Lieutenant Chambers looked at Frank. 'That's thoughtful of you. If you could get a dictionary, I'd be very grateful. And perhaps when they stop giving me this medicine that makes me so damn drowsy, I'll be better. I can't cope with the Greek though, from your cave. I'll have to get a copy made and send it back to my old chum from college. He's a classics man. I was always a bit of a dimwit at Latin and Greek.'

His voice was slurred, his eyes half-closed, and Frank wondered if he should leave and not tire him any further. He was a very sick man, but he seemed keen to talk in spite of everything, and the drugs had loosened his tongue.

'You know, I wonder sometimes how I even made it to university,' he continued. 'It would've been far better to give a place to someone like you.'

He was obviously raving a bit, and his face looked waxy and strange. They'd shaved off his moustache.

Frank got up, making a move to leave. 'I'll have a go at copying it, if you think I can.'

'Course you can, Nixon, clever fellow like you. Would you do it?' said Lieutenant Chambers, his eyes opening a little more. 'That would be splendid, then I can get it sent off to Bertie.'

Frank stood awkwardly, wondering whether to ask for the notebook, but not wanting to seem too pushy.

Lieutenant Chambers tipped his head back slightly, staring at the ceiling. 'I haven't told Millicent yet,' he said. 'I'm a bit of a coward. What is she going to do when she hears I'm coming back a cripple?'

Frank was glad that the officer wasn't looking at him, as he had no idea whether an answer was expected, though he thought it would be rude not to offer something.

'Get ready for when you arrive, I suppose,' said Frank, aware that their conversation was straying again, as it had on a few other occasions since the officer's hospitalisation, into personal territory.

Frank didn't know if other officers spoke so candidly to their men on personal matters. He suspected not, but Lieutenant Chambers was very ill and might die, and Frank was deeply sorry for his horrible bad luck. Frank enjoyed their conversations, found them interesting, enlightening and felt himself becoming less embarrassed by his questions and remarks. He looked forward to the times he could visit. He sincerely wished that Lieutenant Chambers would recover from his paralysis, but after these months, he doubted it. There had been an epidemic of the disease, with over forty cases among servicemen and about a hundred civilians. More than twenty people had died so far, according to 'The Times of Malta'. This officers' ward contained a number of other cases too, some worse than Lieutenant Chambers.

'I think your wife will most likely be very glad to have you back alive, sir,' said Frank, thinking immediately of Manwela. 'Probably a lot of widows would envy her.'

Lieutenant Chambers turned his head, his eyes still half-closed, with the hint of an amused smile. 'You've met many widows, have you?'

Frank coloured deeply. 'Well, only one, sir.'

'And who is she, Nixon, if I may ask?' It could have been a coarse barrack room question, but for the officer's refined accent and delivery.

Frank found himself spilling out what he'd thought best kept to himself. 'She's a woman I met in Naxxar. She's Maltese, and her husband was killed serving in the Royal Navy in 1939. She gave me some water once when it was very hot. We got talking and then, you know, I started visiting her and her boys, just now and then, when I had a day off.' He couldn't hold the officer's drowsy but clinging gaze and looked at the floor, feeling his face burning.

'So, you're having relations with her?'

'No, sir,' said Frank, looking back quickly, annoyed at this questioning. The officer had gone too far. It was none of his business. But Frank's anger fell away when he remembered Lieutenant Chambers' sharing of personal confidences, realising that he was talking to him as he might to a friend. There was also the fact that men needed the permission of their commanding officers if they wanted to get married. One of Marshall's section had met a Maltese girl and he'd then had to go to the CO to ask if he could get engaged.

Frank felt his confidence crumpling like wet newspaper. Talking about Manwela made him twitchy and awkward. He wished he could go. He couldn't remain clear in the head when he thought about her, and he regretted his confession to the officer. What did he think was going to happen? Was he going to marry Manwela? Some hope. Some fucking ridiculous hope.

'There's nothing wrong with admiring a woman,' said Lieutenant Chambers, 'but the Maltese are strict and devout Catholics for the most part. They tend to guard their women very closely. But if you're polite and utterly respectful of her wishes and she welcomes you to her home, what harm is there in that? You're a presentable, decent chap, after all.'

Frank was amazed at this side of his platoon commander. His old-fashioned, gentlemanly advice, like he was Frank's father or a vicar or something, seemed actually to be encouraging him to pursue Manwela, unless he was reading it wrongly.

'You'll have to go now, Corporal,' said a nurse, who had appeared out of nowhere. 'The doctor's coming round, and you've been here over an hour.'

'Sorry,' said Frank, getting up.

'Come back again, Nixon, when you've got the time,' said the officer. 'I'm sorely in need of distraction, and I want to discuss with you this notion of history as the story of great men.'

Frank left the hospital with a strange and puzzling mix of feelings: elation that he had enjoyed another good discussion, sorrow for the plight of the man and delight that he, his platoon commander, should actually have sanctioned Frank's visits to Manwela. It was strange and exhilarating. The officer's advice that he should be 'utterly respectful of her wishes' struck him as entirely fitting for his meetings with Manwela, though he wondered if he could bear the frustration of his desire for her. Lieutenant Chambers hadn't said anything about lust.

'Yes, all right,' said Frank to Chalky as they ran for the shelter. 'It was a bit of a stupid bloody thing to do, coming here.'

The siren howl filled the air around them, rebounding off the mounds of jumbled stone in the street. An air-raid warden stood by the entrance to the shelter, trying to hurry people along. Though the bombers' engines crackled overhead and the street piled with blocks of ruined buildings, the people moved with their familiar resignation, their resilience hardened if anything by their state, which for many meant that there was nothing else to lose.

An explosion sounded somewhere on the other side of the harbour, and most of the queue entering the shelter disappeared inside. Frank and Chalky were nearly the last. A woman in front of them, with three or four children in tow, turned round at a squeal from a little girl who had just tripped and fallen on her face. Frank stepped forward and scooped her up, the shock of which had stunned her into silence. Frank smiled at the child, a waif with a filthy smeared face and dusty black hair, then followed the others into the shelter. He handed the child back to her mother, who smiled her thanks at him.

'Sorry, Chalky,' said Frank as the two leaned back against the wall, the wardens pulling the door closed behind them. 'Someone said there was a bar still open on Strait Street. I just wanted a beer, that's all.'

Frank had persuaded Chalky to come with the promise of beer, though his true motive was to see if the bookshop was still standing and report back to Lieutenant Chambers on the state of Valletta. It would be a dismal description. Even Floriana was a heap of rubble. The view from the Upper Barrakka Gardens over the Grand Harbour revealed a blackened pool with the hulks of broken ships, the flattened buildings of the three cities on the other side. Amidst the wreckage stood a tall skeleton wall, its empty windows like the eye sockets of skulls. Miraculously, however, the massive walls of the fortifications built by the knights stood firm and solid at the core, like the people's faith, which held them upright under the punishing, relentless barrage. They'd got the George Cross for it, for their bravery, and deserved it too, but the prospects were still very grim.

'Let's go down to the harbour,' said Chalky, 'once we're out of here, see if that caff's got any beer.'

An old woman sat on a stool behind them, muttering prayers, and some children nearby punched each other in a mock-serious argument.

'Yes,' said Frank. 'All these folk are going about their business with the bombs flying, so we can too. Just duck down and pray to God, that's all there is to do.'

'You turning religious or something?' said Chalky.

'No, only fatalistic.'

'Fatalistic, that's a big word.' Chalky jabbed Frank's arm.

'You know. If your name's on it. Look what happened to Chambers. You go to war, expect to be shot or blown to bits, and you get polio instead.'

'Do you reckon he'll pull through?' Chalky said.

'Hope so.'

'He's all right, Chambers,' said Chalky, 'but he's a lousy platoon commander.'

'Yes,' said Frank. 'I think he's just always got his mind on other things.'

As soon as the all-clear sounded, they headed out onto the ravaged streets. As they walked down Triq San Kristofru, they saw a cluster of people forming an untidy queue. Women and children talked, laughed and argued as they waited, holding jugs, tins cans and pots. The front of the queue disappeared through the door, and a sign in English announced the presence of a 'Victory Kitchen'. A smell of onions hit them as they passed the place, and Frank thought of Manwela and her Widow's soup. He'd go there this evening, when they'd got back from Valletta. This thought lifted his spirits and his hopes as they picked their way through the wreckage of the city.

They descended the steps to the quay and found, to their amazement, some fishing boats. These boats were painted in lurid stripes of blue, green and red—they didn't go in for camouflage. It was astonishing that some intrepid and foolhardy men were still willing to risk their lives for a catch, going out in mine-filled seas. Three men were unloading boxes of vegetables from the boats, purposeful, deliberate and unperturbed, in their usual working clothes of shirts and black waistcoats. They piled the boxes on the quayside as though it were a normal peacetime market day.

'Bloody hell,' said Chalky. 'You have to hand it to them, they don't give up. How the hell did they get through? Where's it come from?'

'Gozo, probably,' Frank said. 'That's the place they grow most fruit and veg. The Jerries probably don't think it's worth bombing carrots.'

They stood and watched for a moment.

'The Maltese are used to running the gauntlet. They've been raided by just about everyone over the centuries,' said Frank. 'Barbary corsairs, Arabs, Normans, Turks. But this is different. If they start rationing bread, that's the end of it.'

Chalky screwed up his face. 'So, surrender's on the cards, is it?'

'Quite possible, but who knows. The Jerries took Crete. Malta might be next. People say if we can get more Spitfires here, then we might be able to take on the Luftwaffe. And you can always look at history. Napoleon got his comeuppance and so did Kaiser Bill. Plus, the Turks didn't manage to break this fortress in 1565.'

Chalky grinned with a mock yawn. 'Here we go again.'

They drank some watery beers in a small, sad-looking café, then made their way to Triq il-Merkanti and the alley with Mr Falson's bookshop. The face of the stone was badly scored and puckered, but it was still standing, though the windows were boarded with their wooden shutters.

'I'll knock anyway, just in case the owner's inside,' said Frank, stepping up to the door and banging on it a few times.

There was no sign of life from the building, however, nor anywhere else in the street, and Frank knew that his mission was to be unsuccessful. Both he and Lieutenant Chambers would have to wait and be patient.

Patience, thought Frank, if there were only a quick way of learning that virtue, he'd sign up for it. Though he'd learned to hide the signs of disappointment and anguish in relation to Manwela, this didn't stop the rawness of his feelings, like a blister cramped into an ill-fitting boot on a long march. He longed to see Manwela, but dreaded frustration again.

The walk back to the barracks was slow, with planes droning overhead almost continuously, so in the end, he and Chalky didn't bother to look up at them. It was only low-flying ones that presented a risk to them on the ground. It was strange how they could almost ignore the roaring of the attackers, the thudding of more breaking buildings, the cackle of anti-aircraft guns.

Back at the barracks, there was an outbreak of Malta Dog, so the latrines and washrooms were full of the stench of sickness and diarrhoea. Frank washed with clenched nostrils and prayed that he would continue to avoid the affliction. After changing his shirt, he checked under his mattress to make sure that Lieutenant Chambers' notebook and his spare paper were securely stowed. After the incident with Green's destruction of the history book, Frank was extra wary and made sure that Green never saw him with anything valuable, certainly nothing combustible.

The sun was setting as he went on his way to Naxxar on foot, as he'd returned the bicycle to Manwela a few weeks ago, the last time he'd visited. This time, he was determined he would ask Manwela to come for a walk. The cousins could surely look after the children, and he could go with her to a little rocky path he'd seen not far from her house. He would tell her about his feelings for her and know for certain whether he had any hope of her. He remembered Lieutenant Chambers' advice and decided that to be bold but respectful was the best approach. He hurried, though this made him break into a sweat again. Over the rise beyond Naxxar, the sky was a blood red stripe near the horizon. A solitary aircraft rose from Ta Qali airfield. He restrained himself from running as he approached Manwela's yard, where he found Joseph, David and two of the other children playing.

'*Frank*,' said the children and clustered round him, he handing over his only bar of chocolate to Joseph.

'Remember to share it,' he said, laughing.

'Grazzi, grazzi hafna,' they said in a chorus, following Joseph over to a large stone for the delicate operation of the division of the treat.

He knocked on the door of the house, and one of the cousins appeared, smiled and greeted him, stepping aside to let him in. Did he detect a certain coyness in the woman's manner? He couldn't be sure.

Manwela looked up from her seat at the table, smiled and rose. Beside her sat a man, whom Frank had never seen before. He was of middling years, with a solid, square face and tight curling black hair. He too got to his feet with the scrape of his chair on the stone floor.

'Frank,' said Manwela, and he saw that she was colouring slightly. 'This is Mario. He has a farm near Mosta.'

Frank, feeling his stomach clenching, stepped forward and offered his hand to the man. 'Corporal Frank Nixon, Second Battalion, the Devonshire Regiment, stationed at St Andrew's Barracks,' he said, knowing that this announcement was the best way to keep his voice steady.

The man took his hand with a quick, limp handshake and stared back with eyes so dark they were almost black.

'Sit down, Frank,' said Manwela.

The other cousin was holding a cup for the old grandma in the corner, and Frank felt his heart sinking slowly, his hope of some time alone with Manwela dissolving like salt in water. Though inside he felt shrunken, he hoped that he had managed to present the confident air of a welcomed guest. Mario spoke little English, and Frank, with his few words of Maltese, engaged in a stilted exchange, though one which seemed to amuse the old lady. In the corner, she chuckled and rocked in her chair as she watched them.

'The Germans come, you think?' said Mario.

'We'll be ready for them if they do,' Frank replied, assuming the forced confidence that had been drilled into them on coastal defence exercises.

The man nodded, and the old woman giggled again. Mario glanced round at her and said something to Manwela. Frank realised that the cause of the mirth was the presence of two suitors for her beautiful granddaughter, vying with each other here in the kitchen. The grandmother was enjoying the spectacle of these two men in their state of hope and uncertainty. Frank wished he could have laughed with her, but he was too wretched for that. His situation was hopeless; he was a foreigner, an invader of sorts, who had as little chance of securing the affections of this woman as a passing Luftwaffe pilot on his return from a bombing raid. His fantasy of making his respectful declaration of love now seemed laughable, his self-important introduction a pathetic attempt to impress. He would go.

He rose to take his leave, but was surprised when Mario left his seat too. At that moment, the air was strangely charged as the two men stood in the kitchen, neither knowing who should speak or leave first, which one would have the privilege to linger to the last. They both made their own farewells to the others in the room, Frank catching the eye of the coy cousin, who, bizarrely, winked at him. He was not sure, however, as it might perhaps have simply been her expression in the dim light and the disturbance of their leaving. With the children chattering all around in two languages, there was much noise. Frank extricated himself from the children's hands and saw Mario bidding Manwela good night at the gate, then turning left and walking towards the centre of the village.

'Frank, you come tomorrow?' said Joseph.

'I can't,' he said. 'I'm on duty, and I don't know when I'll get another day off. But I'll see if I can get more chocolate by then.'

Manwela spoke rapidly to the children, and they, calling 'goodbye' and 'sahha' to Frank, trailed their way back across the yard and into the house. Frank watched them go, and his stomach surged with hope again. He was alone with Manwela. A moment, only one small moment alone with her. Could he tell her, in spite of his hopelessness, in spite of this Mario bloke, so that she knew?

'Good night,' he said to her, but she said nothing and moved close to him, her body touching his.

To his astonishment, she had taken his hand into hers. He could not believe it. Her head was against his shoulder, and she was pulling him close to her.

'Let me walk with you,' she said in a small voice, not looking up.

They stepped out through the gateway, and Manwela glanced in the direction where Mario had gone. There was no sign of him, though it was dark and with no moon. They set off side by side up the road, leading away from the village, and Frank, his heart pounding, felt Manwela link her arm through his. To the south, the dim moving glow of searchlights could be seen from Valletta and the three cities. Could this be real? Frank wondered. Was it happening?

They had only gone about two hundred yards from her house, but it had already disappeared in the darkness. She stopped. He heard her breathing, felt her body against his, but could only make out her shadowed face. She slid her arms around his waist, laying her head on his chest. This embrace was a seeking of comfort again, of closeness, and he wound his arms around her, his face brushing her hair. Was this a lover's or a sister's embrace? He couldn't be sure, as he had had neither lover nor sister in his life. But his body was roused ferociously for her, and she knew that this was no brother's fondness.

'Manwela,' he said, 'I must tell you something.'

Her arms loosened, and she lifted her head. He responded in turn by releasing her a little. She reached her hand to his cheek and stretched up to him, kissing him on the lips, lightly at first, but when he responded hungrily, she did likewise. Was this real? His body knew that it was no hallucination, that this woman wanted him.

'Respectful'. The word leapt to his mind, and he broke from her.

'Manwela, I love you.'

She kissed him again, pressing herself against him. 'At last,' she murmured a moment later. 'I thought you would never come to me, Frank.'

This struck him like a blow to the chest, that she might want him like this. He kissed her again with passion heavy with disbelief and gratitude. She led him quickly to a hollow behind a low wall at the side of the road and pulled him down on her. Though he longed to rip the dress from her, he felt her breasts through the thin cotton and was thrilled, shocked with excitement, when she undid him and brought him into her. He came quickly with a pleasure akin to agony, hearing her muffled squeal, and was still disbelieving when she kissed him again softly afterwards.

She sat up suddenly. 'I must go. The children. They must go to bed.'

'Manwela,' he said, but she covered his mouth with hers, then broke away, stood up and quickly pulled her clothes back into place in the darkness.

Frank leapt to his feet and buttoned up, reaching for her once more.

'Come again soon, please, Frank,' she said, disappearing into the darkness.

Breathing heavily, his chest tight as he tried not to shout, he stumbled up the road away from her house. He ran, his feet clumsy, tripping and reckless. Oh, Christ, oh fuck, thank you,

God, wherever you are. His cursing was joyous, reckless and physical, and he nearly fell on his face. He had to run another hundred yards before his excitement was tamed and he slowed to a more even pace.

CHAPTER 16

JULY 1942

'*The new measures will help us safeguard our supplies to ensure that they are distributed to all equally. Central food distribution is essential to support the Victory Kitchens and to ensure rations for all...*'

Frank and his section caught the essence of the crackling broadcast from the loudspeaker in the square in Birkirkara, where they stood by the wall of the church.

'*Farmers must comply with the requirements for slaughter of animals. Officials will visit each farm to explain the necessities. No one must hoard. If someone hoards, others will go hungry.*'

The air-raid siren howled, reducing the rest of the governor's message to fizzling background noise. Frank strained to hear, watching as people moved without speed or urgency towards a shelter marked with a ragged sign, the basement of someone's house in the square, close to the church.

'*In these hard times, every man, woman and child must suffer want with patience and endurance...*'

Then the drone of bombers overhead set some people trotting a little faster for cover, but in the centre of the square, a yellow horse-drawn bread van still stood with a few women handing over coupons. An air-raid warden shouted to them and waved his arm, like a semaphore message, and the women, bundling their bread into bags and baskets, made their way towards the shelter. The bread man unhurriedly climbed back into his seat, looked up at the sky, then shook the reins to persuade his horse to lumber forward and pull the wagon alongside the wall of the church.

'Come on, lads, better go,' said Frank, leading the men towards the basement shelter, joining the end of the queue.

They squeezed into a cramped, low-ceilinged room behind the civilians, with the smell of unwashed bodies and the air pressing in upon them. None of his men spoke; they had little energy today for joking. The effects of the soldiers' half-rations were biting now, and the men grumbled and argued, made irritable by constant hunger. It was hard to work, to heave rock and earth into bomb craters all day on food that would barely have kept a small child alive. Frank thought about Manwela, worried about her privations too, wishing he wasn't so powerless to do anything to lessen the hardship. He wondered when resilience, fighting spirit and prayers would lose their power too, though he knew this kind of thinking didn't help.

The all-clear sounded, and they clambered out into the sun and resumed their journey to Ta Qali airfield once again. They moved more like a procession of funeral goers than a professional army, but Frank could do little to speed them along.

'Christ, what I'd give for a fried egg and bacon,' said one of the men, Ken Sparks, a skinny little individual about half the size of Green, who walked beside him.

'Fucking farmers, keeping all the stuff for themselves,' Green muttered.

'Or charging a bleeding fortune for it,' said one of the other men.

'Well, they won't be able to now,' said Frank, irked by their resentful tone. 'Didn't you hear? They'll have to hand over everything they've got stored, and their livestock too.'

Frank had grown used to the presence of Green as an un-avoidable malignancy, like an itchy skin complaint to be suffered and not scratched for fear of making it worse. Frank spoke to him only to give orders and information, nothing more. Green's natural state was sullen and subdued these days, and he took every opportunity to hang back, to lag behind the others, stray from the line, avoid work, start last and finish first. He was one who'd gone down with Malta Dog, or at least that's what he'd claimed, though no one had seen much evidence of that in the bunkhouse or elsewhere. He skulked like a wolf on the edge of a group, sometimes drawing others into his company.

They were to join Sergeant Campbell and the replacement for Lieutenant Chambers, an officer by the name of Perkins, and the rest of the platoon at the airfield. Another formation of bombers roared above, pursued by some of their own Spitfires. They paused to watch as one, then another enemy plane was hit, the first one falling slowly with a trail of black smoke, the pilot's parachute suspended, swinging in the air. A Spitfire was hit too, however, and was spiralling down, with no sign of the airman bailing out.

'Poor buggers,' said Chalky as Frank thought how strange it was that they watched these events like spectators at a football match, groaning at a foul on one of their own, cheering when one of the opposition was tackled. He'd heard how the people in Valletta gathered on rooftops and the ramparts to watch the dog-fights at night in spite of bombardments all around them. Funny kind of fireworks, thought Frank, although, like fireworks, they were far away in the sky and harmless at this vantage point. It was probably the best way to stay sane, Frank thought, rather than let yourself imagine a hit, with the horror of injuries, death and devastation on the ground.

They were approaching a farm, not far from Mosta, a cluster of square, white buildings amidst the familiar small fields, partitioned by stone walls. Some of the patches were green with crops and others with dried, churned earth. Another long stretch was full of olive trees. There was no sign of anyone around, working in the fields or in the yard, as they passed. Even a tethered dog was not roused by their approach as it dozed in the sun. Just past the farmyard, over the low wall of the nearest field, sunk below the level of the road, were several clumps of tomato plants dotted with ripe fruit.

'Corp, look at that,' said Ken Sparks, his eyes wide with wonder at the red dots, as though he'd come upon some treasure, rubies set with emeralds, extravagant riches not of this world.

Frank's mouth was pained with salivation as they all stopped and ogled the tomatoes.

'Is there anyone about?' said one of the men.

'No, don't even think about it,' said Frank. 'If we nick these, someone else'll go hungry, remember.'

'Blimey, ain't they just delicious,' said someone.

'But haven't the farmers been storing up stuff, weaselling it away?' Chalky said.

He was standing at Frank's side, and Frank knew he must get the men moving at once, otherwise he couldn't be responsible for anybody's actions, even his own.

'Come on,' he said, 'at the double.'

He looked down the line of men and saw to his consternation that Green was not there. 'Where the hell's Green?'

The men's faces looked blank or bewildered, all except Sparks', whose sheepish kick at the dust betrayed him.

'Where's he gone, Sparks?' said Frank.

Sparks didn't have time to reply, as the crack of a gunshot burst through the air. All eyes flicked back to the farm buildings and the yard, the source of the noise.

'Bloody hell,' said Chalky under his breath.

'What the fuck?'

'Tell me that's not Green, please,' said Frank. 'Come on, Sparks. We'll go and see. The rest of you stay here.'

Frank and Sparks ran back along the road to the farmhouse, Frank dreading hearing another gunshot. The dog was barking hysterically now, splitting the air with noise. There was a yell, then Green's voice shouting curses as they drew closer and the sound of boots scuffling in the dirt. Frank and Sparks charged in at the opening to the farmyard, to find Green on top of a man on the ground, punching him in the face with a vicious right hand. Green's rifle lay some yards away from them.

The tethered dog was jumping up and down, nearly strangling itself on its rope, suddenly stopping to cough and writhe for its breath.

Frank leapt forward and grabbed Green's shoulders, yanking him back from his victim. 'Get off, you bastard. Sparks, give us a hand.'

Sparks ran at Green, who was rolling on the ground, and wrenched one arm behind his back while Frank did the same with the other.

'You're on a fucking charge, you are,' said Frank. 'Sit on him, Sparks.'

Sparks obliged by jumping down heavily on Green's back and securing him on the ground. His legs stopped struggling, and he lay with his cheek crammed into the dirt.

Frank was now standing up, the hoarse barking of the dog subsiding as it, exhausted, lowered its head and sank down, growling. The man Green had attacked lay groaning and bleeding from his nose and one eye. Frank crouched next to him and saw, in spite of the facial injuries, that this was the farmer, Mario, the one he had met at Manwela's.

'Are you all right?' Frank said, praying that his wounds were not as bad as they looked. The blood was everywhere, pouring from his nose, soaking his shirt front.

'He tried to fucking shoot me,' croaked Green from his pinioned position, jerking his head up. 'He took my fucking rifle.'

Frank, ignoring Green's protests, grasped the injured man's arm. Mario, however, threw off his hand, twisting away, then staggered to his feet and spat out a mouthful of blood into the dirt.

'Haqq il-bagħal. He steal,' said Mario, wiping his nose with his shirt sleeve, pointing at Green.

Now that Mario was standing up, Frank could see that, fortunately, his injuries were only cuts, which had produced a dramatic amount of blood.

The man's black and furious eyes fixed on Frank. 'He steal from me. In the barn,' he said again.

'He's a fucking lunatic,' shouted Green, stopping to cough, his face in the dust.

Frank turned round. 'Did you steal from him?'

Green's face twisted. 'I was taking a look, just going to buy something off him, that's all. But he didn't listen. He just grabbed my fucking gun, the bastard. I had to go for him, else I'd've been a gonner, I'm telling you. Self-defence, it was. He should be bloody locked up, him.'

Frank's anger was bubbling, his desire to kick Green in the head almost overpowering. But he went to him and grabbed his arm, nodding to Sparks to pull him up with the other. Green squirmed, trying to free himself.

'Don't try it, Green,' said Frank. 'Now, apologise to the man.'

'You're fucking joking,' said Green.

Frank called to the farmer. 'Skużani, dak ħalliel!' He hoped that this was on the right lines to explain Green's nature. 'Bad man. He'll be punished for this.'

Mario wiped his bloody face with his shirt sleeve and spat another gobbet of pink froth at Frank's feet. 'Itilqu min quddiem għajnejja, ja demel!' Mario said with a snarl, which didn't need any interpretation, adding for good measure, 'go away, you Britisher pigs.'

Frank and Sparks hauled Green away, out of the farmyard, back onto the road to join the others, who were standing with their backs to the low wall, gaping at them as they approached.

'Chalky, you take Smith and Warner and go on to Ta Qali,' said Frank. 'Tell the sergeant what's gone on here. Sparks, Mulholland, you're with me. We're taking this tosspot back to the barracks.'

Frank pushed Green ahead of him. The two parties split to go their separate ways. As the men moved off, Frank glanced over the wall at the tomato plants and the trampled soil around them. They had all been stripped of their fruit.

Though Green was gone, held in custody on a charge of assault and attempted robbery, awaiting a court martial hearing, Frank did not feel relieved. He was uneasy, mostly because Green was in his section and he should have kept the man under control, particularly as he knew his tendencies. The other source of his unease was that news of the fight with Mario and the stealing of the tomatoes was bound to get back to Manwela, as well as his own involvement in it. Though he knew that thieving could not be tolerated, Frank had sympathy for his men. Their desperate, gnawing hunger was bound to drive them to actions that they'd never contemplate with full bellies. He could excuse the theft of the tomatoes, but he couldn't excuse Green's entry to the farmer's property in search of food to nick from his stores, nor his violence against the man. God knows what would have happened if they hadn't stopped it.

They were all summoned to the parade ground early, on Captain Miller's orders, and Frank knew that the matter was going to be food, or rather the lack of it. The whole battalion stood there at attention for some time, awaiting the arrival of the CO and the other officers.

'At ease,' shouted the sergeant major.

Captain Miller, 'Dusty' as he was known by the men, was a short man whose upright posture was his way of projecting authority and rank.

'Men, as you well know, we have had to cut the rations to preserve food stocks,' he said, with his chin up in an effort to throw his voice. 'Things are pretty grim for all of us, and we must all make sacrifices, like the civilians. You've heard Lord Gort's announcements, and it's up to us to hold up our side. From now on, while you're on half-rations, when you're off duty, you must use the time purely as rest breaks to conserve your energy and food demands. Resting by lying down and not exerting ourselves will prove an effective way of maintaining ourselves as a strong fighting force. In addition, I must issue a serious warning against any man who steals or dishonestly acquires goods, food or consumables. Any man found guilty of such crimes will be severely punished. Two years imprisonment or hard labour is what any miscreant can expect. I'm relying on you men to prove what the British army is made of.'

'Fucking skin and bone,' muttered someone behind Frank.

'And he'll be having a half inch of corned beef tonight, I don't reckon?' said another whisperer.

Frank tried not to wolf his portion of tinned cabbage and corned beef too quickly, to make it last, instead filling up on water to cheat his belly into thinking it had eaten well. They were all confined to barracks for a week, so Frank knew he'd have to wait some time for another pass. It was their punishment for Green's misdemeanour as well as a convenient way of coping with the effects of half-rations. That evening, in the meagre light of the bunkhouse, Frank continued with the copying of the Greek writing from Lieutenant Chambers' notebook. He'd had to scrounge a pen from Sparks, who wrote to his mother every week. Frank had never written a letter in his life and had not, until recently, felt the need to own a pen or paper. It was a slow process, however, as he was striving hard to avoid blots. Crouched on the floor, leaning on his kitbag, he was uncomfortable and awkward as he wrote. Sometimes he couldn't be sure of the exact formation of the officer's letters, particularly near the end of the text. In spite of this, Frank finished the copy to his satisfaction and laid the paper on his bed for the ink to dry. He hoped that this was a good enough record of the writing, and he wondered when he'd be able to deliver it to Lieutenant Chambers. Perhaps he could ask one of the other officers to take it, if they were visiting the hospital soon.

He thought how he'd like to write a love letter to Manwela. That's what people did when they were in love. Some of the blokes wrote to their wives and girlfriends regularly. Writing something down made it a permanent declaration, a tangible object, a record of what had happened or what was thought or felt. The man in the cave had done that more than a thousand years ago. Frank would like to have done something to prove his love as durable as the carvings in that hard rock. Would expressing his love for Manwela make her understand how serious he was and how he felt for her? But he couldn't do it. His pen hovered over the paper for some time. He didn't even know how to begin. What if he were killed the next day without telling her how she filled his thoughts and how his only hope of happiness or even of life would be if she agreed to marry him?

Even as he contemplated this, he knew their situation was hopeless. The imaginary futures he made up in his mind were fantasies. He could hardly leave the army and become a farmer in Malta. The other dream was to take her and the boys back to England when the war was over. They could get married quarters and have a secure life and a future there. But she wouldn't want to leave her family, her home and her country, would she? In his heart, he knew that it was wrong to indulge in such thoughts, with the great blot of the war, heavy with danger and death hanging over them. Others lived only for the moment, the present, with no thought of consequences, of hopes and aspirations. He could do that when he was with Manwela, and he needed no more than the pleasure, the pride in knowing that he could satisfy her and that she wanted him. When they were apart, however, his imaginings pained him with their impossibility.

A week later, the passes were being issued to those with leave, and Frank waited along with the others for Sergeant Campbell to appear. Standing in line, thinking of Manwela, he overheard some snatches of conversation behind him.

'Easy enough... I know a bloke... typewriter.'

Frank turned round to see two men from Marshall's section. Their eyes met his and they, like boys discovered scrumping apples, looked away guiltily. Frank had heard about the forging of passes to enable men to get rations from several different food stations when on a day's leave. He saw that these men, who might have shared this confidence before, were not inclined to now. Since the incident with Green and his removal, the men had been more wary of him and more respectful to his face, which produced a feeling of regret tinged with a small measure of pride. When it came down to it, he could take command of a situation and do the right thing. The captain had commended him for his action, as he had with the retrieval of the stolen goods some months ago and his prompt action in helping out the gunners at Ta Qali. Chalky alone maintained the same irreverent camaraderie.

'Going for two stripes, are you, Nix?' he said. 'Or is it officer training next?'

'Not bloody likely,' said Frank, deciding to keep his head down and just do his job, avoiding unwanted attention.

Frank wished he had brought Manwela's bike back with him. He could have got to her so much quicker. His desire for her was almost agonising to him, and his hopes were high for some time alone with her. It was late afternoon, and the raids had continued relentlessly until now. They'd just read in 'The Times of Malta' that a convoy carrying supplies had been forced to turn back to Gibraltar because of murderous attacks and losses in the Mediterranean. Some people said that the island had only enough food for another month, some said less than that. Frank regretted that he had nothing to bring Manwela and suffered the rawness of hunger himself most of the time. There were no spare rations going, even for money, not that he could get hold of anyway.

His other anxiety, a niggling one, was the incident with Green and Mario. He hoped that the man had recovered from his injuries and intended to ask Manwela if he should go to Mario to apologise and try to make peace. What would she think of the behaviour of his men? Would she blame him in some way?

Coming close to her place, he couldn't stop himself from rushing to the gate of her yard, bursting through in his eagerness. There were no children playing there today, but he could see through the window that there seemed to be a crowd inside. He knocked, and Manwela came to the door, her face solemn, but she slid her arms around him and sank her face into his chest. He sought out her lips and kissed her gently. Thank you, God, thought Frank, she doesn't blame me. But he knew something was wrong.

'Come in, Frank,' she called aloud for the benefit of the others, then looked at him with her troubled dark eyes, touched his arm in a gesture like an apology. He followed her into the kitchen.

The room was full of people. The children were all gathered around a small cooking pot balanced on the kerosene stove. They stared at it, like expectant small sorcerers, waiting for a genie to appear. One of the cousins was cutting up a piece of patterned fabric, a curtain, which was spread out on the table. The other was sitting by the grandmother, whose face was pasty and her head drooping to one side. Frank wondered for a moment if she'd had a stroke or something, as her body was slumped and lifeless as a sack of potatoes, but he saw her stomach rise and fall in sleep. The cousin at the table looked up at Frank and nodded, saying something to Manwela. The children, even David and Joseph, seemed uninterested in his arrival, glancing up briefly at him, then returning their attention to whatever was cooking in the pot.

'My cousin's asking if you have brought any food with you,' said Manwela to Frank.

He felt the heat rush to his face. 'I'm sorry,' he said, 'we're on half-rations. There's nothing extra. We're all pretty starving too.'

'You soldiers steal food,' said the cousin at the table, straightening up, brandishing the large pair of dressmaking scissors in her hand like a sword.

'Mario told us,' said Manwela in a flat voice, picking her way through the crouching children to stir the contents of the pot. She spoke to them sharply, telling them to move further away from it, and they shuffled back obediently.

'I'm sorry,' said Frank, his stomach sinking.

'Sorry is no good,' said the angry cousin. The other woman stood up and stared at him too.

Manwela snapped a reply at them, which produced a pursing of the lips in one and a shake of the head in the other.

Frank shifted on his feet. 'The thief's been charged. He'll be punished,' he said, hearing his voice diminish as he uttered this half-truth, recalling the stripped tomato plants. 'Is Mario all right?'

Manwela nodded. 'He's very angry.'

'He has reason to be. I know that,' said Frank, his earlier hopes and optimism fleeing from him. 'Look, I'll see what I can get for next time. Some of the blokes have got contacts.'

He thought of the forged passes and resolved to find out how he could get one. At that moment, he knew he'd do anything to help Manwela and her boys. He'd have to set aside his qualms, those curiously troubling forces, which had, all of his life, made it impossible for him to be dishonest. He'd never been able to steal and could no more thieve an egg than he could stop breathing. He didn't know where this came from, this unshakeable sense of right, as most of the boys he'd known in the home had been petty pilferers and skilful shoplifters from birth, it seemed. He knew well enough what it felt like to have nothing, to covet possessions that others happily took for granted. But still there remained a sort of block of moral rightness inside him. When others had taunted him, bullied him, he had sometimes pretended that his few bought objects were stolen. But for Manwela, he'd rob a bank, sell his soul.

'I don't know what we'll eat tomorrow,' said Manwela. 'We've only got this soup, which is more water than anything, and a scrap of bread each.'

'Mario will bring food,' said the cousin, with a sour smile at Frank.

The silence was heavy in the air, then Manwela broke it with some words to the cousin, who shifted the cloth from the table in a sweep of the arm, gathering it up and draping it over a chair in the corner of the room.

'And we have no clothes. The boys grow so quickly,' said Manwela. 'We are making shirts and trousers out of anything these days.'

The children rose listlessly, and Joseph went to the shelf for bowls to lay out upon the table. He placed them one by one on the table and looked up at Frank, laying one for him.

'No,' he said, 'I won't have any.'

Manwela glanced at him with a look of sorrow and apology, and he wondered whether he should leave now or endure the guilt and anguish of witnessing their frugal meal. His stomach twisted with hunger too.

'What can I do?' he said to Manwela, desperate and miserable, as the children started sucking up the watery stuff with their spoons.

'Can you make shoes for the boys?' said Manwela with a shrug.

Frank frowned, thinking she was teasing him, but she went outside into the yard and returned a moment later with a strip of a car tyre. Next, she picked up some pieces of the mangled, half-unpicked leather uppers of a shoe.

'The boys have grown too big for their shoes,' she said. 'They go barefoot most of the time. David cut his foot the other day.'

Frank took the dead bits of leather and the strip of tyre from her and puzzled for some moments about the feasibility of the task. He didn't mind the idea of stitching, having done his fair share at St Augustine's, mending the charity clothes that were donated by benevolent local people and repairing holed shoes with leather or even cardboard. It was the occupation of many a Sunday afternoon and evening.

'I'll do my best,' he said and sat down on a stool in the corner.

Manwela brought him a knife, needles, thread and scissors.

'Whose feet are these for?' he said, looking at the boys.

'I,' said Joseph, tipping up his bowl and sucking the last drop from it.

'Let's have a look at your feet, then,' said Frank.

The boy's friendliness returned as he sat on the floor in front of Frank and held up his bare foot. Frank placed the piece of rubber flat against his sole, nicking the rubber all around in the places where he needed to cut. The other children, seeing the spectacle, jumped from their places. In a circle, they watched the proceedings. The next thing Frank knew, they were on their backsides around him, holding up their feet and giggling.

'Hang on a minute,' he said, laughing. 'I can't do you all at the same time.'

He tickled each of their soles with his fingers in quick succession, setting up a stream of laughter from the children. Manwela was beside him, joining in with the happier mood. He felt her hand upon his shoulder. Even the cousins smiled and shook their heads. Manwela chased the children away outside while Frank set about the task, revelling in this change of atmosphere.

It wasn't easy, though the cutting was quickly done. The stitching strained his fingers and drew blood where he had to force the needle through the rubber. He was reasonably pleased with the result, however, a pair of eccentric but sound shoes with neat but crudely stitched soles upon the repaired uppers. He called Joseph for the final fitting, lacing the shoes with string. Joseph, delighted, paraded around the kitchen in his new shoes before an appreciative audience. Only the groaning from the grandmother drew the women's attention from the admiration of Frank's handiwork.

'I'll do another pair next week if you want,' said Frank. 'But perhaps supplies'll get through soon so the kids can have proper shoes.'

Too soon, he knew he'd have to go back. He took his leave of all in the kitchen, Manwela coming with him into the yard.

'Take the bicycle,' she said. 'We do not need it.'

'Are you sure? Manwela—'

She would not let him finish, taking him by the arm and hurrying him out of the yard and onto the road. She said nothing as she walked beside him quickly, urgently, as though she wanted to run from the place. Then she suddenly stopped.

'If it were not a war, what would we do, Frank?' she said.

He, alarmed by the tension in her face and movement, stopped and lowered the bicycle to the ground, then took her in his arms. He couldn't think of anything to say. He wouldn't dare articulate his fantasies to her. It wasn't right. It was too dangerous to tell her of the future he'd imagined, to expose it to the chance of rejection.

'I love you, Frank,' she said. 'You will remember this always even though—'

'What?' he said, suddenly afraid, aware that she was trembling.

'I don't want to think of the future, Frank, but now, these days are so difficult. I must hope for this to end, for my sons. There must be something better for them than this.'

He tightened his arms around her, longing to offer her comfort but with no idea how beyond holding her. 'It will end. It must do.'

She looked up at him, her eyes filling. 'If only you were not a soldier. I wish you were not a soldier.'

He felt this like a blow to his chest. 'I'll leave the army. I can leave in a few years' time. I want to be with you, always. I'll do anything.' He knew he sounded desperate, pleading, but he couldn't control the urgency in his voice.

She kissed him softly on the lips. 'Thank you for your love and kindness, Frank,' she said, grasping his arms to make him release her.

His heart pounded. What was she saying this for? Was she finishing with him? Was this her way of breaking it to him gently? He felt his eyes sting and a lump rise in his throat. He was going to cry, a thought so embarrassing to him that he looked away, half turned from her.

'Frank,' she said, reaching her arms around his neck, pulling him back. 'Whatever happens, whatever I have to do, I have loved you. It's true. Please, Frank, say you believe me. Tell me you love me.'

He couldn't speak, couldn't look at her. He buried his face in her hair and knew that he was crying. Nothing had touched him like this before, no harsh words, no bullying, no neglect, no

callous indifference, all of which he had suffered, had made him
sob like a baby. Manwela was weeping too, he realised, feeling her
body shaking in his arms, though she made no sound. Then she
spoke quietly, almost in a whisper, not looking at him.

'My boys must have a future.'

'But the boys like me, don't they?' he said quickly, thinking
that they must be the obstacle.

'Yes,' she said, shaking with sobs. 'They love you, Frank, but I
can't let them. They need a father who will not go away, a father
who will not be killed in a war. And I could not bear that a second
time, not again. I have to think that they will have a future. It is
for them, not for me.'

There were bombers overhead, one wave, another, heading
south for the harbour, then next swinging inland for the airfields.
It was not dark, but the sun was dipping in the sky. Frank heard
the droning, the throaty roar, and looked up as he pedalled along
the road. He was going in the wrong direction. He was going
south, but he didn't care. He'd just keep going till he went over a
cliff into the sea or got blown to bits. What did it matter?

He craned his neck and looked up at the planes in the sky.
'Come and fucking get me, then, you bastard Huns,' he yelled.
'Drop your fucking bombs here.'

His eyes were sore, his face tight with the dried salt of his tears
and his chest was heaving with the effort of his frantic pedalling.
He braked and stopped suddenly, putting his feet down, leaning
over the handlebars to heave in some deep breaths. Standing
straight again, he saw a low-flying plane swooping down and a
bomb dropping like a turd in the sky and landing about a quarter
of a mile ahead of where he was. He waited for the explosion, his
body and mind expectant, conditioned to receive the assault on
his senses. But none came.

He continued on, wheeling the bike now, though the effort
was like wading in a thick swamp of mud, made worse by his

misery and the weeping, which he'd failed to control. He'd never recover from losing Manwela. It was over. She couldn't marry a foreign soldier, and how could he blame her for it? He couldn't. He didn't. She'd be better off with Mario. But he would never be able to forget her unless he could stop thinking altogether.

He moved on mechanically, wondering whether he should mount the bike again and coast down the slope in the road just ahead of him. He wanted to reach the sea. Perhaps he could plunge into it, swim until he hit a mine and was blown away for ever or drowned. On he went, stumbling over the stony ground until it exploded with a terrible crack. Stones and dirt and stuff were raining down hard as hail, but bigger bits too until he was knocked off his feet and into blackness.

He was lying down with something hard against his shoulder. He stared up at the sky for a clue about where he was for a few moments. There'd been a bomb. He knew that much. He didn't move, except his hand, which slowly explored each part of him to see whether he was whole or whether there were bits not there. Head, there but wet and bleeding a bit on the side. He could see as well, so his eyes were all right. Ears, nose, both arms. This was good. Legs, feet and his privates too. Yes, thank you, God.

He wasn't thinking straight. He couldn't remember exactly what he was doing here. There was a bomb, but it hadn't exploded, had it? He wasn't thinking straight. No, it must have been a timed one, you idiot. He lay there trying to remember. Manwela. Perhaps he'd just dreamt what she'd said. Her bicycle? He still had it. She couldn't have meant never to see him again. There it was, only a few yards from him. He'd take it back to her. He'd rest up a bit before going on. Everything was quiet now. He'd get up in a minute.

He lifted his head and peered down the slope of the country-side below where he was lying. Far over there was a burning thing in the sky, a beacon of fire. It looked as if it were balancing on the top of the walls of a town or a fort. Frank couldn't make it out. Then a muffled blast boomed, followed by another from the same place. The ground had started rumbling too, and a furling cloud of dust came rolling towards him. Through this cloud, he saw small streaks of flashing colours, red and yellow flickering like flags. There were sounds too: the whinnying of horses, trumpet blasts and rhythmical, marching drumbeats. Over the land, a dark mass was spreading, like a huge shivering wave: an army advancing.

CHAPTER 17

MDINA, 1565

T he crash of the door flung open against the wall woke Grezzja from her half-sleep. Sunlight shot in with a yellow streak across the floor.

'Arise. Wake up,' called a hollow voice. 'Everyone must come.'

Grezzja looked up to see an armed man in the doorway. The huddled shapes of sleepers, strewn across the floor of the monastery hall, started shifting, some leaping up, quickly wakeful, frightened.

'What is it?'

'What's afoot?'

'Mary, Mother of God, is it the Turk? Quick, get up.'

Outside, beyond the noise and movement in the long hall, a drum struck up an urgent beat, then came the sound of many running feet.

The soldier at the door called again. 'Come, move yourselves. You are all summoned to the Pjazza San Pawl. There is a signal from Fort St Angelo, a beacon.'

Grezzja heaved herself sideways from her mat, feeling the weight of the child in her belly, as though it resisted the movement. At her side, her two young sisters sat up and rubbed their eyes. Grezzja raised herself to her feet and joined the others around her, stumbling over the clutter of everyday life—blankets, cooking pots, baskets of foodstuffs—in this crowded sanctuary where all the fleeing country folk had been lodged.

Her mother and father were already standing by the door with a group of others. Next, the church bell started a doleful clanging, and Grezzja, dragging her sisters by their hands, made for the door. Everyone moved in anxious obedience to this call, mindful of the threat, this dread, which had hung over them for so long.

Outside, an officer, fully clad in a corselet of armour and helmet, watched and chivvied his men to speed the people along. Grezzja and her sisters joined a stream of others funnelling into a narrow street, meeting a blockage caused by a cart piled high with weapons and army equipment. They turned and were buffeted and pummelled down another alley. Grezzja kept on, with her young sisters clinging to her, following her mother and father ahead in the crowd.

The people pressed into the Pjazza San Pawl, standing shoulder to shoulder and crammed against the walls of houses, their balconies packed with onlookers. In the centre of the square was a hefty stone bench, the place of proclamations. The governor's standard bearer stood beside it alongside two other officers. Suddenly, the feathered helmet of Don Mesquito, the governor, appeared through a split in the crowd, forced open by his henchmen. The knight's tunic was emblazoned with the white cross of the Holy Order of St John. He leapt up upon the bench, standing like a preening cockerel, casting his eye over the crowd below him.

'Gentlemen and people of this noble city,' he started in his strange foreign accent, 'we find ourselves in great peril, but by the mercy of God and his blessed Mother, we shall triumph. The grand master, Seigneur de la Valette, has sent us a signal from Fort St Angelo. The enemy, the infidel Turk, is advancing with his army to attack us and take our city. But do not quake with fear, for it is my belief that the Turk has grown desperate in the face of the true faith, our brave sacrifices and our stalwart resistance. We will stay strong in our fortress Mdina and meet the infidel with strength and the knowledge that God is with us.'

Babies and small children, ignorant of the import of the governor's words, uttered little cries or murmurings. The rest of the crowd stared, and Grezzja felt fear loading the air.

'The Ottomans are sending a great mass of their army against us, but do not quake at the sight. God has shown me the way to meet this force of evil. But we must be quick about the business.' He grinned, revealing yellowing teeth, like a dog intent on a mischievous theft of meat.

Grezzja wondered for a moment if the governor had lost his wits, for everyone knew that the garrison contained only sixty soldiers and a handful of officers and knights. He did not seem like a madman, however, as he swept his arm over the heads of the crowd towards two carts, which bore piles of weapons and soldiers' garb.

'Bring the arms. Make way,' the governor commanded, and the driver of the first cart whipped his two mules. 'Listen well, every man, woman and child, to my plan.'

A rumble of anxious whispers broke out in the crowd. Grezzja saw her father shrugging, shaking his head and growling some words to her mother.

The governor's voice swooped upwards, gathering speed. 'Each full-grown man and woman, and sturdy boys too, must don helmets and tunics. All must take up arms and become soldiers in our cause. Halberds, pikes and swords are here for as many as can hold them aloft. Take children, babes and the feeble to the churches or places of safety. All armed persons will then put themselves under the charge of my officers and stand upon the ramparts here, according to instructions.'

'What nonsense is this?' Grezzja heard her father say. 'He is mad. The Turks may be infidels, but they are not stupid.'

'Peace,' said a man at his side. 'It is a plan. Do you have a better?'

'Go to it, and with speed,' called the governor, swinging around and pointing in the direction of the plain beyond the town. 'We have seen the dust of their cavalry yonder. It is the enemy host advancing. Make ready. Everyone to the battlements, in the name of God and Christendom.'

A drummer started up again in short rapid beats, and the surge of bodies moved towards the carts, where two soldiers stood handing out breast plates, red tunics, helmets, weapons, all the provisions from the armoury. Grezzja was jostled back by the crowd and lost hold of her sisters' hands. Her mother was calling to her.

'Go, girl. Take your sisters. Get you to the church. You cannot stand up there with a child swelling in your belly.'

Her mother came to her and grasped her by the arm in a tight grip, but Grezzja writhed to throw her off.

'No, let me be, Mother,' said Grezzja. 'Let my sisters run to safety. I will do my part, as Filippu did. He did not want to be a soldier, nor more do I, and he has most likely perished in this cause. I would rather die than live without him.'

'You fool,' said her mother, tugging at her husband's sleeve as he came pushing towards them. 'Tell her. Tell her she must go.'

Her father's face twisted with scorn as he answered, not looking at Grezzja, but at his wife. 'She may do as she pleases, for hasn't she done that already, the whore, with a bastard inside her belly?'

Grezzja, with the old shame and anger burning her face, pushed past her mother and father and elbowed her way to the cart. If it was God's will that she should die, so be it. Her sin was great and her child was tainted by her act, but she would not cower in a church, awaiting the marauding enemy. She would stand up and be cut down by them, as Filippu might have been for all she knew.

'Ho, ho, here we have a soldier and a half,' said the man who handed Grezzja a heavy pot helmet and a red tunic. 'Make sure the infidel does not see your belly, for he will pluck out the warrior within. They are godless savages.'

Grezzja shuddered at his words, but she put the metal helmet on her head and draped the red tunic around her shoulders. A spiked halberd was thrust into her hand, and she clutched the shaft in her fist.

Two officers were ordering, pushing, pulling and shouting to the townsfolk and the peasants, dispersing them along the ramparts, around the circle of the wall, to the east and west. Grezzja found herself thrust close to her parents again, being shoved on to the De Redin bastion above the main gate, already crowded with people mixed in with the regular troops. At each corner of the bastion stood gun crews of four men, surrounded by wicker gabions, their canon ready, with piles of heavy shot, powder, rods and other instruments of their trade. Real and counterfeit soldiers now stood two lines deep all along the ramparts as far as could be seen.

'Jesus and Mother Mary,' said Grezzja's mother, 'they do not mean that we shall fight.'

Her father let out a snort. 'The infidel will die of laughter when he sees us as defenders: women, peasants and old men.'

'Hold your tongue and stand over here,' shouted an officer, overhearing this comment. 'We will not let them come near enough to see.'

From the ramparts, Grezzja looked out over the sweep of the countryside, the fields and dotted farmsteads that lay between Mdina and Fort St Angelo. Somewhere over there, beyond the empty countryside where no peasants toiled in their fields, no goats wandered, where dark patches of abandoned enemy camps and the burnt remains of peasants' houses lay, somewhere, Filippu might be watching, if he still lived. He might be patrolling the ramparts of the fortress of St Angelo or resting maybe in the safe depths of the soldiers' quarters. Grezzja would only allow these pictures of Filippu to enter her mind. She would not conjure other images of his fate. She knew of the fearsome attacks on the forts in the south, the forces of the Turks battering at the strongholds. Messengers had brought stories of terrible towers and war machines that breached the fortifications, bodies piled high in the trenches outside the walls, soldiers dying in agony of their wounds inside.

'There, look, there,' someone yelled.

The talk and clatter died to near silence. All faces were trained on the sloping plain, and Grezzja's eyes made out many slow-moving wagons drawn by oxen, carrying the great engines of war, and a wide carpet of bristling pikes of foot soldiers. The army was moving over the terraced fields, spreading about 500 paces across. At the sound of a trumpet, some sections broke free from the mass, troop upon troop of cavalry, their red and blue pennants flying above their heads, rounding the slower moving foot soldiers and wagons, cantering ahead of them.

'Holy God, how many are there?' said Grezzja's father.

The governor was now standing upon the top of the parapet, sword aloft, staring ahead at the approaching cavalry. Grezzja saw the plume on his helmet quiver. All on the ramparts stood as stone, watching the horsemen advance. Grezzja heard the murmur of prayers around her and added her own, placing her hand upon her belly, feeling the child shifting and kicking inside her. The drummer on the governor's bastion started up a steady beat.

'Stand to, ready to fire,' shouted an officer, and the gunners, who had been frozen in place until then, jerked into action. The grind and crunch of shot, the scent of raw gunpowder, pungent burning fuses assailed the people-turned-soldiers upon the battlements.

'Fire!'

A blast like thunder sent a shudder through Grezzja's body. Smoke swirled from the guns, and her eyes wept.

'Fire!'

The crunch of a canon recoiling on its wheels and the curses of the gunners mixed with the thickening smoke.

'Fire!'

Grezzja's head was dulled, numbed by the thundering, her sight dimmed by the smoke. As the fog of it cleared, they could see the enemy cavalry halted. Then the moving mass of the army became visible again, though it was hard to know whether it had truly halted in its advance. All along the battlements, as far as Grezzja could see, musketeers pushed forward to the edges of the parapets, positioning their stands and weapons ready to fire.

'They're too distant for a hit; the shot's fallen short,' muttered Grezzja's father.

'But it's halted them, taken the wind from their sails,' said someone.

'The governor's a wily one.'

Upon the Palazzo Bastion opposite, the governor's pennant flapped proudly, and he stood with his officers, staring at the scene of the enemy host. He sliced down with his sword, and the musketeers fired, in a chorus of cracks and smoke, the smell of gunpowder again.

Grezzja thought of Filippu again and how, if he lived, she was sharing a little of the excited terror with him, the sounds and smells of war. She, a feeble woman, now knew something of what it was to be in battle. She might know soon too what it was to be cut down by a sword or pierced by a musket ball if the Turks advanced and took the town. She would have this death rather than the other fate suffered by women in war. They were so few, and the enemy were thousands. She closed her eyes and prayed, for there was nothing else to be done.

Perhaps, if Filippu were dead and in heaven, he might be looking down upon this sight, wondering and laughing at it, this bold and foolhardy masquerade in which she was a part. He would rejoice too if the might of the enemy were held back by trickery, if it were God's will that the ruse would work.

Filippu, she murmured in her mind, where are you? Mary Mother, take him into your arms.

The firing ceased. The governor had climbed down from his perch on the parapet, and the gunners and musketeers, more slowly, more routinely now, prepared their weapons for firing again. The vast Turkish army lay spread before them, but it was no longer moving. Behind the bastion where Grezzja stood, a drum started up, a slow, dead thump, and she turned to see some soldiers dragging two slack-limbed, filthy men behind them, Turkish prisoners hauled from the dungeon, now forced to stagger ahead, prodded by pikes. The soldiers drove the two bloodied men up the steps to the bastion.

'Make way,' shouted one of the soldiers, and the people on the bastion pressed backwards to create a space to allow passage for the wretched men and to better view the spectacle of their arrival.

'They'll pay. Let the infidel pay for Christian blood,' called a man behind Grezzja.

'Their blood for the blood of our men. Let them out there see their fate.'

This chorus was swelled by the people around Grezzja, and she found herself joining her voice to theirs for a moment. She thought of Filippu's strong and handsome face, his body made tough by toil but tender to her, cut down by these enemies, these Turks. Filippu, her husband in the sight of God, who, but for the invasion by the Turks, would have been blessed as such in a church by the priest. At this moment, Filippu might be lying bloodied and dead in a ditch, shot or hacked down from the walls of the stronghold. She prayed for a miracle, for Filippu to be another Lazarus. Would these infidels' deaths make him alive again? Might he rise up from the corpse of a Turk? But her prayers choked her throat and sickened her stomach.

The prisoners were jabbed and prodded forward into the bastion. Over the edge of the parapet, two heavy iron hooks were positioned with ropes coiled beside them. One of the prisoners collapsed, crumpling on the ground, and an officer standing by rammed his halberd into his back, as though skewering a goat upon a spit. The spiked man screamed in agony as he was hoisted up, impaled. Grezzja looked away, feeling her gorge rise, but her horrified eyes strayed back again. The spiked man's face was twisted with pain, awful to look upon, the more so because he was young and because his agonised eyes had met hers for a brief moment.

She wanted to run from there but knew she could not move, her gaze returning to the face of the young prisoner. The spike of the halberd was wrenched from his body, and he was dragged, along with his comrade, to the edge of the parapet and the iron grappling hooks.

'It is their due. God will have justice.'

The soldiers bound the prisoners' arms behind them, then looped the heavy ropes around their necks. The young man's face had slackened. He was barely conscious, but he suddenly opened his eyes, looked at her again, as though somehow he had found her in the crowd.

The soldiers speedily thrust the two men's bodies to the edge of the parapet, then, as the drumbeat slowed, pushed them over with the points of their pikes. The iron hooks grated and crunched on the wall as the hanged bodies tugged taut the slack of the ropes.

A loud cheer went up from all around, and Grezzja, weak with a dizzy sickness, swayed on her feet.

'Are you ailing?' said a woman at her side, glancing at her belly. Grezzja shook her head, unable to speak.

The guns on the ramparts did not fire again, the gunners wiping their brows, the musketeers cleaning their weapons. They waited, standing in their positions for a long time, many hours. An officer ordered some of the people to walk along the ramparts, shouldering the weapons in a show of patrolling for the enemy to see. As the sun dipped in the sky, the heat still beat upon them in their metal helmets, and Grezzja wondered how long she would be able to keep standing. Some youths were sent to bring flagons of water to those who manned the ramparts so that no one left their posts. Grezzja's back ached, her eyes too, with staring ahead at the enemy host for any sign of movement or advance.

'Look, look. Are they retreating?' said a woman at Grezzja's shoulder.

So it seemed. The cavalry were on the move, the whole vanguard sweeping around, wheeling away, slowly at first and then, in a dust cloud, gathering speed. There was murmuring all around, a low cheer, but the officers spoke sharply, ordering everyone to stay in place.

Some time later, the great swathe of the army appeared to be shrinking back into the distance. Grezzja's sight had blurred by the time the sun had dropped low in the sky, but there was hardly a sign of the enemy forces, save one or two slow-moving wagons. The governor had left his post, though his standard bearer remained, the colours floating gently in the light breeze. The officers continued patrolling the ramparts, keeping the people and soldiers in their places until finally the order came for the citizens to stand down.

'The holy saint has watched over us. We are saved from the sword of the infidel. Let us give thanks,' called an officer. 'This is a sign from God that the Moslem will be defeated. We will drive him from our island.'

'Kill them,' squealed someone as the stream of people, climbed down from the ramparts, took off their soldiers' garb amidst the wild laughter of relief.

Weary but rejoicing, people started back towards the narrow streets leading to the cathedral. Grezzja followed unsteadily behind her mother and father, her body a dead weight and her mind barely capable of thought. The crowd ahead of them slowed, then parted in the middle to let pass a group of soldiers pushing their way back to the ramparts. They were dragging something after them, the bloodied bodies of two more Turkish prisoners, hacked to death. Cheers rose as the soldiers ran to the parapet, mounted the lowest part of the rampart and tossed the bodies over, one at a time, as the first clang of the cathedral bell rang out.

CHAPTER 18

'May it not be a boy,' Grezzja thought as she woke in the dead of the night with stabbing pains some weeks after their salvation from the Turkish army. 'Please, God and Mother Mary, not a boy, who will have to fight, kill others or die by their swords.' She clutched at her belly, writhing with the tightness that tore across it.

'But if it is a girl, her fate will be to mourn her dead husband, brother and father. Which is worse?' She wept to think of this and, rising between her pains, went to her mother, who was lying not far away.

'Mother, it is my time,' she whispered.

Her mother rose quickly, calling for light and pulling blankets from beneath her to make a place for Grezzja's travails. Other women came to help, and an old toothless midwife was there. In the far corner of the long chamber, surrounded by the women, Grezzja's body writhed, she with no sense of anything except her agony. The toothless old woman thrust her hand between Grezzja's legs while her mother spoke into her ear, prayers to the Holy Mother of God. Grezzja knew that she had screamed Filippu's name many, many times. Was this to be the manner of her death, her fate, dying for her child born in sin? The women around her knew of her shame and watched her agony with faces of stone.

But then her belly was tugged, as though a rope was around her innards, tearing the child within her, bringing it forth.

'A boy. A son.' Grezzja's mother held the red, wriggling infant to her.

He was tiny but took to the breast greedily. Grezzja prayed, gave thanks as she looked at him, called him Filippu, then wept with grief.

'Mother,' she said as soon as she could form the words. 'Bring the priest.'

The next time the bells of the cathedral rang, it was in triumph and relief. The guns from Fort St Angelo and messengers riding in a sweat to Mdina brought the news that the Turkish army was retreating. Their fleet was gathered near the harbour and off the bay of San Pawl, foot soldiers and cavalry moving rapidly to the coast. God had brought them a Christian victory against the infidel horde. The army of the heretic Sultan was defeated.

Grezzja, with her baby son in her arms, climbed up to the ramparts. Her mother stood by her side, along with her sisters. The bald countryside, dry and dusty, lay beyond, more desolate now than ever before. The infant Filippu snuffled at Grezzja's breast as the main portals of the town swung open below them and a troop of cavalry ventured out.

'Can we go back home now, Mother?' said Grezzja's smaller sister.

Her mother looked down at her. 'We will wait until it is safe to go out, until the soldiers have told us there is no enemy left upon our soil.'

'I must find him,' said Grezzja, speaking the secret thought that had festered in her mind for so long.

'Find him? What do you mean?' said her mother.

'Filippu, whether he is dead or alive, I must find him.'

'You witless girl,' said her mother. 'You must wait. If he is alive, he will come to you.'

'Yes, but if he is wounded or dead, he will need me. I must heal him or mourn for him. I must know where he fell.'

'Leave the child with me, at least,' said her mother, turning a stern and unforgiving face to her.

'No, his son must come with me. Filippu must see his child, and the child must see his father.'

'You are mad. God knows what you will find out beyond the walls.'

Her mother was gripping her by the arm, her fingers digging hard, but Grezzja pulled free of her and, clutching the baby to her breast, stepped down from the ramparts and made her way to the gates.

The first signs of battle, of death and destruction were not far from the town walls. At only five hundred paces, Grezzja came upon a scatter of bones, picked clean by birds or dogs, scorched white by the sun. She crossed the rocky fields on paths dusty and baked dry, towards the stronghold of St Angelo, where the fiercest battles had been fought. More bodies, dead mules and broken carts lay at the side of the track, and then, like a strange burnt crop in a field, bodies lay more thickly.

There were other people too, picking their way between, stooping, plucking at the dead. One ancient bent woman pulled a coloured belt from a corpse, drawing it up like a dead snake pelt. A man nearby was hacking at the finger of another dead man with his knife to claim a ring or jewel from a hardened finger. Grezzja's stomach turned at the sight. The island people would not rob their own dead, surely. It was infidel booty and treasure they sought.

Her feet were sore with walking, her eyes full of grit and dry of tears. The baby whimpered, and she sat on a rock to give him suck and calm him before rising again and walking on. Ahead were others, some women with a donkey cart scouring the land, searching as she did. From a distance came a weeping, keening

246

sound as a woman wailed. Then Grezzja saw him. The body was dark-haired, half-clad, stripped of all but a bloodied linen shirt and torn breeches, lying with his face in the dirt, wedged at the foot of a low wall.

'Filippu,' wept Grezzja, grateful beyond words to have found him, her love, though he was cold and stiff and dead. She ran to him, the small warm press of the child against her chest. The stench made her retch, but she bent down to the body, touched the unyielding shoulder and turned it to her. She recoiled. It was not Filippu's face, but the grey, waxy, bearded one of a stranger, an infidel. She wailed in grief for Filippu and for this man, whose woman would never be able to kneel beside him and pray as she could for God to have mercy on his soul.

CHAPTER 19

AUGUST 1942

'Well, if the bloody convoy doesn't get through, we're done for,' said Chalky.

The last syllables of the broadcast died away on the radio set in the crumbling ruin where they were quartered. The power had given out again amidst a chorus of groans.

'What odds do you give them? Four merchantmen sunk already and the aircraft carrier too,' said someone.

Chalky picked up the pack of cards and shuffled. 'What'll we play?'

'What about Black Maria?' muttered someone.

Frank felt the weight of their gloom add to his own low spirits. The elation of discovering himself alive after wandering in among a load of timed bombs had gone, swamped by his misery over Manwela. He must have been really losing it too, close to the edge of his sanity, thinking an army was invading. The memory of that mad vision was still vivid in his mind, like a recurring nightmare. It hadn't been a modern army he'd seen, not with horses and pikes and trumpets. Now, some weeks later, he certainly felt saner but much sadder.

The fact that Green was back in the platoon after serving his sentence of a month's hard labour didn't exactly cheer Frank either. Green's presence was a troubling menace, but it was something he'd just have to deal with. There was also the real possibility of the fall of Malta, that they would be starved into surrender and be prisoners of war and that this, all this death and suffering and destruction, would have been for nothing.

The loss of Manwela hurt him more than all of this, however, though he didn't dare admit it. Chalky had stopped joking about her after he realised the depths of Frank's depression. Frank withdrew into his reading, re-reading the account of the Great Siege in 1565. The Turks had given up and gone home. Pity the bloody Germans wouldn't do the same.

Sometimes, he allowed himself to think about Manwela, convincing himself that he really had an excuse to go and see her again, to take her bicycle back. It had been pretty mangled up in the last bomb blast, which had nearly got him, but he'd brought it back and stowed it in the cycle workshop. The men in the workshop repairing motorbike engines had laughed at the wreck, saying it was irreparable. Frank knew this too, but he left it there anyway in the corner, wondering if he could get some kind of replacement, imagining, in his weak moments, how he might take it to her.

The shrunken rations and resulting weakness of the men meant an end to exercises and training, but there was still urgent work to do on the airfields. The Spitfires were in action day and night, and Frank's platoon were at Ta Qali again to help with re-arming the aircraft, filling ammunition belts and conducting endless repairs to the airfield in between the raids, which still battered all day and much of the night. Some of them had even been drafted in to help the RAF ground crew with refuelling the aircraft. Frank's section had been there for a week, bunking down in a dilapidated old leper hospital near the airfield to be on duty round the clock.

As Frank and his men ran for cover yet again in a slit trench, he wondered how many times he'd done this, how many bombs he'd seen falling. He watched an enemy plane trailing black smoke and flame as it ducked towards the ground. Insignificant lives cut off, the unremembered dead, like the heaps of Turks and Christians piled up together in the trenches of the knights' besieged fortresses or floating in St. Paul's Bay at the end of it all. Pilots shot down, merchant seamen drowned, infantrymen machine gunned, bombs dropped. These would be the stuff of the history books, but only in numbers, not in lives. History books didn't tell the stories of ordinary lives. They couldn't. There were too many people, too many stories. It drove you crazy even thinking about the multitudes of the dead.

The next night, all the men hung around the buzzing radio set again for any news of the progress of the convoy, which was crawling its way through hell towards the island. It had left Gibraltar with thirteen ships, and many had been hit or sunk, but the remnants were fifty miles from the island and it was touch and go. Frank knew it was irrational to put his hopes on the island's previous history, but it gave him a measure of comfort. The besieged knights and the Maltese people had feared the worst too, but when the Turks eventually withdrew, they saw in this the hand of God. So, if religious conviction was what was needed to win or at least survive, the Maltese people had that in bucketloads, and nobody seemed to doubt whose side God was on.

The skinny, brown legs of barefoot children standing on the wide top of the parapet blocked Frank's view of the arrival of the first ship into the Grand Harbour. He stood with his shoulders pressed against Chalky's on one side and a thin, elderly civilian on the other. Behind them were swathes of bodies pushing in upon them. A huge American flag on a stick swung and weaved in the air, brandished by one of the boys standing on the parapet. The air was filled with chatter and laughter and the sound of a band belting out 'The Stars and Stripes Forever', then 'God Save the King'. Forces personnel and civilians mixed in delight at the arrival of the longed-for convoy.

'It's a tanker. Look, it's nearly sunk,' shouted someone.

'Santa Marija, Santa Marija,' some children chanted, and a spontaneous cheer drowned the music for a moment, Frank joining in. One convoy wouldn't save the island, but it gave hope, which was sometimes almost as good as food to a starving body. Frank had lost Chalky in the crush, and there was no sign of any of the others he'd come with. It was most likely they'd gone in search of liquor of any sort, though nowadays it was only contraband and black-market stuff available to those in the know and officers.

He pushed back from the press of people near the parapet of the Upper Barrakka Gardens and made his way through Pjazza Kastilja, past the wrecked shops and houses of Triq San Pawl, deciding to try once again to visit Mr Falson's bookshop or at least find out if it was still standing. He knew that this was probably a fruitless quest, but one he wanted to undertake for his own and Lieutenant Chambers' sake.

He collided with a group of drunken naval ratings and dodged his way through the bundling people, not minding, glad to be part of history in the making. The convoy had got through, the island was saved, at least for the moment. What would historians make of this? It might disappear into the welter of other more important, significant events and complications of the war. But in the present, it was something worth glorifying. Photographers had captured some of these scenes, and perhaps he was there, in one of these in profile or retreating in back view, but it didn't matter. The now became immediately the past, to be transformed into history, in books and memories, noted or ignored depending on the importance later placed on it. He would go now in his search for stories of more distant events, old battles, old sieges, old suffering, frozen and distanced like a mountain range, which would be there for ever, for the next generation and the next.

Rubble was piled high on the sides of one street he had to negotiate, with only a narrow central passageway in the middle. A rickety karozzin, like an ancient pram pulled by a skeletal horse, trundled down the centre, bearing two RAF officers singing drunkenly. Frank reached the corner of the street and looked down the alley to see that the line of buildings, which contained the bookshop, was still, miraculously, standing. Better still, the windows of Mr Falson's shop, though dark, were unshuttered.

Frank approached the door, looking up at the stone facade puckered on the upper floors, with windows black and empty of glass. He knocked on the door but heard no sign of life. Another knock and he tried the handle. It yielded in his hand, and he pushed it open, stepping inside into the dust-smelling gloom.

'Bonġu,' he called. 'Anybody there? Sir? Mr Falson?'

There was a shuffling sound from behind the cluttered central shelves, and the bookseller appeared, a look of puzzlement on his face, as though he had recently awakened from a heavy sleep.

'Sorry to bother you,' said Frank, taking off his helmet. 'Are you open for business, sir?'

The man's face changed, his wrinkles tightening into a smile. 'Welcome, welcome, Corporal Nixon,' he said, which startled Frank. Either the man had an astonishing memory or no other customers. 'Your commander, Lieutenant Chambers, is not here today?'

'No, he's not. He's ill, I'm afraid.'

'Oh dear,' said the bookseller, coming towards Frank and holding out his hand.

Frank took it, gratified to find such a welcome.

'I hope it's not serious,' said the bookseller.

'It is, sir. It's polio.'

The man's face fell again. 'I will pray for his recovery.'

Frank was unsure what to say next, as they had both slumped for a moment into the silent reflection that often follows the breaking of bad news.

'But it's good news today too,' said Frank. 'I mean, the convoy arriving.'

'Yes,' said the bookseller, looking up. 'It is the feast of Santa Marija. Yes, there is much reason to give thanks.' The man seemed a little cheered and smiled again.

'Now, Corporal, you have come to do business, I think? And to collect your books that you left last time. In all the commotion of the bombing, they were forgotten.' He went over to the desk, which stood near the window of the shop, and picked up a dusty pile of books from the place where Frank remembered leaving them.

'Thanks very much,' said Frank, delighted. 'How much do I owe you?'

The bookseller peered at him and smiled again. 'You are a young man, without much money, I think. If you have five shillings, I would be most happy with that.'

Frank blushed, fumbling in his pocket. 'But they must be dearer than that.'

'Take them with my blessings on this feast day of Santa Marija and of our salvation,' he said.

'That's very kind,' he said, remembering his other commission. 'And Lieutenant Chambers would like a French dictionary, to help him to translate the journal.'

'Ah, yes,' said Mr Falson. 'Let me have a look.'

While Frank waited, thrilled to have a chance to accomplish his mission and to have his own books, he leafed through the first, a nineteenth century translation from the Italian by a Frenchman, Pierre Gentil de Vendome, *The History of Malta and the War between the Holy Knights and the Grand Turk Suleyman 1565*. His fingers trembled as he turned the flimsy pages, peering at the close, dark print. All of these for five bob. He could hardly believe it.

A few moments later, the bookseller returned, carrying a large volume as big as a couple of bricks, with a smaller book balanced on top.

'It is big,' he said eagerly, 'but it is very good. English-French, French-English. See, Cassell's, a very good dictionary. And I have a grammar here too. He will need this too, I think.'

Frank glanced at the books, in some doubt about whether he'd have enough money to pay for them, having parted already with five shillings. He wondered if Mr Falson would let him have the books on tick.

'How much?' he said, rather more abruptly than he'd intended.

Mr Falson had put the books on the desk, raising a puff of dust as he did so, and started rummaging in a drawer.

'These are a gift for the lieutenant, with my kindest wishes for his health and recovery,' he said.

'Really? He'll be very grateful,' said Frank, thinking the bookseller the most generous person he'd ever met.

'I have no paper to wrap these for you. But I have string,' he said, pulling out a length from the drawer.

Frank couldn't hope to find Chalky or any of the others again in the crowds in Valletta. He heard the thumping of the band still playing and people were still thronging the streets as he made his way along with the heavy bundle of books slung across his shoulder. He felt like a ridiculous overgrown schoolboy, but at the same time, triumphant.

There was, amidst the terrible destruction, real joy on the faces of the people filing into a church on the Strada Reale, or Kingsway as the British had named it. There was probably a Maltese name for it too. Poor little island, thought Frank, passed like a parcel from one sovereign state to another, colonised, governed, imposed upon, stuck at the crossroads of conflict for centuries. No wonder the people took to religion.

A small, ragged procession trooped along, led by a large lurid depiction of the Virgin Mary and Child, carried by two men. There would be little to feast on tonight and little enough from the ships that had made it through, only five out of thirteen, with all the mouths on the island and the enemy's presence in the Mediterranean. The threat of starvation or surrender had not disappeared. But for today at least, there was scope for rejoicing.

Frank thought of Manwela and her boys, discovering this a little less painful now. He wondered if the longing for her would ever leave him entirely. He knew that he would never be the same again, never be contented. He couldn't imagine what it would be like not to want her, though he imagined that the pain might fade a little, like the island landscape blurred soft pink after a violent red sky.

CHAPTER 20

He had to stash the books under his bed at the barracks, taking only one with him to their next posting on the coastal defences.

'It's a beach post up north, Mellieha Bay,' said Sergeant Campbell.

'How long for, Sarge?' said Frank.

'Christ knows.'

Sergeant Campbell was scouring a piece of paper, a faintly printed map. 'Nix, you and Marshall go and sign out the rations. Come on, lads. No, you're not sick, Forest. It's just a touch of the scabies or something. Green, get a move on.'

Although the oil and petrol supplies had been replenished by the miraculous survival of the tanker 'Ohio', which had limped into the harbour, half underwater, there was still strict rationing of fuel. The two sections of the platoon marched, fully laden with rifles, rations, kit and equipment.

'Not even a fucking donkey to carry stuff,' said Chalky as they marched along the coast road.

'No, they've all been eaten,' said one of the men.

The defence post consisted of a blockhouse, a rectangle of concrete and limestone blocks stuck on the rocks above the level of the shore, two gun emplacements and a searchlight on the cliffs above. Frank's and Marshall's sections descended to the blockhouse from the cliff path and found eight men from the Devonshires packing up, ready to depart.

'It's all yours, chum,' said their sergeant to Frank. 'Enjoy yourselves.'

They inspected their new quarters, discovering a bleak, dark interior with eight bunk beds. They would work their system of two hours on, four hours off day and night, taking turns in the bunks.

'All the home comforts,' said Frank.

'Sarky bastard,' said Chalky.

'It's Buckingham fucking Palace for the likes of orphan boy,' Green muttered in an undertone. Frank pretended he hadn't heard, wishing that Green would drop off a cliff somewhere.

Frank and Marshall ordered the equipment, the machine guns in the slits of the blockhouse wall looking out to sea and drew up the rota of patrols.

Up on the cliff, by the circular stone walls of the gun positions and the searchlight, Frank and three others were the first patrol. Frank had chosen Green for this one, knowing that he shouldn't avoid the man and hoping to keep him under surveillance. Green still smouldered with bad feeling, and Frank knew that this was unlikely to disappear. Only the threat of more serious punishment, if he committed another offence, seemed to be keeping him quiet. He was Frank's cross to bear. There would always be people like Green to be endured, managed or avoided. At least Frank knew he could rely on the others in his section. They were all good blokes. He'd just have to watch Green and his own back.

It was good up on the cliffs, though. With the autumn rain, it seemed the arid land had greened up almost overnight. Grass and foliage were draped over the white-stoned landscape like net or chiffon, a floating scarf he'd seen a woman wearing once. There were little pockets of colour too, pink and purple flowers dotting the cliffside. In spite of everything, the defacement of military equipment, barricades, barbed wire and pillboxes, it was beautiful in the dusk.

As night fell, it became cooler, with only a slit of moon appearing as the sky changed to navy blue. Frank walked the short distance along to where the cliff curved around, beside Bert 'Ramrod' Ramsey, a solidly built conscript who'd joined the platoon just before the siege. A builder in civvy street, Ramrod had proved himself a tireless labourer on all the heavy work. Behind them came Green and Sparks.

Frank heard it before he saw anything, a rumble from the distance somewhere out to sea.

'They're bloody coming,' he said, stopping suddenly. 'Get back and get the lights on them.' He turned quickly, finding Green with a cigarette cupped in his hand.

'Fucking put that out and get back to the guns.'

They all ran the fifty yards back to the gun position and the searchlight.

'Wake the rest of them,' shouted Frank to one of the men.

Frank and Ramrod stumbled over the rough ground to the searchlight, mounted on blocks of stone, and Frank kicked the generator into action, took hold of the handle and turned the beam upwards.

'There they are, Corp,' said Ramrod.

'Get ready,' Frank shouted to Green and Sparks, who were manning the gun.

There were five or more of them, black shapes, fish-shapes over the sea, about a quarter of a mile away.

'Bugger,' said Frank, 'out of range.'

'Let's have a pop at them,' shouted Green.

'Wait, for fuck's sake,' yelled Frank. 'Don't fire. Wait.'

But a rapid cracking broke from the gun, and Green swerved, recklessly losing one round, then another, tearing into the lit-up sky. Frank waved furiously at Green to stop, but he wasn't looking.

Dark shapes, the black silhouettes of the other men, were scrambling and swearing up the path from the blockhouse as Green still fired. Frank signalled at Chalky to take the controls of the gun, and two others piled into the emplacement to reload and push Green out of the way. The firing stopped, and Frank swung the light around to try and find the aircraft again, seeing them swerve in towards the land. They were still flying parallel to the coast, heading for Valletta and the Grand Harbour, but closer than before in spite of Green's reckless and useless bursts of gunfire.

Chalky fired but didn't hit anything until the last round, when they watched as black smoke and a trail of fire came from one of the planes.

'Fucking brilliant,' shouted one of the men. 'Got him.'

They watched the unharmed aircraft growing smaller in the sky and the stricken one veering wildly now towards the land.

'Nice one, Chalky.'

Frank cut the searchlight, and the sky was lit only by the flame of the aircraft drifting towards the shore. Then the faint pale shape of a parachute billowed out.

'Bastard's coming in to land.'

Frank squinted through the dark. From its trajectory, it looked like the plane was going to crash into the sea or on the shoreline, and the pilot, if lucky, might land on the lower part of cliff, to the south of where they were standing.

Marshall and his section took over the patrol, and Frank took Ramrod, Green and Sparks with him to search for the enemy airman. Frank knew it would be difficult to find anything in this light. The bloke could be anywhere. Still, they had to look for him.

'It'll be getting light soon, so we'll be able to spot him maybe,' Frank said, looking at his watch.

As the sky lightened, Frank sent Green and Ramrod up on the cliff top path, telling them to search about for half a mile to the south, then head inland before returning to the blockhouse. Frank didn't think the bailed-out airman would be up there, so that was probably the best place to send Green. He and Sparks took the lower path down towards the shore. Down near the shoreline, the pale rocks along the coast showed no sign of the pilot or the plane, which must have disappeared into the sea. Frank and Sparks stumbled over the stony edge by the sea for another half an hour before heading up a track again towards the top of the cliff.

About halfway up the slope, they saw, down in a hollow, a piece of the white floating shroud of the parachute ballooning out.

'Christ, there he is,' said Sparks as they picked up their feet and puffed on up the stony slope.

Frank peered ahead, unsure for a moment if he was seeing things, but as they came closer, about 500 yards away, he made out two dark figures moving towards the parachute, with rifles and bayonets pointing at what Frank assumed must be the German pilot. It was Green and Ramrod.

'Oi, you two,' Frank shouted, half hoping that the German airman had scarpered and that the parachute had got caught on a bush.

'Let's hope for his sake he's dead,' said Sparks.

Frank started to run, alarmed by Sparks' tone, jumping over the stony ground. Frank saw Green leaning over the body, with the bulge of the parachute behind as a backdrop to the action. Ramrod was standing a few yards from them.

Frank ran up. 'Is he dead?' he called.

'Yes, Corp,' Ramrod answered, turning round.

What Frank saw next brought a lump of rage to his throat. Green was standing over the body, tugging at the man's wrist, removing his watch, then pulling at his hand, trying to remove a ring.

'Stop that, you maniac,' shouted Frank, leaping the last few steps and tearing at Green's shoulders, pulling him off and throwing him to the ground. 'You fucking scavenging bastard.'

'He's bloody dead,' said Green, lying back on a rock, as though relaxing in the sun. 'He doesn't need them.'

'So it's OK to thieve from the dead, is it? You'd bloody sell your grandmother for sixpence. Give me the stuff back.'

Green didn't protest nor resist when Frank grabbed the watch and gold ring from his hand. He laughed instead, but Frank breathed deeply, turning away from him, disgusted to his stomach. He looked at the face of the German pilot, a young man, with no mark on his face, but his arm had been severed above the elbow and the rocks around his body were dyed a deep red with his blood. He wouldn't have made it. Then Frank saw a slit in his chest, a neat, blood-fringed cut and a ragged tear in his uniform where the insignia had been hacked off.

Frank told Chalky when they were alone in the blockhouse later that day.

'He'd probably have died anyway, Nix, loss of blood,' said Chalky. 'That's war.'

'I should have looked at Green's bayonet, but he'd wiped it on the uniform when he cut off the Luftwaffe insignia. It's a wonder he didn't try to take a finger off too. He's a sick bastard.'

'Yeah,' said Chalky, 'and I'll bet he gets through all this just fine.'

Frank was depressed by the incident and found little consolation in his reading that night by the meagre light of a small oil lamp when he was off duty. The plundering of the dead on the battlefield was an age-old practice, he knew, but one that sickened him.

They had to stick it out for another week of this posting but saw no action of any sort after this incident. Their main problems were boredom and hunger. The sea washed scraps of the crashed plane to shore, and Green and some of the others found themselves more trophies. The rain started again and refreshed the land, turning it greener each day. Frank finished the book about the Great Siege and looked forward to talking to Lieutenant Chambers about it as soon as he had some leave. He had to deliver the hefty dictionary and the grammar book too. He was heartily glad when Sergeant Campbell brought the rest of the platoon to relieve them and news of the state of play.

'Good news, boys. Perkins says you can all have passes for two days when you're back.'

Frank wanted to tell Sergeant Campbell about Green, but he didn't. Ramrod Ramsay said he thought the German was already dead when he and Green had found him and he hadn't seen any bayonet wound on the man. Frank knew that loyalty to mates was more important than the welfare of prisoners of war, but he felt tainted by his knowledge of what had happened. The dead German was buried. There was nothing he could do. It troubled him still and, in his fitful sleep for several nights, he imagined the drone of aircraft engines, rose in a sweat but found only a darkness and silence outside. He realised truly for the first time that to carry these things in your mind and your memory was the burden of being a soldier in wartime.

Frank walked to Imtarfa Hospital on his first leave day, shouldering the books for the lieutenant. It was windy and, for Malta, quite cold, and he was feeling the effects of his poor diet—sluggish, hungry and weary—before he'd even gone halfway. As he passed the ridge of Naxxar, he was afflicted by that longing sadness again, thinking of Manwela, with no excuse to call upon her, knowing that it would be foolish anyway. He wondered if she was married to Mario yet and tried to wish them good luck in his heart. He hoped that the boys were well, missing their chatter and their welcoming smiles. He trained his eyes ahead on the path and kept going.

Lieutenant Chambers was not at the hospital, Frank discovered to his disappointment. He'd been transferred to a convalescent home in a former monastery near Qrendi, about eight miles to the south. The thought of more trekking dismayed him, though having come so far, he couldn't consider anything but finishing his mission. He remembered also, from his reading, that there were some prehistoric temples in that area near the coast and some mysterious cart tracks in the stone. The possibility of seeing them boosted his flagging energy a little. While he stood for a moment or two in the reception area, gathering himself for a continuation of his journey, he was greeted by a friendly female voice behind him. He turned and found the pretty Maltese nurse he had met when he'd visited Chalky.

'Hello,' she said warmly, as though he were some long lost friend. 'Here again.'

'Yes, I came to visit my platoon commander, but he's been transferred,' Frank said, looking into her smiling face, finding himself quite glad to see her.

'To Qrendi? Are you going now?' she said.

'Well, yes. I suppose I should be on my way.'

She smiled again and came closer. 'You look tired, Corporal. And you've got such a heavy load to carry. Would you like a cup of tea?'

The nurse led him to the staff canteen and gave him two cups of tea in the dingy Nissen hut in the yard of the hospital. There was even a piece of hard cake, but Frank found the refreshments and the girl's company reviving. She was a pleasant, talkative woman, who told him all about her large family, all girls, and their work for the war effort.

'I like the independence,' she said. 'It's good to live your own life, but I suppose you're used to that.'

'Well, the army has pretty tight rules and regulations,' Frank said, considering for a moment the lack of anything he could call independence in his own life apart from in his head. He recognised that if circumstances had been different he might have asked this girl on a date to the pictures or for a walk or something. She clearly had no reservations about being with a British soldier. His feelings were too raw, however, from Manwela and the effect she'd had on him.

He took his leave of the friendly nurse, thanking her, mildly guilty that he couldn't like her more and respond to her advances.

He set off on the route to Qrendi, seeing the lurid deep blue of the sea ahead from the higher ground around Imtarfa. Only once or twice did he hear the distant drone of aircraft overhead and found himself enjoying this solitary walk. An ambulance came chugging up behind him after a few miles, and he was glad to accept a lift the rest of the way from the cheerful Maltese driver, who was bringing two wounded RAF officers to the convalescent home.

'We win soon,' said the driver to Frank. 'We beat the Hun with God's help.'

Frank nodded and thanked the man, then helped to wheel the injured men into the cool, stone-floored hallway of the ancient building. The nurse on the desk told him where Lieutenant Chambers could be found, along the end of a corridor, around a cloistered square. He found the officer in a small room, a monk's cell, with one small window high up, like in a prison, with an iron bed in the corner. Lieutenant Chambers was sitting in a wheelchair, engrossed in a book. His face was clean-shaven, with a sick greyish sheen about his complexion.

'Afternoon, sir,' said Frank.

The officer's head jerked up in surprise. 'Good heavens, Nixon,' he said, his face brightening. 'Jolly good to see you. Come in and er...'

The lieutenant looked around the room, as though wishing to indicate a comfortable, easy chair in his parlour. There was only a wooden three-legged stool on which stood a cup and saucer and a candlestick.

'Yes, take that, so sorry,' he said. 'A bit short of home comforts here. Good God, Nixon, what have you got there?'

'A French dictionary and a grammar book, sir,' said Frank, trying not to look too pleased with himself.

'Really? How absolutely marvellous. How did you manage it?' The officer was beaming now.

'Mr Falson sends his compliments and his best wishes for your recovery,' said Frank, glad that he'd lugged the things here after all. He handed the dictionary to the officer, wondering whether his knees could stand the weight, but Lieutenant Chambers grasped the heavy book firmly.

'Can't feel a damn thing in these legs. Might as well use them as a table,' he said, opening the dictionary.

'I'm sorry, sir,' said Frank, holding the small grammar book.

The officer was too intent on flicking through the pages of the dictionary to answer, so Frank dragged the stool closer to the wheelchair and sat down.

'This is a marvellous dictionary. Top class. Well done, Nixon. I'll be able to refine the translation, and you've got a grammar there too. This will do very nicely indeed. I've just read the part in the poor chap's journal where he's been torn off a strip by a very forceful Maltese woman. It's most interesting, but unfortunately it doesn't end well for him. He must have been one of those who was massacred, judging by the date his entries finish. Now,

Nixon, tell me what you've been up to. But wait, let's see if there's any food to be had. Are you hungry?'

'Just a bit,' said Frank.

Officers' rations were clearly a step up from the men's, but Frank's hunger overcame any misgivings he may have had about this privileged indulgence. The officer had a tray of lunch brought to the room: sardine sandwiches and tomatoes followed by tinned peaches and condensed milk, a real feast.

'Aren't there some prehistoric temples near here?' said Frank, collecting and stacking the empty plates after they'd finished eating.

'Yes, there certainly are,' said Lieutenant Chambers. 'You must go and have a look. If I weren't such a damnable cripple, I'd come with you.'

Frank glanced at the contraption of metal and wood to which the officer was now confined. 'What are the roads like round here?' he said. 'I mean, to get to the temple of Ħaġar Qim. It's not that far, is it?'

The officer raised his eyebrows. 'You *have* been doing your reading, haven't you? Yes, I think there's a reasonable main road down there.'

'Right, let's go, then. We've got a few hours of light left, haven't we?' said Frank, amazing himself at his audacity.

The lieutenant looked back at him, frowning. 'But, Nixon, it must be at least two miles. You go there and tell me about it.'

'No, I don't think it's that far. And I need a proper commentary, sir. I don't understand about archaeology,' he said, feeling bolder and rasher by the minute.

'I can't, Nixon. The idea's ridiculous.'

'But, sir, we might never get another chance,' said Frank, with a genuine sense of urgency.

'Well, yes. You're right. I'm going to be invalided back home as soon as it can be arranged.'

266

'I can easily wheel you, sir.'

Frank was surprised at the force of his insistence, and it was not until he was wheeling the officer out of the hospital gates in the rattling chair that he realised his suggestion might be foolhardy or even dangerous to the officer. However, it somehow didn't feel like that and, as they struck out along the road leading east, with the sea on the right-hand side, Frank heard Lieutenant Chambers whistling. Frank tried to push forward with greater speed, but the wheelchair creaked and complained on the gritty surface of the road.

'Bit of a rough ride, sir,' said Frank.

'It's fine. In fact, it's perfect,' said Lieutenant Chambers, and Frank had no more doubts.

The land rose towards the coast and the pathways to the temple, but the tracks were smooth and well-worn.

'There, look,' said the officer, pointing to the tip of a stone column just visible on the crest of the hill where they were heading.

As they drew nearer, they came upon a cluster of stone ruins, massive blocks, some above roof height, arranged in circles, curved into a complex of chambers and passageways.

'They think it was several temples or holy places,' said Lieutenant Chambers as they approached. 'Carefully crafted doorways, pedestals, altars. It would probably have been much taller originally and roofed in.'

Frank pushed the wheelchair right around the outside of the complex, the curved outer walls, amazed to see its solid and huge reality, the grandeur impossible to convey in ink sketches and gritty photographs. They found a main entrance with enormous supporting columns and huge flat lintels of yellow stone. Inside, the massy stones had been cut and piled up to form thick walls, rooms and passageways, some with crusty pitted surfaces, some with carvings. Frank was overwhelmed with wonder at the place, at his presence in it. He heaved the wheelchair up the uneven stones and into the smaller spaces of the temple. They said nothing for some time, Frank leaving the officer to examine the strange, pocked surface on one wall while he wandered through the maze of the ruins.

'Pretty marvellous, isn't it?' said Lieutenant Chambers when Frank rejoined him. 'The original carvings and statues have been taken to the museum, of course, the Fat Lady and other figurines, fertility goddesses, phallic symbols and the like.'

'But how could they do all this without metal tools?' said Frank.

'Good question,' said the lieutenant. 'There are theories, of course, well-documented in the works on the Tarxien period, three thousand to two thousand five hundred BC. I'm no expert, but it's fascinating.'

They spent another half an hour or more in the place, Frank gazing through the window hole of a massive stone at the blue of the sea. What a site for a temple, he thought. No wonder the people who came here, whoever they were, chose this as a holy site.

'Nixon, it's getting dark,' said Lieutenant Chambers.

The sun had turned the sea a red-bronze and the pale temple stones stood pink-lit and glowing. Frank could have stayed there all night, to sense more of the ancient world inhabited by the people who had first discovered this island of rock and built these places of worship. But that would have been asking for trouble, maybe, given his overactive imagination. It was a rough, slow journey back in the dusk, which turned quickly to dark, Frank rebuking himself for staying too long, but still in thrall of the experience.

A metal bracket on the footrest of the wheelchair snapped off, then one of the wheels came loose and hit a boulder at the side of the road, which tipped Lieutenant Chambers rudely out onto the dirt.

'Sorry, sir. Are you all right?' Frank said, appalled at his inattention.

The officer laughed as he lay on the ground. 'Don't worry,' he said. 'I think we've done pretty well. Didn't think I could do an archaeological expedition in a wheelchair.'

Frank had to lift the officer from the ground and into the chair again, remembering how he had done this in the cave all those months ago when he had first been struck down. He felt no embarrassment now, knowing that Lieutenant Chambers himself would have to grow accustomed to this kind of dependence on others. When they finally rattled back into the hospital, they were met by a furious matron.

'Where on earth have you been?' she said, advancing on them.

'Back in about three thousand BC, Matron,' said Lieutenant Chambers with a smile.

'For goodness' sake, Lieutenant, in your state?'

'Sorry, it was my idea to go and see the temples,' said Frank, not minding the woman's anger. It was a small punishment to pay for the success of their outing.

The matron turned to Frank, her face softening a little as she scrutinised him, her voice less loaded with blame.

'Lieutenant Chambers should not be stressed or overtired. Don't you realise how ill he's been?'

'Matron, I feel fine,' the officer said. 'In fact, I feel much the better for the trip. And by the way, I wonder if there's a bed somewhere for Corporal Nixon. He can't go back to St Andrew's at this hour.'

'Oh really,' she said, with an exasperated sigh.

The next morning, Frank awoke on a camp bed in a storage room where the matron had let him spend the night and leapt up when he realised the time was nine o'clock. He found a toilet and washed quickly in cold water, feeling grimy but surprisingly full of energy. He decided to seek out Lieutenant Chambers, then take his leave and not overstay his welcome by expecting breakfast, particularly so late; however, he found himself directed to the canteen, where all the men were eating. There was one long table shared by officers and NCOs, a fact that surprised Frank and even more when he was invited to sit down. The men were all physically disabled, with amputations or polio by the look of them, but there was much laughter and joking. Frank helped himself to a hunk of bread, a greasy string of bacon and a mug of tea.

'Nixon, come and join us,' called Lieutenant Chambers to Frank.

He took a seat at the end of the table, beside a sergeant with one arm and an officer in a wheelchair, opposite Lieutenant Chambers.

'This is Nixon, a budding historian,' said the lieutenant.

'Oh no, not another one of these boffins,' said the officer. 'Off we go on a lecture about pagan gods, fat ladies and fertility rites. Snore, snore.'

'Sounds quite interesting,' said the sergeant, with a grin.

'Oh dear, there will always be philistines, Nixon.' Lieutenant Chambers laughed. 'Eat up, then. I want you to take me to see the prehistoric cart ruts.'

After visiting the mysterious long ruts gouged in the rock on the coast at a place laughingly named Clapham Junction, Frank knew that he would have to get back to barracks, his journey likely to take a good few hours on foot.

'So, there's really no satisfactory explanation for these things,' said Lieutenant Chambers from his fixed wheelchair. 'These are just some of the theories.'

They were still debating this when Frank wheeled the officer back into the hall of the hospital.

'I can take over from here,' said the lieutenant, gripping the outer wheels of the chair and swivelling round to face Frank. He looked up with a serious expression.

'Thank you, Nixon. Jolly decent of you. I've enjoyed your company, and I'm deeply grateful for your help. There's a life to be lived, even for a cripple.' He paused for a moment. 'And I've written to Millicent, told her the worst, and she's answered. She's being such a brick about the whole thing. She's keen to meet you.'

He extended his hand to Frank. 'We've still some unfinished business, haven't we?' he said. 'You've got some of my books and I've still got a translation to do, plus there's old Bertie's work on that cave inscription. You have our address, so I'll look forward to seeing you when this wretched war is over.'

Frank took the officer's hand, gripped it, shaking it vigorously, eager to show his gratitude but unable to put it into words.

CHAPTER 21

JANUARY 1943

'Here we are, lads, fill up,' shouted the cook from the kitchen. 'An extra pile of mash for everyone.'

Sergeant Campbell, at the end of the table, chomped on a piece of bully beef, stopping to pick his teeth, then looked down the line of men, with his usual thinking frown. 'What do you say we do something for the poor bloody civilians?' he said. 'They're still on starvation diets.'

'Yes, and we're dining like royalty,' said Chalky, nudging Frank and holding up a piece of grey stringy stuff on the end of his fork.

It was true, Frank thought, that rations were still necessarily very stingy. The ending of the siege had allowed more merchant ships to get through with supplies, but it would be a long time before there would be any real feasting, for them or the civilians. He thought of Manwela's two skinny little boys.

'What about a party for the kids?' he said. 'Just a bit of a treat. It'd give them and their families something to look forward to.'

'Yeah,' agreed Chalky. 'It's a bit late for Christmas, but I reckon the kiddies won't mind as long as there's a bit of grub and some games.'

'Simpson does party tricks as well, don't you, mate?' said one of the men to his companion.

'Jim plays the piano. We could have pass the parcel, musical chairs, you name it.'

These ideas brought back the few bright spots in Frank's memory of childhood, of Christmas parties at the local church hall, when the boys, the waifs and strays, were allowed to mix with the normal children from proper homes.

The platoon was soon enthused by this concoction of childish excitement, nostalgia and relief of their boredom, to plan the party, which coincided neatly with another increase in rations and a reduction in the bombing. They put Sparks and Ramrod in charge of the food, sorting out the parts of the rations that could be saved, asking all the platoon to give up their bread on the day to make sandwiches. Even some jelly had arrived in the latest delivery.

Frank was in charge of the entertainment line-up and so contacted some of the concert party members who were free that day to come along with their instruments to sing and play. Simpson, the magician, in need of a costume, found an old top hat and a blackout curtain in a cupboard. The canteen was to be decorated too. Invitations were produced on the CO's office spirit duplicator and then men set off on bicycles to deliver them to all the surrounding villages.

Frank would dearly have liked to go to Naxxar, to take the invitation to Manwela, her sons and the other children, but he didn't offer. He didn't want to reopen the wound that was healing over now, paining him less; however, he hoped that David and Joseph would come and that she would bring them. It would be easier to see her with other folk and children about.

The day approached, and Frank grew nervous, in part because he was anxious that all the arrangements should run smoothly and partly because of the chance of seeing Manwela again. He'd briefed all the acts, made up a running order with timings and assembled a wooden platform for the performers. He'd even written out a bit of a welcome speech in Maltese and practised saying it when there was no one about. Streamers and paper bunting made of painted pages from 'The Times of Malta' were strung up all over the canteen.

Some of the more idle men, who had absented themselves from the allocation of duties, were ordered to put up directional signs for the children and their families to find their way round the barracks complex. One of these was Green.

Sergeant Campbell approached Frank as he was securing the end of the wooden platform to the floor with a bracket. 'We better watch out for that bastard again, Nix,' he said, nodding towards Green.

Frank and the sergeant watched as Green picked up the banner he'd been told to attach outside and, turning to glance around at the buzz of activity, quickly left by a side door.

'He's up to something,' said the sergeant. 'He's been sneaking about. Let's follow him.'

Frank, annoyed that Green was about to disrupt the start of the event, followed the sergeant through the doorway where Green had disappeared. A path inside a wire fence led along the building to the right, with various entrances to storerooms and kitchens leading off this, which were all generally locked. Thrown to the side of the path in the dirt was the sign that Green was supposed to have attached.

'I'll put this up, Sarge,' Frank said, bending to pick up the discarded banner.

'OK, then come on down there. You know, I think that bastard must have nicked a key from somewhere. He's bloody got in somewhere. There's no sign of him.'

Frank ran back and tied the strings of the banner hastily onto the fence. The sergeant had gone quickly down the path and had vanished into one of the side doorways to the kitchen. Frank, aware that the sergeant's temper was up, followed quickly.

Coming into the kitchen, he found the tables and workbench-es spread with plates of sandwiches, large bowls of jelly trifle topped with lurid pink blobs of something, biscuits and cakes. It was quite a banquet, given the limitations of the ingredients available. At least Green hadn't tampered with any of this. There was no sign of him or the sergeant, but then he heard voices from behind the door of a storeroom-cum-larder.

'You fucking tosspot, Green. Where did you pinch the bleed-ing key from?'

There was the sound of scuffling feet and more cursing as Frank leapt to the door, flinging it open. Green and Sergeant Campbell were squaring up to each other, surrounded by shelves of tins and packets of food.

'Here, grab hold of him, Nix,' said the sergeant as Green charged like a bull at Frank, who was filling the doorway.

Frank side-stepped quickly as Green's head and body shot through the doorway, but a quick kick to his knees floored him, bringing him crashing to the floor.

'Nice one, Nix,' said Sergeant Campbell, jumping on top of Green.

'You thieving bastard. You're fucking for it this time. No more chances. We've had enough of you in this platoon. Hold him, Nix.'

As Frank and the sergeant knelt on the struggling man, they heard children's high-pitched voices outside.

'Bugger it. They're here already. What are we going to do with him? We can't have him spoiling the party,' said the sergeant.

'We could tie him up and keep him quiet in here till it's over,' said Frank, seeing a ball of thick twine on one of the shelves in the kitchen.

'Good thinking. Lock him in as well, just to make sure.'

'Fucking let me go, you wankers,' said Green. 'This is intimi-dation. It's against the rules of war, Geneva rules or whatever.'

Frank reached for a tea towel that was draped over a chair and stuffed it into Green's mouth. Then they tied his wrists and ankles tightly, trussing his legs together with string and more around his torso, reducing him to a red-faced, writhing worm. Next, they dragged him back into the storeroom and pushed him under one of the shelves. They slammed the door, and the sergeant locked it behind him.

'That'll hold him for a bit, unless he's Houdini,' said the sergeant.

Frank grinned at Sergeant Campbell, who gave him a friendly punch on the shoulder, and they went through the kitchen and into the canteen, towards the growing din of children's voices.

The room was packed with chattering children, some mothers and grandmothers and even a few men. They were packed on all sides of the two long trestle tables. The noise was like a pen of hysterical monkeys, and Frank had a moment of panic.

Sergeant Campbell nudged him. 'Go on, Nix. It's your show. Tell 'em what treats they have in store.'

Frank swallowed, his stomach skittering, but there was nothing for it. No one else was going to do it. Sergeant Campbell was standing back with his arms folded and neither the CO nor Lieutenant Perkins had turned up. Frank took the folded piece of paper out of his pocket and saw that his hands were shaking, but he grabbed a tin cup and a spoon from the table and clanged them sharply together, jumping up on the platform and facing the crowd.

'Merħba, lil kulhadd. Qegħdin niedhu pjacir narawk hawnhekk,' he said, but he couldn't finish the final part of his short address in Maltese because of a deafening cheer from the children. He waited a few moments, then called them to order again, amazed that they fell into silence. He told them about the entertainment and games to come, announced the band and signalled that the food should be brought in.

The kitchen door swung open, and a team of men came through, their arms laden with the plates. Frank stepped down from the platform to join Chalky and Sergeant Campbell.

'Pretty good show, Nix,' said Chalky. 'Very professional.'

'It's hardly started,' said Frank, feeling relief and a little pride that at least it had got going well. But he was disappointed too. Manwela and her boys were not there.

Amazed, he watched as the children said grace, most crossing themselves before their eager hands darted at the plates of food. The band struck up a relaxed jazz number, and Frank, feeling a little superfluous, turned and saw some more children standing at the door.

He recognised David and Joseph immediately as they spotted him, held themselves back doubtfully for a moment, then rushed for him, clutching him around the legs. The other children, Manwela's cousins', followed sheepishly, but Frank, with the two boys still clinging to him, went to usher them in. He wanted to ask if Manwela had brought them, but he knew that he must first find the children places and some food.

'Frank, can we have something to eat?' said Joseph.

'Come on, then,' he said, moving towards the far away table. The children scrambled around, and Frank found them some seats and managed to snatch up half a plateful of sandwiches and cakes for them.

'Your mother?' said Frank to Joseph, unable to contain his anxiety.

'She's at home. Mario come with us. Outside,' said the boy, his mouth full of a sandwich.

Frank left the children and went to the door, stepping outside to find Mario on the path about ten yards away, leaning against the wall, smoking. He looked up when Frank appeared, straightening himself from his slouch. Frank hesitated for a moment, seeing the morose expression on the man's face, but he had to make the first move.

'Merħba,' he said, approaching and holding out his hand. What was there to lose? The worst he would get would be a punch in the face, but he thought this unlikely, as there was nothing aggressive in the farmer's manner.

Mario mashed his cigarette butt on the ground with his boot, then took Frank's hand in a brief, loose shake.

'I'm sorry,' Frank said, 'about that time, at your place. Sorry about the tomatoes too. Are you doing all right? I mean, have you got enough...'

He knew that he was spewing out words in a nervous ramble in his genuine wish to apologise to the man, another of Green's victims. But it was his need to know about Manwela that most flustered him. He couldn't utter her name.

Mario shrugged, and his body seemed to slacken, his eyes losing the last hint of suspicion. 'Not worry,' he said. 'Manwela tell me to bring children. She can't come. She say sorry, but the grandmother has died three days.'

'Sorry to hear that. Please...' Frank faltered and knew that he was colouring, but there was nothing he could do about it. 'Please give her my best wishes.'

Mario nodded.

'Why don't you come in and have a beer?' said Frank, in a sudden desperate inspiration. 'If you can stand the noise.'

A slight smile appeared on Mario's lips, and he nodded again, following Frank into the buzz of music and chatter.

It took some time to clear up the aftermath of the party. Captain Miller arrived just as the last of the children were leaving. 'Splendid, splendid gesture, men,' he said, sniffing the air and looking at the piles of dirty plates, torn bunting and wrappings from the pass the parcel.

THE DUST OF MELITA

'Come on, lads,' said Sergeant Campbell, 'just another bit of bomb damage.'

The men were in a hearty mood.

'There's another crate of beer in the store,' said the sergeant.

'Sarge,' said Frank, suddenly remembering, 'Green's still in there.'

The sergeant turned to the CO. 'Sir, we've got a man on a charge in there.'

Captain Miller pursed his lips. 'Not that chap Green again?'

CHAPTER 22

Frank was smoking a cigarette outside the barrack gates, staring at the vast expanse of the sky. After denying himself during the shortages, he was enjoying the way the smoke made his head dizzy.

He'd been stupid to wish for another leave-taking from Manwela. It would simply have renewed his grief, he knew, but yet he had wanted it. Why was he such a fool that he couldn't forget her, as other men seemed to do after encounters with women they would never see again? She had said she loved him, and he believed that she had. Did she think about him at all now? He hoped so, but not with pain, perhaps with some fondness. That would do. He hoped too, now that his jealousy had dimmed, that she would be happy with Mario, a husband and a father to her sons. She certainly had a better chance now of a decent life, even on this pulverised little island. They were tough. They would survive, as the Maltese people had done for centuries.

His own story was infinitesimal in the huge sweep of the war, and this small speck of it, his encounter with Manwela, so intensely felt, so charged with love and pain, would fade eventually. It was the fading sting of an insect bite upon the vast plain of the human skin.

And what were his chances of getting back alive, of having some kind of a life? Better, he thought, than an Iron Age tribesman, an Ottoman foot soldier or a Napoleonic infantryman. Was life dearer now than in the past? He hoped so, though he was far from sure and knew that war changed how life was valued.

He'd found some Maltese proverbs at the back of a guidebook and one that seemed apt in wartime: 'Żgur il-mewt,', meaning 'Death is the only thing that is certain'. His own death if it came in this war would, like those of the tens of thousands, millions of past unknowns who had suffered and perished in conflicts, be recorded in history books, subsumed in such phrases as 'the losses were heavy', 'more than 2,000 men were killed in the assault', 'only half of the troops survived'. If he lived, he knew what he wanted to do: explore some of these hidden histories.

He wandered back to the workshop, remembering the mangled machine, which he had imagined he might be able to beat out straight again, mend and take back to Manwela. A couple of men were in there, smoking, pausing in their work on a dismantled motorbike. Frank nodded to them, looked around, his eyes lighting on the place where he thought he had left the bicycle, but it wasn't there. The only bikes were the army issue ones, standing in neat rows in the racks.

'Seen an old scrap bike, have you?' said Frank to the men.

They looked around vaguely and shrugged.

'Don't think so, mate,' said one.

Frank looked briefly again, but he knew that the broken thing had gone.

Later that evening, Frank was reading a book from Mr Falson's gifts to him about the Maltese and Gozitan temples, but the single lightbulb in the room flickered and went out.

'Another bloody power out,' said someone.

Sergeant Campbell came in and stood at the end of their row of beds. 'Green's got six months in the clink, then a dishonourable discharge. Good riddance, that's what I say,' he said. 'We don't want scumbags like him in the British army.'

No one disagreed.

'By the way, we've got a field training exercise tomorrow, lads. Up at six,' the sergeant continued.

A few of them groaned.

'Well, some say the Hun's going to have another shot at the island, invading it, I mean. We've got to be ready. But let's look on the bright side; if we beat them, we'll be on our way to Sicily. Mussolini's in the shit.'

'Sicily?' said Frank. 'They've got some fantastic ruins of antiquity there.'

ACKNOWLEDGMENTS

I would like to thank my writing group: Helen Chambers, Sue Dawes, Philippa Hawley, Pauline Rendall, Sue Whytock and Eleanor Young for their encouragement and feedback on early drafts, Steve and Viv Goldsmith for their enthusiastic responses, Caroline Phillips for her detailed comments, my husband Roger and my brother John for their unfailing support and my Maltese son-in-law Chris for his help with the Maltese language.

My thanks also go to Cassandra Davis and the team at Cahill Davis Publishing, for their constructive editing, helpful guidance and advice in the production of this book.

If you enjoyed The Dust of Melita, I would very much appreciate it if you left a review online, if you can. If you post a review on social media, please feel free to tag my publisher, Cahill Davis Publishing, and use the hashtag #dustofmelita so that we can find your post.

About the Author

Clare was born and brought up in Scotland of an English mother and Irish father and has lived in several different regions of England throughout her adult life. After a career teaching English, among other subjects, in every sector of education (except primary), and raising two lovely daughters, Clare at last found time to write. A distance learning course in novel writing soon had her hooked on historical fiction and she has produced about a novel a year for the last ten years. Clare loves the background reading and research and often locates her novels in regions known to her, exploring the lives and experiences of ordinary people caught up in larger historical events, in a range of different periods. Clare and her husband of 45 years are now thoroughly enjoying the experience of being grandparents to four young children.

You can find out more about Clare and the other titles she had published on her website www.clarehawkins.co.uk

Printed in September 2024
by Rotomail Italia S.p.A., Vignate (MI) - Italy